THE OUTCAST

From the Swedish of
Selma Lagerlöf

Translated by
W. Worster, M. A.

Garden City   New York
DOUBLEDAY, PAGE & COMPANY
1922

PRINTED AT THE COUNTRY LIFE PRESS
GARDEN CITY, N. Y.

First Edition

CONTENTS

BOOK I

BOOK II

CONTENTS

BOOK III

BOOK I

THE OUTCAST

GRIMÖN

ON THE island of Grimön, among the rocks and reefs of the western coast of Sweden, there lived, some years back, a man and his wife. The two were much unlike each other.

Joel Elversson, the husband, was the elder of the pair by fifteen years or so. Ill-favoured to look at, heavy and slow, he had always been, and age had not improved him. His wife, on the other hand, was still as neat and pleasant a little body as ever; far from having lost her looks, she seemed almost as pretty now, at fifty, as she had been at twenty.

One fine Sunday evening the couple were sitting on a big flat rock just outside their house, chatting together at their ease. Joel was a man who enjoyed hearing his own voice, and delivered his words with care. Just now he was giving his wife at some length the contents of an article he had read in the paper. The little woman listened, but her thoughts were not following very closely.

"Eh," she thought to herself, "he's a wonderful head has Joel, to be sure. How he can get all that out of a bit of print in a newspaper. . . . Pity he can't put his learning to some use for us both, instead of others."

Involuntarily she glanced across at the house. It was a good-sized place in itself, but in such a state of dilapidation as to be largely uninhabitable; the pair lived now in one small outbuilding, which the previous tenants, sea-captains all, had used for kitchen and larder.

"If only he'd had a liking for the sea," went on Mor Elversson to herself, "like his father and grandfather before him. He'd have laid by something now, and we'd be able to look forward to old age in ease and comfort. But he's always been set on farming and field work and such, and little enough it's brought us."

She did not move from her place while her husband was speaking, but her little head, that moved quickly and easily as a bird's, turned slightly as she glanced over the patches of cornfield and potato, little islands of growth among the barren rock that formed the greater part of the island.

Every little strip of cultivation was her husband's work; the very soil was, in a manner of speaking, his creation. He had brought endless boatloads of earth and manure to Grimön, in the firm conviction that he must one day reap a rich reward for his pains.

"All that trouble for so many bits of earth, and poor at that," thought his wife to herself. "Needs but one good northerly gale at Whitsuntide, and all the sowing and planting'd be nowhere Nay, 'tis to the sea we should look for our daily bread, living here as we do. There's neither right nor reason in it else."

Another movement of the quick little head, and she was looking out through the space between the tumble-down old house and the cottage, over the broad, gleaming surface of the water beyond.

"Ay, the sea," she sighed. "'Tis different with that. Freights and cargoes and good money paid. If I'd been a man, I'd have gone to sea from the first, and never taken up with the farm work at all. And here we're getting old and older, and what's to become of us when we're past work? There's none of the children 'd stay at home to toil and moil that away—and small blame to them for that."

The last words must have been spoken aloud, for her husband turned sharply toward her. He had been describing the perils and hardships of an English expedition recently returned from the Arctic, and broke off now in the middle of a sentence.

"You're not listening," he said. But it was doubtless not the first time he had found himself talking to deaf ears, for he seemed neither surprised nor annoyed.

"Indeed I was," his wife assured him. "I was thinking this very moment how fine you talk, and how you'd do for a preacher."

"I don't know about that," said the husband, with a laugh. "If I can't keep one listener from thinking of all and sundry when I'm preaching, how'd I manage with a congregation?"

"But I was listening," his wife protested, somewhat discomfited. "I've got it all in my head now. How they lost their ship the very first winter and managed to build a snow house, and had to stay and live there for over a year, till all their food was gone, and they were chewing bits of hide."

There was a note of vexation in her voice, and her mouth twitched in a way it often did when anything troubled her.

"Wonder how it would feel," suggested her husband, casually, "if 'twas one of our own blood had been there starving in a snow hut."

The woman glanced at him sharply. What did he mean by that now? Something, surely. But Joel sat staring before him, with no trace of expression in his rheumy eyes.

"Well, if we were to spend all our time sitting thinking of other folks' troubles, there'd be little pleasure in life," she said, apologetically. "And, anyhow, they were saved in the end."

"That's true," Joel admitted. "There was a ship went out to find them, and they're safe back in England now."

"And all the honour and glory, and live happy ever after," concluded his wife.

To her mind, there was nothing to be so serious about when all had come well at last. But her husband went on without changing his tone.

"I dreamt last night about our boy Sven," he said. "Dreamt he came and stood by my bed and said I'd done him a sore wrong. I won't say if I've any gift of dreaming true as a rule, and I don't know if there's anything in this or not. But it's a queer thing, all the same, to see his name in the paper here to-day."

The last words were spoken carelessly, as if the

speaker were thinking only of himself. But from that moment he had no reason to complain of want of attention in his listener. His wife came close to him and deluged him with questions: Where was the name? What was it he had dreamt? Was there really anything about their boy Sven? Her voice grew shrill, her nose flushed, and tears stood in her eyes.

Had it been any other of their children, she would have been less easily moved. But it was different with Sven. They had given the boy away, when nine years old, to an English gentleman and his lady, who had come sailing along the coast in a yacht. The strangers had simply fallen in love with the child, and had promised, if he were entrusted to them, to bring him up as their own, as a rich gentleman, and make him their heir.

It was a wonderful prospect for the lad; his parents had felt that for his own sake they dared not refuse. If he stayed with them, he would have none to help him but themselves. And he was a bright child, with a clever head; they had often agreed that he would surely get on in the world if he had but the chance in his upbringing.

Seventeen years now since they had let him go, and during all that time they had heard nothing from him. Never a letter, never a word of greeting. They knew no more of him than if he had lain at the bottom of the sea.

"See there," said the man, handing across the paper to his wife. "List of those saved. Here it is. 'Sven E. Springfield.'"

"Yes, yes. 'Sven E. Springfield'—it's there, right enough."

"And that can't mean anything but Sven Elversson Springfield," Joel went on. "His own name, mine, and his foster-father's. There's no mistake about that."

Mor Elversson crushed the paper close. At that moment she felt that the son she had given up to others of her own free will was dearest of all her children.

"Why didn't you say straight out at once that Sven was there?" she said, reproachfully. "I wasn't listening. Now you'll have to tell it all over again."

Joel seemed somewhat at a loss. He had thought to tell her the whole story before saying a word about Sven; it would have been easier so. Then he could have seen how she took it, and acted accordingly.

However, he must tell her now. And he went on to explain all she wished to know. What was meant by the eightieth degree of latitude, for instance. And she listened, growing eager on her son's behalf for the honours to be won, and thinking surely he and his comrades must have reached farther than any before them. And what had they lived on after the ship had gone down with all their stores? The story of how the relief expedition had found them that summer, on the shores of Melville Island, had to be repeated over and over again.

"Oh, what he must have had to go through in all that time!" she exclaimed. "No, 'tis a wicked thing to give away one's own child to strangers."

"But he's made his fortune now, I suppose," she went

on, relieved. "And they'll give him a host of medals and orders and all."

Soon she began to wonder how the boy had been received in England on his return.

"Millions of people came out to see them," said Joel. "'Arctic explorers' homecoming.'"

He felt ill at ease, anxious, and in fear. All their future depended on how he framed his words now; if he could say the thing as it must be said.

"If only we could have been there too," said his wife. "If I could but have stood at a street corner and seen him go by."

"No need for you to have stood at street corners," said Joel. "It says here there was a special steamer for parents and relatives to meet them."

The look of joy faded suddenly from her face. "Eh, Joel," she sighed. "Little good it would have been if we'd been there. They'd never have let you nor me go on that steamer boat. *She* wouldn't have let us."

"*She*" was Mor Elversson's word for the English lady that had taken away her son. She had never forgiven her for forbidding her son to write to his parents. And in her thoughts this stranger woman had become a monster.

"I doubt but they'd have let us see him, all the same," said Joel.

It was some relief to him, in a way, that his wife laid stress on little details such as this. He needed time to collect his thoughts before he could break the news to her. All their future depended on how it was said and taken; he told himself this again and again, as if to urge his mind to the effort.

"Never believe it!" cried the woman, stubbornly, with a toss of her head. "When she never so much as let him write a line all these years. And I doubt but he's little thought for us, anyway. Nine years old he was, when he went away, and sense enough, if he'd cared, to write without her knowing. But it's plain enough; she's put it into his head how we were common folk, and not the sort for a little young gentleman to be asking about."

All her joy was gone and vanished now; the thoughts that had plagued her so often in the past came back with renewed force.

"I'll admit," said her husband—"I'll admit it's a strange thing Sven shouldn't have written a single word to us all that time. And it may well be 'twas their fault that wouldn't let him. I heard something up at the church to-day."

The woman said no word. She was too sick at heart to speak.

"This is going badly," said Joel to himself. "If she's in that humour, there's little hope anyway."

"The Pastor's had news from England," he said aloud. And now again he was touching on a matter he had thought to leave until his wife was more prepared, and in the mood to take it better. But there seemed no help for it now. "Pastor asked me to go along home with him. 'Twas he that gave me the newspaper here."

"The Pastor?"

"Yes. Wanted to talk to me about Sven."

"Huh! What do I care! 'Tis all the same now, the way he's turned out."

Joel made no reply to this, and they sat for a long time in silence. At last the woman burst out violently:

"I never knew the like of you for making a poor body curious. What was it Pastor's heard from England?"

"It was news of Sven. And Pastor's coming himself to tell you about it this evening."

The woman sprang to her feet. "Pastor himself—coming here! Well, of all the wonders. . . . And you sitting there and never said a word of it till now!"

She took a pace toward the house, thinking to look round and see that all was clean and in order. Then suddenly she stopped.

"What's he coming here for?" she said. "There must be something wrong."

She cast a keen glance at her husband, as if trying to look into his mind and read the thoughts within.

"Maybe Sven's turned softer now," she said, "after being up there in the ice and chewing bits of hide. Maybe he's wishful to come and see us, after all. But, mark my words, this time *I* say no! If we weren't good enough for him before, we're no better now."

"Be careful of your words," said her husband, warningly. "You never know but you might be sorry after." He felt a growing anger toward her for speaking so violently, and taking the whole thing differently from what he would have done himself.

Mor Elversson had forgotten all about seeing to the house now. Her husband's last words could mean but one thing—she had guessed rightly.

"And do you know what's the news Pastor's coming to tell?"

"I know something—yes."

"Was it himself told you to read out all that in the paper for me to hear?"

"Well, no. He was going to tell you himself, I take it. But I reckoned it was best you should know a little before he came, and be prepared."

"And just as well," said his wife. "Well that I knew of it in time. I might have been forgetting myself and saying good-day and welcome before I knew, and been sorry for it after."

Joel felt his anger increasing. "She'll spoil it all beyond mending," he thought to himself, "and it's all our future to think of. Eh, she'll never be wiser, only growing worse and worse for every year."

"I fancy Pastor 'll be glad to hear you can talk so careless like about Sven. All one to you . . . well, 'twill make it easier for him to say what he's got to say."

"Easier? . . ." repeated the woman, and her voice seemed harsher even than before. "What d'you mean by that?"

"Why, it looks as if Sven's in trouble after all. That procession, when they came home, that was to be last Sunday, and so it was, as fine as could be. Next day, too, there was banquets and invitations and things— and then all of a sudden it stopped. They'd come back from the Arctic all right, but folk were beginning to say strange things about them. Ugly things."

The woman's face set hard.

"You mean to tell me he's done something wrong?" she murmured between clenched teeth.

"Took down all the flowers and flags and stuff, and put a stop to everything. One day they could hardly make a way through the streets for folk crowding round to cheer the sight of them; and the next, those same folks ready to spit on them."

Mor Elversson raised her head.

"Well, I never heard . . ." she cried. "I doubt it would have been better for him to have stayed with his own flesh and blood after all."

"Remember," said her husband, speaking more forcefully now, "it's not the first time such things have happened away on expeditions like that. They were starving, and mad with hunger, and didn't rightly know what they were doing. And then one of them couldn't stand it any longer, and took and cut his throat, and after that, well . . ."

"Well? They ate him up, I suppose you mean?"

She spoke the words coldly, without a trace of excitement. Her heart was full of bitterness and disgust.

"They were no more accountable, really, than folk in a madhouse," said her husband. "And it says here in the paper they couldn't bring themselves to go on. Only started like."

"And Sven was in it, too?"

"When anything like that happens, they take good care all's in it. They made him do like the rest. But that was all."

"And now," cried his wife, with an indescribable contempt in her voice—"now I know what it is Pastor's got to say. Sven's not good enough for *her* now, and so he's got Pastor to come and persuade us to let him come back here. Isn't that it?"

"I daresay that would be best, if it could be done," said Joel, slowly.

"But I say no!" cried his wife. "I say no! He shan't come back here because he's nowhere else to go. He forgot all about us as long as he was well off and comfortable; don't let him think we're anxious to have him now. Poor and old we may be, and needing help. But we'll not have a son that's done things so nobody else will own him."

Joel Elversson looked at his wife, with anger and impatience in his eyes. He was old and weak, and it would have been a grand thing for him to have a son at home able to work. His wife's feeling seemed to him childish and unreasonable; she was obstinate; she was downright wicked. "Wait," he thought to himself. "Wait, and you'll soon hear something more to your mind."

"Just as I said," he went on aloud. "Pastor won't find it so hard, after all, to tell you what was in the letter."

"It—isn't it what I thought, then?" asked his wife in a milder tone. Her stubbornness was shaken by his evident anger and disapproval.

He looked at her sternly.

"Would you like me to tell you myself, or wait till Pastor comes?"

And in his impaitence to punish her for her want of affection, he did not wait for an answer, but went on:

"They live in London—the Springfields. And Sven had gone back home to them there. But when the ugly stories began to get about, the father sent a paper with the news up to him—and a loaded revolver with it."

"And the mother—what about her? Did she know he'd sent it?"

"She knew—yes."

"And—and what then?"

"Then—why, it came about as they wished. That's all."

"And now—he's dead."

"Now—now you know what Pastor had to tell you," said her husband.

"And she," cried the poor mother—"she that was not his mother at all, but had had him with her all those years, she let him kill himself, when he'd done no wrong?"

She turned on her husband fiercely.

"You lie!" she cried. "It is not true!"

"I'd have said those very words myself an hour ago. I wouldn't have believed that a woman could be so heartless. But since I've heard you, now, I can believe it."

"But—but he hadn't only them to look to. He'd his mother and father here."

"Most likely he thought we'd take it the same way. And he wasn't so far wrong, it seems."

Mor Elversson turned away, and sat down on the rock. The tears ran down her cheeks. "Sven's dead," she said, "dead. No mother but a woman with a heart of stone—and she let him die."

She sat awhile, weeping and moaning.

"O God, why did we ever let him go? And that woman to send him to his death for nothing! When it was the others that made him . . ."

"You'd better try and be calm a bit," said her husband. "Here's the Pastor coming. The boat's just putting in."

"Tell him I know all about it. He can go back again."

"Can't very well do that, when he's been at the trouble to come."

Joel walked away, and came back a moment later with the Pastor and a young man.

The priest walked up to the weeping woman.

"Joel tells me you've heard already, Mor Elversson," he said. "About Sven. He was concerned in a very unpleasant business, and his adopted parents sent him away."

Mor Elversson had risen to curtsey to the Pastor. She still held a corner of her apron to her eyes, but, for all her weeping, she caught a glimpse of the stranger with him.

"It's Sven," said a voice within her. "Sven. . . ."

A host of thoughts crowded into her mind. She realized that Joel had lied to her, in his anger at her heartlessness. She felt, too, that she would never be able to overcome the sorrow she had felt on hearing that her son had tasted human flesh. She saw that they would have to keep this son at home with them now, since no one else would have him in their service. But in the midst of all these cold reflections she saw how thin and pale the boy looked, how his eyes begged her sympathy, and a wave of pity and love rose in her heart.

"Eh, Joel, Joel," she thought. "Always strange in his ways. He's shown me now what I am; made me see what I really feel. I know now, that for all the boy's been away from us all these years, and come back in disgrace, I can't but love him all the same."

And, without a word to the Pastor, she stepped forward to her son and bade him welcome, her husband watching her anxiously the while.

"Surely," she said, in her gentlest voice, "it was just for this that the trouble came—that Joel and I might have you back again."

IN GOD'S HOUSE

SVEN ELVERSSON, the man who had been greeted as a son by the two old folk at Grimön, sat in the church at Applum, thanking God that he had found a place of refuge where he was not looked upon with horror and disgust.

On the lonely, rocky little island with its two poor inhabitants, he had no fear of encountering that downward curve of the lips that signified loathing. His father was an old man, and felt no disgust toward him, having no strong feelings any longer in that way. His mother was sensitive as ever, but she loved him.

The church in which he sat was an old wooden building, the ceiling decorated with a great picture of the Judgment. And every time he looked up he found himself involuntarily gazing at a big, black, grinning devil, who was thrusting fuel under a cauldron filled with sinners boiling in a sulphurous broth. Sven Elversson knew that particular fiend of old, from the time when he had been in that very church seventeen years before. A striking feature was the long tail, cloven in three at the tip, which he used with great dexterity to stir the boiling mess.

As a child he had often let his fancy play about the figure of this master cook, who managed so skilfully to tend his fire and his pot at the same time. Now, however, other thoughts were in his mind. If all those who every Sunday looked up at that merry spirit of the infernal kitchens at his boiling were suddenly told that there, in their midst, sat one of their fellows who had actually tasted human flesh, they would hardly let him remain there long.

There was one thing—he could find no other to compare with it—which civilized human beings could not do. Murder, adultery, cruelty, theft; these they could commit. They were not above such things as drunkenness, rape, treason, espionage. Such things as these were of daily occurrence. There were, no doubt, those who would shrink from any such crime, but the things were done. *One* of mankind's ancient sins there was which no longer existed in civilized countries—a thing too loathsome for any to contemplate. And that he had done. Yes, he was more to be abhorred than any fiend.

The only soul in the church, beyond his parents, who knew the reason of Sven Elversson's homecoming was the Priest. But the Pastor had received him kindly on the previous Sunday, showed him sympathy, and spoken with his father; had gone with him out to Grimön, and been pleased to see his mother's affectionate welcome—and had approved the idea of his remaining at home with his parents. The Priest had shown himself throughout as a tolerant and generous man.

To-day, as the Pastor entered his church, his eyes fell on Sven Elversson, the man from the starvation camp at Melville Island. And at sight of him he felt a stifling sensation in his throat.

He had helped this man, and done what he could for him; he had been glad to be the means of bringing him back to his home, and finding a refuge for an unfortunate who was made to suffer for what he had been forced to commit; a fellow creature in such desperate straits that he might otherwise have turned to suicide. But he had not thought to see him here in church.

At the vicarage, he would not have hesitated to receive him if he had come. But this he could not endure. The man had eaten human flesh—had been guilty of something heathenish, abominable. Surely, he ought to have understood himself that his presence there was intolerable.

A moment after, he reproached himself for his thoughts, accused himself of uncharitableness, and called to mind how Christ had bidden all sinners come to Him. He strove to rouse more sympathy in himself; he thought of the poor sinner's gentle, kindly bearing, and checked his first impulse to send the verger with a message asking him to leave the church. He went through the service, and delivered his sermon as usual, but could not free himself from a feeling of abhorrence.

The words he had to speak clung to his palate; he had to pause once or twice in his sermon and clear his tongue before he could go on. It was as if the taste of something loathsome actually filled his mouth; he seemed to be witnessing the scene as it had happened: the group of starving men flinging themselves upon the body of the suicide.

He would have felt nothing of this had it not been for

the presence of the man himself there in the church. But the feeling had come upon him now, and he felt himself helpless in its grasp. He clenched his hands in strife with himself, turned in the pulpit so as to keep the figure of Sven Elversson away from sight; he strove to read the sermon as he had written it, forced himself to concentrate his thoughts upon his words, and suddenly the trouble was gone, and he felt at ease once more.

But now it chanced that he came to a passage in the sermon dealing with falsehood, and how far it might be justified in certain cases. And at once his thoughts turned to Grimön, and the manner in which Joel Elversson had brought his wife to realize her true feelings, It was his custom frequently to illustrate his sermons with episodes from real life, and in doing so, he did not write down the story beforehand, but told it in such words as came to him at the moment. And now it occurred to him that the little happening at Grimön might be used by way of example.

He had had no thought before of using it, but now, carried away by his subject, he took it up.

He had not been speaking long before a warning thought crossed his mind—it was perhaps hardly well to make the matter known to the whole congregation. True, no one had asked him to keep it a secret. Nevertheless, he felt uneasy, and sought for some way of altering the story as he went on, but could find none, and told it as it was. He tried to emphasize only that part which bore on his subject, of falsehood and justification, but here again he failed, and told the very thing that should have remained unsaid, making known the entire affair to all those present.

At first, he felt ashamed of what he had done, then suddenly he was seized with a sense of exultation at thus treading underfoot the unclean spirit that had dared to appear in the church itself. "Despicable worm!" he thought. "That such a creature should ever presume to enter into my church—into the house of God."

He had struggled against the sense of loathing; now, it had crept upon him unawares and overwhelmed him.

All next day the Priest was ill at ease. He had not acted as a man should, with proper self-control. He had behaved like a child, like a savage, giving way to instinct at once.

In vain he tried to find some way in which to repair what he had done; it could not be altered now. He must wait until some opportunity offered. The more he made of the affair just now, the worse it would be.

But what a power—what a terrible power—lay in this sense of loathing, that it could thus overwhelm a man, as it had done with him, at the very moment when he stood as teacher and spiritual guide in a Christian church, speaking to Christian souls!

The little party from Grimön left the church as the preacher descended from the pulpit.

Once outside, they stopped involuntarily, and stood a moment by the church door, looking around.

The church stood in the middle of a level, open plain—an unusual thing in that part of the country

Not of very wide extent, but still considerable. One could see from one side to the other, and mark the doings of one's neighbours, yet, for all that, it was large enough to furnish ground for church and vicarage, and a score of homesteads and farms round about.

The plain was walled in by gray, rocky hills on every side—not very high, but still considerable. Both the north wind and the west could force their way across the barrier, yet it sufficed to shut out the view of everything beyond, even to the mountain peaks.

The whole plain was cut up into field on field of cultivated ground—and these were neither large nor small, but of a size to suit the standing of honest peasant farmers. And here and there among the fields were buildings, red and blue and white, likewise of an equable, respectable size. No big mansions dominating all the rest, and, on the other hand, no poor cottages such as might serve to exalt the appearance of the others, and make for pride in those who dwelt there.

As for the vegetation, it could not be called luxuriant, for there were no trees to be seen, whether as woods on the hillsides, or in groups on the plain, or set in rows along the waysides. On the other hand, it could not be denied that it was a fertile soil, as it lay there now in its autumn glory—a waving sea of wheat and grass and peas and beans and clover.

Almost in the middle of the plain stood the church, from which the Grimön folk themselves had just, as it were, been driven out. It was an old-fashioned wooden building, that could not be called altogether ugly, for it had a slender little tower rising up boldly, and leading the mind heavenward. On the other hand, it was hardly beautiful, by reason of its dark, heavy nave, that weighed down the soul to earth.

And in the stone-walled enclosure about the church itself, a gray-striped cat wandered to and fro while the three stood without. A handsome animal, well marked, with close, fine fur, and a pleasant softness in all its movements.

But as they watched it, there seemed to be something uncanny about the way its limbs moved under the soft skin. It was not only that it moved so silently, or that its green slits of eyes, as it looked at them, were so veiled and without expression. The thing was hateful because it was so smooth and soft and pleasant-looking, while all the time it thought of nothing but stealing and killing.

And as they looked, the cat seemed to grow and stretch itself and expand, until it rose so high as to shut out sight of the wall of hills. And as the creature grew, it purred and hummed and made all manner of playful, easy movements—and the horror of it increased.

And they saw that the beast was the loathing that had arisen about them—the loathing that was to grow and grow till it spread over all the plain, that could find no better soil for its growth than here, shut in within narrow bounds, where all things were level, equable, even. . . .

Mor Nathalia Elversson faced round toward the church, and, scraping with her nails at the red-painted wooden wall, tore loose a few splinters, which she laid between the leaves of her prayer book.

"Here in this church I was christened," she said, "when I was a week old. And here I was confirmed as a young girl. Here I was married, and here, like as not, they'll read the burial service over me. But, till that day comes, I'll enter there no more, as long as the shame of this day's left to endure."

FATHER, MOTHER, AND SON

AS THE two old people at Grimön came to know their stranger son, they wondered at him for many things.

"I tell you this, Joel," said Mor Elversson to her husband one day, "that if *I*'d been taken away and brought up amongst gentlefolks as one of themselves, and then all suddenly had to lay it all by, and come to live on such fare as we can give, after being used to all manner of dainties; if I'd had to leave all that and turn to helping you in the fields and never so much as time to read in a book, nor ever change a word with finer folks, but only a pair of ninnies like you and me—if it was me was come to that, I'd be sullen and hard from morning to night, that I would. And I doubt but you'd be the same."

Joel agreed that he would find it hard to be otherwise in such a case.

"And then look at Sven," went on his wife. "As if there was never a thought of such in his head. And he's not grieving over money and friends he's lost or that sort. Never seems to trouble him that he's no sort of pleasure nor enjoyment to turn to. He can go about here laughing and chaffing with me, and arguing with you, as if he'd never thought nor longing for better company. Every day the same—gentle and humble and glad as any God's lamb. There's but one thing I can see that plagues him."

"Well, as for that, I can't think any the worse of him for feeling so. It's the disgrace that's ever on his mind—and that's a sore thing for any man to bear."

"Ay, that's true. And a cruel thing it is that folk can't get used to him like, so he can't go over to the post, or into a store, but there's some that curl lips at him or let out an ugly word. And I'm as sure as can be in my heart he's innocent all the time. Sven, he's far and away above the rest of the children as the sun and the moon, and it's in my mind he's fretting for nothing at all. Ung-Joel might have done what they say, but never Sven."

Day after day Mor Elversson talked in the same strain. As soon as she and her husband were together, she would fall to praising Sven.

"You don't understand him, Joel," she would say. "And his ways, and how he's different. But I'd have thought you might have seen it by the difference in me. Washing and doing my hair neat, and sweeping and scrubbing and cleaning about the place. You don't suppose it's for your sake I do it?"

"Why," said Joel, "as for that, you've always been a great one for keeping things clean and neat beyond other folks." It was a way Joel had, of saying nice things to people whenever he could.

"It's not only that," said his wife, "but it's changed me in other ways. I'm never angry about things now—I've turned soft as an eiderdown. Did you ever see a smile like Sven's? When other folks look kindly at me, I'm glad enough, but when Sven looks at me that smiling way of his, I just feel I could fling myself naked into the sea if he said the word."

Joel laughed.

"I don't see there'd be any great gain in that if he did," he said. "But there's something in what you say there. To my mind, the boy's like one of the stones that lie down on the shore, and always being rolled about by the waves. He's got worn and smooth from all the hard knocks he's got, till there's not a sharp edge nor a corner anywhere."

Truth to tell, Joel, was at least as interested in his son as was his wife. But, pleased though he was with the lad, he could not but be anxious about him. It seemed as if he were resigned now, to submit to the judgment that had been passed upon him, and keep away from his kind for ever. There seemed little chance of his leaving the island. But even there, he would not be cut off from all communication with his fellows, unless he wished it so. Joel had been clerk to the magistrate's court for thirty years past, and in the course of that time had gained much knowledge of laws and regulations. In consequence, his help was often sought by neighbours wishing to make a will, draw up a contract, or arrange some similar matter in proper order. But when such visitors appeared, Sven Elversson never came in for a word with them. On the contrary, he would go off to the farthest part of the island as soon as a boat came in sight.

"Well, what's he to do?" said Mor Elversson, when her husband spoke of his anxiety. "To begin with, he's almost forgotten to speak his own tongue in all these years, and it's only just beginning to come back to him. And when folk themselves turn shy of him as if he was a monster, what's he to do?"

Joel threw back his head, drew in his breath audibly, and uttered words that his wife found it hard to understand.

"If I'd been born to be a musician," he said, "I doubt but I'd manage to find me something to play on."

"Well, and what then?" said his wife. "What do you mean by that?"

"I mean that, if it's as I think, and our Sven's meant to be a picture and example and show the way to others, then it can't be right for him to live here on this bit of an island like a hermit."

Mor Elversson looked at her husband, and a wealth of tenderness shone in her eyes.

"*You've* lived on this bit of an island all your life," she said. "But there's folk enough have been able to come and learn from you and plague you with no end of things."

Joel waved his hand impatiently.

"What's that compared to Sven? I never learned things when I was young, but Sven—he was set to it in time. There's nothing to stand in his way."

"There's one thing. . . ."

"There's that, of course. . . ."

"And that's everywhere, where you'd least expect it. Like a cat lying in wait, and before you know, it's at his throat."

"Ay," said Joel. "That's just the trouble. And

what's done can't be undone. There's no sort of miracle could keep that cat from flying at him."

"But, Joel, remember, if it hadn't been for the trouble, he'd never have come back home to us again. Though I know in my heart he's innocent," she added.

And again and again she said the same. So overjoyed was she at having her son back home that she could hardly understand why he and his father troubled themselves about what other folk thought. "Never heed them," she said to Sven. "They're just foolish. You're better than all of them. The one that sneered at you the other day when you went to the post, he'd be in prison for forgery if he had his due. Don't fancy he's any call to look down on others."

But as time went on, she could not but feel that Joel was right, and that her son was gradually becoming a recluse, shunning his fellows altogether. And not only that. His manner had grown so humble that it almost made him appear ridiculous. He seemed wishful to efface himself altogether in his misery.

"No," she thought to herself. "This will never do. Something must happen soon. Surely the Lord will not forsake us altogether."

The parish of Applum, to which Grimön belonged, included, not only the level tract of the mainland as seen from the church, but also some dozen little islets off the coast, and the fishing village of Knapefiord, which last, with its boathouses and sheds, long quays and harbour basins, vessels and buoys, seems to spread out as far over the water as over the land.

Mor Elversson often rowed over to the village with

butter and eggs, and in talking with her customers, housewives who had known her for years, she made frequent endeavours to praise this son of hers who had come home, assuring all that he could never have done any wrong.

But she soon found that all her pains were to no purpose. No unkind words were said, but those she spoke to pretended not to hear, as when a person known to be otherwise sensible enough makes some unreasonable assertion.

"Oh, they're over good and holy for this earth," said Mor Elversson bitterly, when she came home. "Full to the brim with faith and righteousness, till there's no room for a drop of mercy in them."

Joel himself met with no better success.

Of late, when people came to ask his help in this or that, he had taken to hinting that he was getting too old for the work, and that his son Sven ought soon to take over in his father's stead. But the suggestion passed unheeded everywhere. Fisher or farmer, whoever it might be, all were as deaf on that one subject as the sternly righteous housewives of Knapefiord.

On Christmas Eve, Joel and his wife and their son sat in the little dwelling at Grimön, talking of the future.

"Look here, Mother," said Sven, who seemed in particularly good humour this evening, "don't you think this kitchen place is dark and uncomfortable? What do you say to moving into the house itself?"

"Heavens!" cried his mother. "What's the boy thinking of! Why, there's neither roof nor floor to the place."

"That's no worse than can be mended," answered Sven. "I've been looking at the walls; they're sound enough. There's fine big rooms there, with plenty of light, and looking out over the sea. It's a shame to let the old captains' house go to rack and ruin."

Both father and mother agreed in this. But there was the question of money.

Sven explained that he had money of his own—not from his foster-parents, but money he had fairly earned. Before starting out on the expedition he had been promised a thousand pounds to be paid on his return. And this he had now received.

But Joel, for all that he had felt no qualms himself, suddenly saw how the old sea-captains who had lived there before would turn in their graves.

"Not with that money!" he cried. "I'd be glad to see the old house set to rights—but not with that money—no!"

Mother and son looked up at him in surprise. But both of them realized in a moment what was in his mind, and no more was said.

Joel sat thinking of the old sea-captains with their weather-beaten faces, their tarry fists and thirsty throats, good-natured, cheery men, not over-careful of their speech, nor dainty in their choice of company. His fathers, no doubt, had been of the same breed—and now he had told his son he was not good enough to live in the house that had been theirs. Told him that the money he had earned at the risk of his life on those same waters where they had voyaged and won their own was not good enough to be spent in mending their home.

There was a strange smile on Sven Elversson's face that evening—a gentle, patient, and forgiving smile. It had been there many a time before, when he had felt how his fellow men shunned him. But now, now that his father had shown a trace of the same feeling as all others had toward him, the smile of resignation seemed to settle on his face as if for good.

When Joel saw that look in his son's face, and marked how it stayed, and did not pass, he rose to his feet, and tried with kindly words to make amends. The boy answered with kindly words in return, but the look on his face remained.

Joel was angry with himself for having reopened the old wound. He understood that the lad had been keeping the news of the money a secret, in order to bring it out that very evening. And the sense of shame grew on him, till he felt unable to stay in the room, and took his hat and went out into the dark. Perhaps in his absence the boy's mother could tell him what were his father's real feeling toward him.

Hardly had Joel gone out, however, when a party of seven wild, drunken fellows came storming into the kitchen. They wanted Sven—Sven Elversson—to come out with them and be merry. They had taken a boat across on purpose to fetch him.

Mor Elversson looked at the men, and saw they were a crew of fishermen numbering some of the worst an wildest men on that part of the coast. And behind the rest, as if trying to remain unperceived, was one of her own sons, Ung-Joel, who was working in a store at Knapefiord.

And, turning from the drunken men with their unsteady gestures and foolish laughter, she looked at the boy, her son, whom they had come to plague and torture. A slender lad, finely built, with soft, gentle eyes and clean white hands. Neatly dressed he was, too, andshaved and orderly. He did not drink or smoke or spit about the place, and never a rough word passed his lips.

The others, who had come to make a jest of one in trouble, knew well enough that he had had a better upbringing than themselves, that he had led a richer life, and had a better understanding. They came because they hated him, because they looked on him as a worm to be trodden underfoot, a despicable creature that should not be let live in any Christian house.

As the strangers entered, a feeling of helplessness came over Sven. Not an ordinary faintness or loss of consciousness: it was simply that he felt unable to move. It seemed as if something were telling him plainly that this must be the end of his life. These men were come to torture him to death. And it was useless to resist. After all, life, as it was for him, now was hardly worth any great effort to preserve.

One of the men had found a dead snake by the roadside earlier in the day. He had taken it home and shown it to his comrades.

"Looks tempting," one of them had said.

"Yes. Anybody like to eat it?"

"Take it over to Grimön and ask Sven Elversson if he'd like it. He eats all sorts of things."

"Ay, just the thing for him."

And thus it was they had hit on the idea of coming to Grimön. They had a vague feeling that a man so vile as this Sven Elversson ought not to be left to enjoy his Christmas in peace; surely that was the very time he should be punished, and without mercy.

They had brought his brother with them to show them the way in the dark; the boy had agreed without any great reluctance. He was by no means as drunk as the others, but his feelings toward Sven were much the same as theirs. He was constantly being sneered at on account of the relationship, and many an ugly word was flung at him for his brother's misdeed. And he asked himself, what right had Sven to come home in this way and make trouble for them all? He stood now behind the broad backs of the rest, chuckling already at what was to come.

"Joel, Ung-Joel," cried his mother at sight of him. "What's all this? What do they want with Sven?"

The boy was used to answering without hesitation when that voice questioned him. And he spoke out now:

"They want him to eat a snake."

Sven Elversson felt even more powerless than before. He could see the whole scene; these men commanding him to eat, and he would refuse. Then they would set on him, with blows and kicks. And still he would say no. There was no power on earth now that could compel him to such a ghastly act—they might torture him to death.

But there was still a little respite left before he would be forced to go with them.

The fellow who had found the snake that morning drew out the long smooth thing from his pocket, and, rocking unsteadily, held it out before the mother's face.

"A rare little feast it'll be for him," he said.

"You call yourselves men?" cried the woman. "And you think I'll let him go with you, that's better than all of you together?"

The men burst out into a shout of laughter.

"He won't have to go farther than down to the shore," said the man who had just spoken. "We'll make a fire and cook it for him there."

Sven Elversson felt his strength returning. "It will soon be time," he said to himself. "By to-night it will be all over. And better so."

His mother glanced toward him, and marked how he sat still, with the same sad, forgiving smile on his lips. No trace of anger or sign of resistance showed in his face; only a gentle, submissive sadness.

"Sven, you're never thinking of going with them?" cried his mother. "D'you know who he is, that man there? Olaus from Fårön, that helped to kill his new-born child—and left the woman to bear it all when she'd most need of him."

The men roared with laughter.

"Don't be afraid, Mor Thala," said Olaus. "We'll look after Sven all right. We'll salt and pepper it for him and make it nice. A snake's nothing to him after what he's been used to."

"Look there!" cried the mother again, pointing to the biggest and wildest-looking of the men. "That's Corfitzson from Fiskebäck. He's done a power of evil in his day—and 'twas him that set fire to a shed full of cattle, to get the insurance money."

"Never mind her talk, boy, you come along with us," said Corfitzson, laying a hand on Sven's shoulder.

But Mor Thala went on without a stop.

"And there's Bertil from Strömsundet. If you'd know the worst of him, he's only starved his grandmother to death. She lived just two months after he came into the house. And him there in the corner—that's Torsson from Iggenäs, that never sold a fish but what he stole from others' nets, and those two there that can hardly stand for the drink in them, that's Rasmussen and Hjelmfeldt. They drink up all their earnings and leave their wives and bairns to starve."

Her voice had risen almost to a shriek; she was quivering with rage and terror. Even the men shrank back a moment before her fury, and forgot to laugh.

"And that one there, behind all the rest," she went on, bitterly. "Can you see who that is? Your own brother, Ung-Joel, it is. He's done no more harm as yet than leaving his father and mother to perish for lack of a helping hand. The times I've begged and prayed of him to come out here and help us, but he'd never hear. There, lad, that's the men that have come to bid you go with them—but you won't; you can't. . . ."

But as she spoke, Sven rose to his feet, gentle and forgiving as ever, ready to submit and suffer.

The men lauged again.

"That's right, my son," said Olaus, who was evidently the leader. "Just as well to come with a good grace. You'd have little chance against the lot of us."

But Mor Elversson was not the one to give up without doing all in her power. With a rapid movement she grasped the body of the snake that Olaus still held in his hand, wrested it from him, and flung it into the next room, placing herself before the door.

At that moment the outer door opened, and Joel came hurrying in.

"What's here?" he said, looking round. "What are you rioting here about? What do you want with Sven?"

Two of the men had sprung forward to force Mor Thala aside from the doorway; two of the others had gripped Sven by the shoulders and were thrusting him before them.

Without a moment's hesitation the old man flung himself upon them.

"Out with you! Leave the boy alone," he cried.

And suddenly Sven Elversson was himself again. Something within him was whispering: "Now, now is the time! Father and mother are fighting on your side."

"Ung-Joel," he cried to his brother, who was still keeping away behind the rest. "Open the door there, quick!"

The boy obeyed instinctively; it was as if he could not disregard an order given in that house. In a moment Sven had gripped Olaus by the middle, lifted him off his feet, and flung him out.

Corfitzson rushed forward to the rescue, but found himself gripped in turn by a pair of strong arms, lifted, and flung out after his leader.

Then it was that Ung-Joel stepped forward and stood by his brother's side. There was a moment of wild tumult, and the place was cleared.

Ung-Joel bolted the door behind his former comrades. Then, solemnly, he stepped up to his brother and offered his hand.

"How did you manage it?" he asked, after a pause, with frank admiration. "I'll get you to teach me that throw."

The elder brother's face was flushed with the fight; his look of patient resignation was gone.

"You've given them a lesson, you may be sure," went on the younger. "They'll know better than to trouble you again. But what made you take it so patiently all this time, when you're a match for the worst of them?"

Now for the first time Sven Elversson lost his self-control. Sinking down in a chair, he buried his face in his hands.

"What's the use?" he cried, desperately. "How can I defend myself when all the time I hate myself more than any of them can ever do? Hate and loathe myself worse than you can ever think. Horrible, horrible. No one knows as well as I do what it is I've done—what it is I've sinned against. Is it any comfort to me to stop the mouths of a drunken crowd when all the time I've that on my mind that's ghastlier than all?"

THE "NAIAD"

A FEW days after Christmas, Ung-Joel came back to Grimön with a message from Olaus, to ask if Sven would take a share in the herring fishery on board the motor-boat *Naiad*, belonging to his crew.

"He says it's hardly likely you could get taken on with any other crew," said Ung-Joel; "but seeing that you're my brother, I was to tell you. They'll not be the best of company, I doubt, that sail with Olaus."

Mor Elversson declared at once that it was out of the question; Sven should never have any dealings with any of them. But his father thought otherwise.

"It wouldn't be a bad thing, perhaps, if Sven tried to pick up the ways of the fishery on the coast here," he said. "And it's true enough he'd hardly get taken on with any other crew."

"Joel! How can you talk so!" cried his wife. "Who knows what they've been plotting and planning now, to send for him like that. Some new mischief, I'll be bound."

"Why, I only said 'twas a pity Sven shouldn't have a part in the fishery," said Joel, mildly.

But Sven remembered his father's words on Christmas Eve, and it came into his mind now that perhaps it was his wish to get him away from home.

"You can tell Olaus I'll come," he said to his brother.

"And thank him for offering. I'll go over to Farön myself as soon as I can."

"Why not come back with me now?" said Ung-Joel. "Then you can get the things you want at our store. There was a telegram in this morning that the herring are shoaling thick up at Smögen. By to-morrow they'll be getting away all about."

There was a hurry of preparation for a while, and then the two brothers set off, leaving Joel and Thala alone.

For a week or so they heard no news of Sven, then one Sunday Ung-Joel came out to visit them.

Mor Thala was eager to know how matters had gone with Sven and the crew—for all she knew, they might have killed him.

"I've heard nothing but what folk say," answered the boy. "And that's this. The crew of the *Naiad* before counted one man that had helped to kill a child, and one that had starved an old woman to death, one that had burnt down a place, and one that never sold but what he'd stolen, and two that were fast drinking themselves to death—and now they'd got another to help, and that a man who'd eaten human flesh, so it would be hard to find a rougher crowd on one keel. I've heard nothing from Sven himself, but, from all accounts, he seems to be getting on all right with them."

"That's foolishness," said his mother. But for all her angry looks, she was glad to learn that no ill had come to Sven. "But don't forget as soon as you've word from Sven to come here and let us know. 'Tis the best you can do for your father and me."

A fortnight later, Ung-Joel came out to the island again.

"Here's what they're saying now," he began. "That the *Naiad* men won't be able to stand much more of Sven. They say, here's the dirtiest, meanest, stinking little boat all along the coast getting gradually clean and workmanlike, the motor taken to working properly instead of going on strike when it's most needed, the rags of sails they used to help now and then been patched and put in order, the faded old flag done away with and a bright new one in its place and the name painted clean on the stern with all the letters in gold; the food on board getting that decent you wouldn't know but what you were on shore, and clean pots and pans in the galley. And the way folk look at it is this: the *Naiad* men, they might at a pinch take any sort of scoundrel on board, but clean pots and pans and all the rest, it's more than they can put up with."

"Ah! you're making fun of me," said his mother. But it was plain to see that she was glad at heart. "And don't forget," she went on, "as soon as you've any word from Sven, come out and let us know. He's done no wrong, and we must know how it is with him, that he doesn't come to any harm."

But folk that live at Grimön have need of all their patience, waiting for news. All through another two weeks Mor Thala waited, before Ung-Joel came with news of his brother.

"I haven't seen him myself yet," he explained. "But I've heard what they say, that it can't be long now before there's an end of it with Sven Elversson and the *Naiad* crew. It seems that Olaus—he's the skipper—has taken to seeing the men come on board to time, and more than once he's got his boat away with the rest of the fleet, instead of after, and got up in good time to the fishing grounds and made a fair haul. And what with the nets being sound and whole, instead of torn in parts and rotten the rest; when they bring up full catches, and the man at the windlass isn't dead drunk and tips the whole lot into the water alongside; when they're beginning to earn good money on the *Naiad*, why, it's plain that Olaus from Fårön and Corfitzson from Fiskebäck and Bertil from Strömsundet and Torsson from Iggenäs and Rasmussen and Helmfeldt won't stay long on board. They might bear with a man that's eaten human flesh, but to sail on a well-found ship and make good hauls like all the other crews, and earn good money—it's more than any of them have ever done before."

Mor Thala scolded him roundly for a fool that could never so much as speak one serious word, but she was pleased enough at the news he brought.

"You wait and see, it'll all be well yet," she said. "Eh, Joel, Joel—I wasn't meaning you, lad, but your father. He's surely the wisest man in all Bohuslän. He knew what he was doing when he let Sven go and take a share in that boat, he did."

A week or so later, Ung-Joel came in with a new report.

"I've not seen Sven myself," he said, "for the herring are keeping away up to the north this year. But I've heard what folk say. That when Olaus from Fårön goes spending money he's earned on doing up his house on shore, and Corfitzson from Fiskebäck puts his in the bank, as soon as it's paid him, and Bertil gets his wife a new dress, and Torsson buys a new boat, and Rasmussen and Hjelmfeldt start bringing home food for their wives and little ones—why, there must be something wrong with the *Naiad* lot somewhere. They might take a man-eater with them on board and nothing surprising in that, but to see them now with a clean ship and decently at work and living almost like honest folk, it's more than any 'd believe."

"I never heard your like for talking wicked nonsense," said Mor Thala, but she was happier than she cared to show. And she declared that all would go well with Sven in the end; folk would come to look at him differently before long.

"The trouble is," said Joel, "that folk have always looked on that one thing one way, and it's hard for any to see differently. And it won't be easy for him to win them. We must be thankful if we can but see that it's not too much for the lad himself."

A week or so later, the two brothers came sailing home to Gramön together. They looked ill at ease as they entered the house.

Neither mother nor father ventured to question Sven, but Mor Thala soon managed to get Ung-Joel by himself.

"Now what's happened?" she asked.

"Ay, what's happened," said Ung-Joel, bitterly. "Little use that Olaus and Corfitzson and all the rest of them have turned better than they've ever been

before, and can boast of a clean ship and a good season
and a fine price for their fish, and the money well looked
after, when they can't set foot in their own house but
they're met by crying womenfolk. What's a man to do,
when his own wife comes and begs and prays him and
says better go on in the old way, bad as it was, than
work and share with one that's done dreadful things
like Sven. Says a man can't go near one that's done
things like that without getting such himself that none
can bear the sight of him after. Houses put to rights
and boats and dresses and food and decency and
comfort—they'd give it all and gladly, to be free of the
one ugly thought. When things turn that way, what
can a man do but go to Sven himself and beg of him
to take off his hand from off the ship and crew, and say
he'd better go back to Grimön and stay there, where
there's none that's likely to meet him and be the worse
for it."

THE SCHOOLHOUSE

THAT spring, soon after Sven had come back from the herring fishery, old Joel Elversson was asked by the Priest at Applum if he would care to undertake the building of the new schoolhouse.

Joel had done a good deal of building work before in the parish, and so cheaply that he had made but little for himself. And this was perhaps the reason why he was chosen now, though many might well have thought him too old for the work.

As soon as Mor Thala heard of the proposal, she at once declared that Joel was no longer able to undertake work of such responsibility, and her husband did not altogether oppose her view. But he pointed out that it would be hard if the parish were forced to get in a stranger for the work. And he himself would gladly have had some share in building a new school for the children, who had for long had to put up with the old and dark and draughty building that served at present.

"You should see the plans," he said to Mor Thala. "The things they hit on nowadays to make all fine and easy. They'd no such contrivances in my young days."

"You're set on that building work yourself, that's plain to see," said his wife. "It's my belief you've promised to take it on already."

The old man looked embarrassed.

"I'd not have done it if it wasn't that I'd a grown son in the house," he said.

"But surely you should have asked him first," said his wife. So much foresight and sharpness on the part of her husband was a surprise to her. Sven had been going about for some days looking moody and depressed; it seemed impossible to get him to undertake any work at all.

"I don't think Sven would regret it if he did take to building work," said Joel. "A man that's to live in his own house ought to know a bit about timber and foundations and the like. But if he won't help me, I'll have to say I can't do it after all."

It was a strange thing to her that her husband should ever think of getting Sven to work on a building connected with the Church, in a place where the general ill-will against him seemed stronger than anywhere else.

Sven was present when they talked it over, but said nothing at first. He knew well enough what was in his father's mind; it was his one idea and aim to get him to move about among folk. As to the failure of the *Naiad* cruise, Joel had merely said it had turned out far better than could be expected, and he had nothing but praise for his son. Sven himself had still but one desire, to hide himself away at home, but he felt now that his father would not permit him, until he had seen once more how impossible it was for his fellow men to forget the feeling of abhorrence with which they regarded him.

"I don't think Father ought to give it up now," he said. "I'll lend a hand gladly as far as I'm able."

Joel was highly pleased at this, and that very day he took Sven with him to make a round of visits to the others concerned: merchants, carpenters, masons, and workmen.

Almost against his will, Sven Elversson soon found himself keenly interested in the building, and his father let him take the lead. He was allowed to superintend the work, and to determine how it should be done. Grimön lies some distance from the mainland, and Sven did not care to waste so much time in journeys backward and forward, but lived close to the site while the work was in progress. Joel himself also began to tire of the everlasting trips from the island in to Applum, and for several weeks he stayed at home, leaving his son to take entire charge.

Whenever he went in to see how things were going, he invariably returned well pleased. His wife asked anxiously each time if there had been no expression of dissatisfaction among the Applum folk at Sven's taking over charge, but Joel was always able to reassure her.

"I met Israel Jonsson yesterday," he said, "the head of the council, and I asked him what he thought of the new schoolhouse. 'Well, Joel,' he said, 'I won't deny that we Applum folk were in two minds at first about getting your boy take over the work. But I think I can say now that both the school council and the parish council and all the rest would think twice about giving it elsewhere. When we see how he puts in granite under blocks instead of common stone, as it was thought, and find him building the walls of heavy timber, instead of thin planks that the architect thought would do, why, if there's any that bear him ill-will, they'd better put it in their pockets and do the sensible thing.'"

Mor Elversson began to understand now that Joel had accepted the contract solely and entirely in order to give Sven a chance of proving his worth and making friends. It was a kindly thought, she was forced to admit, but she was less confident now, and dared not believe it would succeed.

Next time Joel came back from the building site, her first question was whether Sven was still getting on, and if he had had no trouble with any of the people there.

"I'll not tell you what I think myself," answered Joel, "for you might not believe me. But I'll tell you word for word what Gunnar Markusson, that lives close by, said to me yesterday when I met him on the round:

"'I'll admit, Joel,' he says, 'that we were a bit uneasy in the parish about letting Sven Elversson take charge and build the new schoolhouse. But I will say now that, to my mind, the ratepayers would do well not to let their feelings run away with them, when it's a case of a public benefactor like Sven. He's putting in smoothed boards now, where we'd agreed we'd have to be content with unplaned wood. And he's using better paint than we'd reckoned on. He's roofing with tiles, instead of the tarred felt that was all we thought we could run to. And instead of cement steps at the entrance, he's making stone. It's this way with that boy of yours, that he'll have nothing but first-class work. and for all that it seems he's asking no more for the building than if he'd followed the plans from the first.'"

Mor Thala was overjoyed to hear that her boy was doing so well, but she felt nevertheless that the dreadful thing which haunted him was not to be so easily overcome.

Joel did not go over to the mainland again until September. He was away for several days, and when he returned, he brought Sven with him, and the news that the place was finished. The schoolhouse was built, and the inspection had taken place; the inspector could hardly find words to say how pleased he was with the result.

Mor Thala agreed that so far all was well. And, looking at her son, she felt that he looked like one released from prison; she understood that he felt he had regained some little of the honour and respect he had lost.

And she was loth to spoil his pleasure, but as soon as she was alone with Joel, she asked if there really had been no one in all Applum who had made Sven feel he was not good enough for the work.

"There's none can say what folk think in their own minds," said Joel; "but I'll just tell you what the schoolmaster himself said to me yesterday, when I spoke to him after the opening.

"'There's no trusting to folk's gratitude,' he said, 'but if I was one of those whose children are to get their schooling in this new place, I'd show no unkindness to the man that built it. When you look at the hall there, the way he's chosen the best colours, and the neat and sound benches he's put up, the fine glass in the windows, well, it's a wonder how he could do it. And then all the fixtures in the *slöid* room, and the kitchen, and heating pipes, and gymnasium fittings and all—it's plain 'twas a lover of children that settled it all. There's many might well wish to be children again just to go to school in the place Sven Elversson's built.'"

Mor Thala could not but be pleased at this, and was glad now to feel that all her anxiety had been unfounded.

THE STONEHILLS

SVEN ELVERSSON had been in to Göteborg to settle some accounts for building materials supplied for the schoolhouse, and came back by train. On arrival at the station nearest Applum, he found that the conveyance which was to have met him there had not come.

It was over ten miles to walk, and he stood in the station puzzling how he was to get back, when a small carriage with two horses drove up and stopped. It was from the inn at Applum, and, on inquiry, Sven learned that it had been ordered by the Priest, who had just married a clergyman's daughter from a distance, far away in Norrland.

Sven Elversson had likewise ordered a carriage from the inn, but it was now clear that his message had gone astray; no carriage had been sent for him. The driver suggested that he should ask the Priest to let him ride on the box, but Sven did not wish to push himself forward, and would not hear of it.

They were still discussing the question, when the Priest and his young wife came out from the station.

They made a handsome pair. The Priest, just over thirty, was a man of middle height, powerfully built, and with a splendid head. He wore a full beard, dark and curling; had a broad, handsome forehead, well-cut features, and fresh complexion, with white teeth. Altogether, he seemed all that a young girl could wish for; a man to cherish and protect her, work for her, and give her a good place in the world. The young wife, too, was surprisingly beautiful. Sven Elversson was reminded of the type so favoured by some English painters: handsome women with tall, slender figure and sloping shoulders, slightly bowed head, rich hair prettily shading the face, straight eyebrows and delicate cheeks, and with a look in the brilliant eyes that seemed looking out of a strange world toward heaven.

It struck him as curious that, as he watched the pair, the Priest seemed gradually to lose all that Sven had formerly found attractive in him. The fine, unspeakably delicate lines and colouring of the woman seemed to render the man coarse and mean, almost ugly, by comparison. And Sven hoped that he was not influenced by ill-feeling toward the Priest from the time of that scene in the church, in feeling now that this was but a poor husband for the slight, dainty creature at his side.

Sven Elversson moved quickly away as the two came up, but he heard the driver asking on his own account if he might take Sven with him on the box, whereupon the Priest came forward and invited him to drive with them.

The Priest had, indeed, always treated him with kindness, and now, as Sven Elversson sat on the box and the carriage drove off, he tried to efface the impression of a moment ago. "I was mistaken, as I often am," he said to himself. "I should say that I have not seen for years a pair so completely suited as these two. And well they may be. Here is the husband sitting and thinking how different life will be now in the little vicarage at Applum, with a young mistress to fill the place with life and gaiety—while she on her part is dreaming of all she will do to make the home so comfortable that he will never wish to leave it, and always be longing for it when he is away."

So completely had Sven surrendered himself to this view, that he was astonished when a little later the young wife exclaimed, in a tone of weariness, even impatience:

"Oh, will they never end?"

"What is it she wants to end?" thought Sven to himself. "What can it be that could trouble her this day of all days?"

Sven Elversson looked round on all sides. And suddenly he understood. It must be the stonehills.

It was indeed a strange-looking landscape they were driving through.

Mountain country one could not call it, for there were neither peaks nor mountain ridges; on the other hand, it was not a level plain, for the ground was broken everywhere by hillocks of rock, large and small. In places, they were so close together as hardly to leave a passage between; then they would lie farther apart, with broad open spaces large enough for homestead and field. Right and left, behind and before, the same —truly a stranger might well ask if they would never end. The road wound in and out between them, and never the crest of a hill so high that they could see across them, to what lay beyond. All along the way were stonehills, and ever more behind. Some were sparsely clad with a poor growth of grass, others were bare, and others again showed patches of bush and heather; save for this, they were all alike.

Now and again, an open space between led one to hope that the ground might be clear beyond, but one had scarcely time to frame the thought before a new hillock thrust itself into view.

"It must be different in Norrland, of course," thought Sven. "And these stonehills of ours are dark and forbidding enough, it is true. A pity they should be the first this little lady sees of Bohuslän."

And next moment he heard her telling her husband that she felt as hopelessly lost among these stony hills as in the darkest forest.

In one place a flock of sheep could be seen grazing, then a couple of cows, or again some children picking berries. And the young wife declared that it was well they were there, for had it not been for the sight of children and homely animals, she would hardly have believed they were in a Christian country.

"Sigrun, how can you say such a thing!" exclaimed her husband. "This is Bohuslän, my own country, and I love every stone and every tuft of heather in it. What would you have said if I had spoken so about the pine forests and the moors of Norrland?"

As was but natural, his words took effect. The young wife was silent at first for a while; then she whispered something, with tears in her voice, and Sven understood that she was begging her husband's forgiveness for having spoken so about his country.

"I'm not like that other days, really. I don't know what can be the matter with me to-day," she said.

Every word she uttered was a delight to hear; so solemnly and sincerely she spoke, with the slightest trace of a lisp in her voice. "God forbid she should be otherwise for my part," thought Sven. "Surely 'tis only beautiful that she should be afraid of all ugly things."

Nothing more was said for a time, but then the little lady began again, with a strange quiver in her voice:

"Edward, I know it's wrong of me to trouble you, but I can't help it. I am so afraid. I've been trying to overcome it by myself, but I can't—it won't go away. And then I just remembered that I shan't need to struggle against things all alone now—that I've you to help me with all my weakness."

There was such a depth of entreaty in her tone that Sven Elversson felt embarrassed at sitting there where he could hear. He felt himself unworthy even to over-hear the thoughts and feelings of this delicate lady.

She was trying now to explain to her husband that she was actually afraid. She fancied she had seen these hills somewhere before—had fled for her life among such a confusion of rocky hills, with some behind that sought to kill her. Or that there was someone even now lying in wait there, ready to fall upon them. Something terrible there must be, close at hand. She had but one desire, to get away from the place.

Her voice told that she was in greater fear even than she would admit, and that this was deadly earnest. Sven Elversson himself could not help smiling where he sat, and the Priest was utterly unable to understand her fear of nothing at all; he tried to answer gaily, and pass it over with a jest.

But his endeavours failed of their effect. She declared, with sudden violence, that if Applum were as cold and shut in as here, she could never live there.

"And it's wicked and wrong of me to say so, I know," she said; "but I've been thinking of it all the time, while we've been driving here; if I cannot find something beautiful at the end of it, something to help me, I shall be haunted by the same fear there as well. I shall be dreading every day that something terrible will happen."

Sven Elversson thought of the plain at Applum, with the vicarage behind the church, set in a little hollow to be sheltered from the wind. And he wondered if she would find any comfort in the evenly divided fields, the dark wall of hills all round, the narrow view, the homesteads painted blue and white and red, and the treeless meadowland.

"'Tis none so easy for him just now," thought Sven. "I'd find it hard myself to comfort her in his place. But he knows her, and loves her—it makes all the difference."

The Priest must have been thinking of the same thing. He sat for a while without speaking.

"'Let me tell you of a dream I had last winter," he said at last. "It made me very happy at the time, that dream, and perhaps it may help you too.

"I dreamed that I was driving along the road to your home at Stenbroträsk, and it was toward the end of winter, bare earth and leafless trees, and the road a sodden stretch of mire. The bridges were out of repair, and the horse was a wretched beast that could hardly move at all.

"There was a keen, cold wind from the north, and everything was gray and dismal, and the few houses here and there along the way looked poor and miserable; the whole country seemed inhospitable and depressing.

"Then at last, coming up over the hill, I caught sight of the steep river-bank, and the church and the house at Stenbroträsk, and in a moment all was changed. The air seemed warmer, the fields were green, the birches wore a veil of leaf, the road was firm and good—everything was kindly and smiling as if in welcome; even the horse came suddenly to life and trotted on bravely.

"But the strange thing about it all was that I felt the spring and the warmth came from myself. They had not been there before, but now, as if by magic, they came—and all because of the warmth that filled my heart at sight of your home. And there seemed nothing strange about it all in my dream—it was all natural and as it should be."

Here the Priest paused, and his wife, in a changed voice, asked what happened after.

"There was no more," he answered. "For the warmth at my heart was so good to feel that I woke." And, having said this, he was silent again.

But those few words of love, the little glimpse of something beautiful, had filled the young wife's heart with joy, and the listener in front heard her whisper to her husband in a voice almost stifled with emotion:

"You mean that if I had but the same warmth in my heart as you, I should find beauty in this country of **yours,** and in your home—even in these dreadful hills."

And then gladly and confidently she went on:

"Do not be afraid for me. There is nothing to frighten me now. I feel now as you felt in your dream."

"There," thought Sven to himself. "See how little one can judge things at first sight. Truly she could not have found a better husband than Pastor Rhånge. He has a good heart and a good head. Who else could have answered her so well?"

THE SEA

THE newly married pair had come home on a Tuesday. On Saturday in the same week, Sven Elversson went up to the vicarage with some papers about the school. He walked straight up the front steps and through the hall into the office, and stopped just inside the door.

It was the Pastor's day for business, he knew, and though it was rather late, he had never thought but that he would find the Priest sitting at his writing-table. But he was not there—was not in the room at all. He could not be far away, however, for the big books that were always used on business days lay open on the table, and a pen was in the inkstand.

It was not Sven's way to push himself forward, and he did not care to go through to the kitchen and ask if the Pastor was at home, or look for him in any of the other rooms. There could be no harm, he thought, in staying where he was, to wait a little.

But as he stood, there was a sound of voices in the next room; the door was ajar, and he could hear every word distinctly.

"Sigrun"— it was the Pastor speaking, in an easy tone—"the post ought to have been here by now. But I can't go down for it myself to-day, in case any one comes."

"Why, then," answered his wife cheerfully, "that's easily managed. Malin will be going down to the store directly, and she can bring back your paper at the same time."

Evidently the Pastor had only gone out for a moment to ask about the post, thought Sven. He would be back now, since that was settled.

But the Pastor spoke again.

"Well," he said, "don't you think now you might go yourself? Wouldn't you like a little walk? It's lovely out just now, and the road has dried after the rain of yesterday. It would do you good to get out in the air a little."

He spoke gently and kindly, as if thinking only for her good. And the young wife answered as kindly again.

"I'd go and gladly," she said, "but look at these curtains strewn all about the room. I can't go till I've got them up."

There was no more to be said after that, thought Sven. But he noticed at the same time how the Priest's voice, manly and strong in itself, seemed to lose its pleasant tone, and become rough and coarse, when heard beside his wife's soft, gentle speech.

And it seemed that the matter was not ended yet, after all, as he had hoped. The Priest began again.

"Oh, of course, one couldn't expect a great lady like yourself to go and fetch a paper for her husband," he said. This must be meant in jest, surely. But it sounded at the same as if he were annoyed at her refusing to do as he wished.

"Oh, Edward, you know it's not that."

"Or perhaps Applum's too dull and ugly a place for you to care to go out at all. Her ladyship doesn't care to take the air unless there are fine houses and big estates all round. Perhaps I had better order the carriage, so that——"

"Edward!" she cried.

"Oh, I know there's nothing here to compare with your own place," he went on, with a little ill-tempered laugh. "But I didn't think you were too proud to set foot to the ground in Applum, for all that."

"Edward, it isn't that at all. I can't go just now."

"You *can't* go?" asked her husband, with an air of profound astonishment.

All this had passed before Sven had time to think. "I ought not to hear," he said to himself. And to make his presence known, he rattled the handle of the door, opened the door itself and closed it again, stamped his feet and coughed. But no one seemed to notice, and the two in the next room went on again.

"No, I can't," repeated the young wife. "There is something in this place that stifles me; I can't breathe. It isn't just longing for home, but something more. I am well and happy enough as long as I keep to the house, but as soon as I go out it comes over me again."

She spoke passionately, flinging out her words in broken snatches.

"But, Sigrun," said the Priest, "what is the matter with you? I meant no harm."

"I'm not so proud, indeed I'm not," she cried. "Ask any of those at home, and they'll tell you it was

never my way to be so. And it's not because the place
is not pretty to look at that I can't bear to go out. No,
it is something else—if only I knew what it was!"

"Look here, Sigrun," said her husband, "you must
tell me what all this means. We must talk this over
seriously, that's clear.

Sven Elversson was at a loss to know what to do. He
had already heard too much, perhaps; it would make
matters worse to let them know he had been there. He
walked to the door, but turned back again. He was
always in doubt now as to how to act. It would be
hard to find a man so undecided and lacking in self-
confidence.

"I didn't want to tell you about it," said the young
wife, speaking breathlessly and impatiently as before,
"for I know it's nothing really. Only something that
comes over me as soon as I go outside the house. Not
anything I can see or hear, but something that makes
me feel miserable and sorry for myself. It is cruel to
think that I must go about here always, and never get
away; I feel as if I had been condemned for some crime.
It is just that—to feel myself condemned to stay for
ever in one place, the same little, narrow, monotonous,
cheerless place."

"Now I know," thought Sven to himself, "she is only
saying this so that he shall say something beautiful in
return, as he did before. And the Priest's a man with
the heart and head to set her right again—'twill be easy
enough for him."

"Oh, if only one could look out and see far away—if
only I were not buried here, in a hole, and had not that

wall of hills all round. But it must be a punishment for something I have done, or I should not have come here. Oh, can't you say something to help me?"

Now it must come, thought Sven. Now surely he would say some beautiful thing. And it would be fine to see how he would help her again this time.

Truth to tell, Sven Elversson was perhaps not sorry to be standing where he could hear all this. The young wife's voice was very sweet. And he was sure the Priest would say something wonderful now; something inspiring and good to hear.

"I have tried again and again," she went on, "to go out. But I can't. You can't think what it is like. I feel as if I were choking; I feel it here in my throat. And I've cried—— "

"But there is nothing," said the Pastor. "Surely, Sigrun, you must know that. There is nothing in the air here that we cannot see. It is all imagination."

"There *is!* There is something here—I can feel it. Something that hates me, and is trying to take away my happiness. Do you know what I have been doing lately? I go and look at that poor little picture of Stenbroträsk, that one of my cousins did for me—I laughed at it then. But now, when I have looked at it a little, the river and the house and the big rowan trees by the gate, it seems to give me courage enough to go on living."

"I am afraid, my dear, you are giving way to a foolish fancy," said her husband. And the listener marked how he slipped into the admonitory tone of the preacher. "You must really try to overcome it before it has gone too far. And I think, really, I must ask you now to go and do as I said—go down to the post at once."

"But I can't!" she cried. "I can't—I can't!"

Sven Elversson knew, of course, that the Pastor was honestly acting for the best. But—he had thought he would have found some other way. Still, perhaps after all this was best. He himself would hardly have known what to do.

"Listen to me, Sigrun," said the Priest. "You must surely understand that it is childish to give way to such ideas. The only thing to do is to overcome it. You are well and strong; you will not tell me that you cannot walk that little way. Anyhow, I must ask it of you, for the sake of our happiness—if you wish it to last for life, and not for a few weeks' honeymoon only."

"I will go another time," she said, humbly, despairingly. "But—won't you let me off for to-day? I will try in a day or two; I will try to-morrow."

Sven Elversson stood listening yet a moment, anxious to hear if the request would be granted. But when the Pastor repeated that he must have his paper now, at once, Sven saw in a flash what he should have done before, but in his confusion had not thought of. Very quietly he opened the door and slipped out. He walked slowly until out of sight of the vicarage, and then set off at a run down to the post.

And so, when the young wife came walking slowly, so slowly, down the road, with tears on her eyelashes after what had passed, and trembling, half-unconscious, as if she had risen from a sick-bed, she had not to go many steps before a young man stepped up to meet her.

He greeted her politely, and said something about having driven with them from the station a few days back.

She made no answer, only stared at him, without understanding at first what he meant. He endeavoured to explain that he had been to the store; she fancied afterward he must have been going to say something about the storekeeper having asked him to take the paper up with him to the vicarage. He spoke softly, and with so much hesitation that she would have found it hard to understand him even had she been herself at the time.

He handed her a newspaper, which she took, but still she walked on, as if unable to realize that here was the thing she had been sent to fetch; that she could go back home now as soon as she pleased.

Then the young man came up to her again, saying something about going another way, if she wished to go for a walk. He begged her humbly to excuse him for the liberty, but seeing she was a stranger to the place, and a fine evening, if she would not rather go down and look at the sea.

In the midst of all her fear and trouble of mind, with the same stifling feeling at her throat, she caught a word of the sea, and stopped, and looked at him.

"The sea? Is there any sea near here?" she asked.

"Indeed there is," he answered. And if she were not above letting him show her the way, it would not take long to get there.

He turned off along a little path running straight toward the west, and she followed. She noted that he was dressed as a workman of the better class, and had a kindly, honest face, though his manner was strangely humble. She felt no hesitation about going with him now.

It was a beautiful evening, with a curious reddish light that seemed to float down from the sky. It was as if the air about her took colour, and became visible. She felt as if it were filled with tiny, delicate rose-leaves, that came falling softly down, like snowflakes, making the plain all round blush faintly, like a bride.

And when they came out toward the western hills, she saw that they did not make one continuous barrier, as she had thought. The wall consisted of huge masses of rock, but with passes leading through in many places.

The young workman led her out between the rocks, and on the farther side there was white sand on the ground, with here and there a shell. Then, after turning a corner of the cliffs, she stopped and drew a deep breath.

Before her was a broad, open expanse. All the rich red sea of air, and all the wide sea of water spreading out and away, with nothing to shut it in. Open, free, as far as the sun itself, that was sinking toward the western verge.

There was no land to be seen out there save a narrow strip of sand with a long stone mole, and, farther out, a few black reefs rising from the pearly water.

And at sight of all this, she felt in a moment that she was saved. For where could she choose to be rather than here, in a place with so much beauty, so near at hand—so much beauty that she could see every day.

How could it be that no one had ever told her of this? She sat down on a stone and rested there a long while, drinking in the light with her eyes. Her eyes wandered over the wide expanse, looking as far as they pleased, like birds released from a close cage.

And she thanked God for her home, and for the sea, so great and strong and clean, so near her.

She must have sat there long without speaking. When she looked up, the young workman had gone.

Truth to tell, she was pleased at this. She could always thank him, another time. It was pleasanter now to be alone.

She felt stronger now, and more hopeful—better able to fight against the stifling sense of something threatening that hung over the plain.

Suddenly she remembered her husband—he might be anxious about her. And she rose to go home, to tell him that she was better now, and happier. And to thank him for his sternness in sending her out to face her trouble boldly.

SAILING

IT WAS a Sunday morning in late October. A heavy wind came sweeping up from the south, from lands where the air was yet warm, where roses still budded and bloomed, where the vines were newly stripped, and the juice of the grape foamed in the presses.

The heavy south wind spoke with a strange, disquieting sound. Listening to it, one felt confused, as if hearing a stranger speak in some foreign tongue. Who could say what it was trying to tell—whether some great secret, or merely a whisper of all the yellowing trees, the fallen wings of butterflies, the empty nests, it had passed on its way?

That Sunday, Sven Elversson had come over in the boat to land his father at the little harbour outside the barrier rocks of Applum; the old man had gone in to service at the church. But Sven did not go with him; as soon as his father had gone, he sought out a cleft in the rocks a little to the right. It was a place he knew well; he had lain there often on the green heather as a child.

This was the happiest time Sven Elversson had known since his return. The patient, sorrowful smile had begun to fade from his lips, and the bitter trouble that had filled his soul no longer tortured him as before.

And as he lay there on a ledge of rock, listening to

the wind, wondering what it was trying to tell him, and staring out over the sea, he called to mind a vision he had seen one day, when he had been lying just as now on a rocky slope by the shore, with a broad expanse of sea spread out before him. The bright glitter of the sunlight on the water had tired his eyes, and he had lain quite still for a long time. Then, suddenly opening his eyes and glancing down at the great water, he had seen a mermaid.

It was only the briefest glimpse; she was gone the moment his eyes fell on her, changed to a fleck of white mist that floated away over the water.

But he had seen her—and the thought filled him with a great joy; he felt himself favoured, honoured beyond others, and supremely happy at having been granted a sight of one of those lovely spirits of nature that fill the air and sea, yet hide themselves so jealously from the sight of men.

He was certain that a whole flock of mermaids had been playing there on the shore, but had vanished the moment he sought to open his eyes. All but that one, who had not been able to escape in time.

He had never forgotten it, and since then he had never sat alone by a quiet sea but he must close his eyes and lie very still for a time, that the mermaids might think he slept, and venture out from the deep. But never since that once had he gained a glimpse of any.

To-day he tried again, though with little hope. And when he felt he had been quiet long enough, and opened his eyes, he started almost in dismay. True, there was no mermaid, no figure half maiden, half a fish, to be seen amid the waves. But there, on a tall rock just at the water's edge, sat a woman. A young, slender creature, clad in white, and seated with easy poise on top of the rock—she seemed as if she might as well have come there from the sea as from the land.

But it was soon plain to see that the woman sitting there was no joyous fairy being. She dried her eyes again and again with a handkerchief—after all, no more than a poor human creature, that could suffer and shed tears.

Sven Elversson sat watching her, wondering what it could be that troubled her. Was it more ugly stonehills again, more prisoning barriers of rock, that made her fear so that she could not go to church, but must sit alone and weep beside the sea?

He saw how her slight figure shook with sobs; her whole attitude told him that it was no light burden that weighed her down. And he understood that she had come to seek for comfort from the sea, having no other to whom she could turn. And this time the sea had not helped her.

A moment later the woman turned at a slight sound behind her. A man was clambering down the slope; she recognized him, surely, as the young workman who had shown her the sea here some weeks ago. Hastily she dried her eyes and went toward him; she had not thanked him yet.

"I saw you sitting there," said he, "and I thought, if I might be so bold . . . I've my boat close by here, a good boat, though not much to look at. And if you'd honour me so far, I'd be very glad to take you for a sail."

Had it been any other day, she might not have accepted. But, just now, she felt so grateful for any little crumb of kindness that she could not refuse. And she did not wish that this young workman, who looked so modest and kind, should think she declined because he had only a common, workaday fishing-boat to offer her, and was himself but a common man in his working clothes. Though it was Sunday, Sven was wearing his heavy sea-boots and rough clothes, with a sou'wester that suited him well; it looked like the steel helmet of some old sea-king.

So they pushed off from land, and he hoisted the sail, and the heavy south wind filled it, sending the boat heeling to one side. Sven put the rudder hard over, heading due west, and the little vessel flew out across the bay toward the open sea.

Fru Rhånge had at first no thought of any pleasure to herself in going out for a sail to-day. She had not thought there was anything in the world that could make her forget the weight of sorrow that burdened her now. But when they had been sailing a little while, she could not help feeling easier; fresher in body and stronger in mind to bear her trouble.

The sky was clear, save for a few little flecks of white cloud. But there was yet enough moisture in the lower air to soften the light and tinge the dry, bare surface of rocks and reefs and islets with shades of grayish red and blue. They seemed, too, now to rise more boldly and strongly from the water, standing out with a certain majesty against the rest. The clefts seemed deep and black, the slopes steep and terrible and perilous; the distances seemed more marked, with ridge upon ridge in a succession of ever softer and more heavenly hues.

And after a little while there came into the young wife's eyes a look of quiet, earnest questioning, and she laid her folded hands in her lap as if in worship of all the beauty spread about her.

She was filled with a single thought—that she was learning to know one of God's miracles. She was learning to know the sea. She had never known before what it was to be so near the sea, to feel its breath in one's ears, to watch the play of expression in its face, to nestle close to its breast and be lulled to calm and peace.

Sven Elversson put the helm over, and they ran across to the north, in between the reefs, sailing close in under rugged cliffs, by little red fisher-huts set among ancient pear trees heavy with red-brown fruit, with glimpses of meadow between the rocks, greener, more brilliantly, livingly green than in the kindliest spring.

He led her from sound to sound, meeting white steamers, heavy, deep-laden barges, and lighter craft that glided over the water like huge sailing butterflies.

Sven Elversson himself looked at it all with something like amazement. Reef and islet, houses and meadows and trees—there was a greatness, a wealth of colour, a beauty over all to-day unlike other days. And he was glad that she had seen them thus, in their festal array.

They must have known, he thought to himself, how deeply this woman loved all that was beautiful.

And it was with Sven as with all the rest, the land and sea. He was seen at his best to-day.

They talked at first of the weather, and of all the beautiful things about them, and he taught her the names of all the rocks and islands as they passed. But after a while they came to speak of other things, of every possible thing, old things and new, as if they had been tried friends.

And he laid aside the barrier of humility and shyness, and spoke freely and naturally, until she wondered, and thought that young men born by the sea, and voyaging early abroad to other lands, must gain an education and experience beyond others who spent all their days on land.

She felt a real trust in him, for he was good and gentle and wise; she wished she knew him better, and had such a man to turn to when her own wits were at a loss.

As for Sven, he had not spoken with her long before there came over him an intense longing to tell her of his sin, to confess it all to this innocent creature who knew nothing of sin herself.

It crossed his mind that all those who had hitherto condemned and despised him were themselves well acquainted with sin and vice. All had no doubt at some time cheated, lied, stolen, borne false witness, been proud and merciless, idle, miserly, revengeful, or cruel.

But this young girl from a pious home had lived a quiet and protected life, untouched by 'passion or covetousness. She had as yet no knowledge of sinful nature, her own or others'. She had never cherished an evil thought, never wished harm to any soul.

He could not expect her to judge him over-leniently, for she was keenly sensitive, and could never control her abhorrence of all that was ugly and evil to her mind. But be that as it might, he would gladly submit to her judgment; she should be his court of appeal. He could not go to the King for justice, but he could go to her.

For some time, however, he refrained, shy and uncertain of himself. And while he sat hesitating, he noticed that she had grown silent again. She seemed to be trying to say something that was hard to begin.

At last, however, she made up her mind and came straight to the matter at once.

"You saw I was crying when you came up before?"

"Yes," he said. "I could not help seeing that."

"It wasn't anything very much," she said. "Only a letter that came. It was from a friend of mine, a rich man's daughter, just married, and her husband was such a good man, clever, and looked up to by everyone; we all thought she would be so happy."

"And now—you mean she is not?" Sven laid both hands on the tiller and leaned forward. He seemed keenly interested in all that concerned this friend of hers.

"No," she answered, looking out over the sea, as if seeking to avoid his glance. "She is not happy. She writes that her husband is always displeased with her somehow. And she can't understand it. She asked if I could tell her what it might be. But I can't. I would gladly help her, but I can't understand it myself. So you can understand I was sorry. That was why I couldn't help crying."

"Yes, I understand," Sven replied. "But your husband, lady. Pastor Rhånge is a man of great experience. Ought you not to ask him about it?"

Fru Rhånge coloured, and gave him a quick glance, almost of suspicion. But his eyes met hers frankly and openly, without a thought of anything to conceal, and she went on:

"I do not think she would like me to speak to my husband about it. It is always when they have been out anywhere and are driving home that he is—displeased with her. Hardly speaks to her at all. And whenever she tries to say anything, he only answers with an unkind word or a sneer."

"But are you sure there is not anything in her behaviour that could offend him? Anything wrong, I mean?"

"No," answered the young wife, eagerly. "That, I am certain, there is not. They are earnest-minded, both of them, and wherever they go, among friends, it is always quiet; no dancing or noisy games or anything like that. But she did think of that, too, that perhaps he found her too gay in her manner, and last time they were out she sat all the time with the old married women and talked sensibly. Only when the host came and wanted to show her the garden did she go out at all. And he was an elderly man, and they spoke of nothing but trees and flowers, and how there were not enough gardens round about. And she was so interested, and asked him if he did not think they could manage a little garden at her home. And he promised to send some of his own people over that autumn to mark out a garden for her, and then in the spring he would send her some things to plant in it. But then in the evening, driving home with her husband, she told him about it, and thought he would be pleased. But he gripped the whip so hard as he listened, she could see the knuckles grow white, and when the horse stumbled he was furious, and lashed it again and again. And he told her that their home would stay as it was, and as it had been, and he'd have no gardener people coming to alter this and that. And told her not to enter into any arrangements of that sort in future without first asking his permission. And she tells me now she was so frightened she could not say a word. Only folded her hands and prayed to God to show her what it all was, what it could mean."

The young wife spoke throughout very slowly, choosing her words with care, and Sven Elversson listened with growing interest. And he could not help thinking that the description of the old man who was so fond of gardens fitted in excellently with a landowner living a little way out of Applum, near the sea; he had a big place, and would naturally have invited the Pastor and his wife some time.

"She must be very pretty, I suppose—your friend," was all he said.

Again she cast a covert, searching glance at him.

"I daresay people would think her quite good-looking," she said, carelessly. "But what joy can it be to her, when her husband has so much to find fault with in all that she does? When it seems as if she were never to have her will in anything; and all that she cares to do is wrong? And never can learn what she may do and what not?"

Sven Elversson was getting the sail over ready to tack, and had not time to answer before she went on:

"Before, when she was at home, no one ever spoke unkindly to her for what she did. Everyone seemed pleased with her then. She was a good example to her little brothers and sisters, they said, and wondered how they would manage when she was gone. And whenever she thinks of that time she cannot help smiling at herself, for now that she has a home of her own, it seems she can do nothing right, and is scolded for all she says or does not say, whatever she does or does not do."

Sven Elversson was at a loss how to answer. "She is all alone," he thought, "and has no one to confide in; helpless and a stranger. And she needs someone to talk to; it helps her a little to talk of it this way."

And he said only that Fru Rhånge seemed to care very much for her friend.

"I wish I could help her," she said, and was very near to weeping again. "For I know she is good and kind, really. She loves to help and comfort old people, and the poor, when they are in trouble, but she must not do that now, and that is almost the worst thing of all. And she may not sit in the pew that belongs to her home in church, though she likes best to sit there, because it is just in the choir, and a little above the rest, so she can see out over the congregation."

Sven Elversson thought of the little pew in Applum church, set aside for the family of the incumbent; it stood a little higher than the others, and one had a view of the rest of the church from there. "But how can I tell her," he thought, "that her husband is jealous? It would only hurt her. Perhaps it will pass over. Better that she should not know."

He turned the vessel now, and made for home. It was as well that her husband should find her there when he came back from church.

And in his pain at not daring to help her—perhaps to turn her thoughts from her own trouble—he pointed to a rocky island far to the west.

"That is Grimön," he said. "That is where the fellow they call Sven Elversson lives. You've heard of him, maybe?"

She nodded. "Yes, I have heard about that—the whole story."

She seemed inclined to let the matter end there, but suddenly she added a few words that made an end of the little happiness Sven had felt that morning.

"You've heard, of course, that the schoolhouse he built over by the church was burnt down last night?"

"Burnt down!" he cried. And in consternation he loosed his hold of the tiller, so that the sail was flung over and the boat nearly capsized.

"Yes," said Fru Rhånge, with perfect calmness, "burnt down to the ground. And a good thing, too!"

Sven brought the boat round again. "Why do you say that?" he asked between clenched teeth. "Why is it a good thing the place was burnt? I have heard that the folk in Applum were pleased enough with the build-ing."

"I have heard so, too," she said.   "But what was the good of that when the children would not go there?"

"Children would not go there?" he repeated, help-lessly.   "I have not been over to the mainland since it started—I knew nothing of that."

Fru Rhånge could see he was astonished at her saying it was well the place was burnt, and she went on eagerly to explain.   From the very first, the children had taken a dislike to the new school.   They had heard it was built by a man who had eaten human flesh, and they feared they would lose all chance of salvation if they sat at their lessons in a place that smelt of Christian blood.

And, as she told all this, she wondered why the man before her sat there so quietly, as if unconscious, with a far-away look in his eyes and a patient, suffering smile on his lips.

And in order to justify what she had already said, she went on to relate how the schoolmaster and, most of all, the mistress in charge of the little ones, had done all they could.   Had spoken kindly and sensibly to the children, shown them how well the new school was built and fitted, and how all had been thought out to make it useful and comfortable for them.   But the children had no ears for that, and persisted all the same: the place had been built by a wicked man, a dreadful sinner, and it was unclean.

Some of them had suddenly begun to cry during the lessons.   Others had fancied they saw visions, and the fear and horror grew day by day. At last the parents could hardly get their children to go at all; it was even feared that some of the more excitable would go out of their minds.

Sven Elversson sat looking straight before him. "I wished her to be my judge," he said to himself. "And so it has come about. She condemns me, like all the rest."

She went on to say that it was of the children she had been thinking when she had said it was a good thing the school had been burnt. The fire had been caused by a pure accident. The woman who came to clean the rooms had upset a lamp: the fire had spread at once, and before she could get help it was beyond control.

The man at the helm looked up. "Well, well," he said. "Now Sven Elversson has been judged by God and man. Now it will be said that God would not suffer such unclean hands to build a house for children."

"Really, it almost seems——" began the woman, and checked herself. By a sudden intuition she felt now that the fellow there, who had been in her company for two hours at least, must be Sven Elversson himself.

Had she not heard his name mentioned the first time, when he had driven with them from the station? She had not noticed it at the time. But now . . .

She looked at him closely. His simple dress had deceived her; she could see now that his face was that of an educated man. And then the curious little accent that she had noticed and wondered at—doubtless a trace of his English upbringing.

He sat with his eyes cast down, and as she watched

the patient smile that played about his lips, she felt desperately miserable at having added still further to the burden he had to bear.

"Must I go back now with the memory of having wounded this poor sufferer against my will?" she thought. "I should have more to sorrow for then than I had this morning when I came down to the sea. He must have been a fine young man, with a career before him, and now he has lost all. And he has spent money, given his own work, on this schoolhouse building, to regain the good will of his fellow men. It is hard. I should not have spoken as I did."

Both were silent for the rest of the way home; neither cared to speak.

But when the boat came in to the stone pier under the cliff, and he rose to help her ashore, she grasped his hand.

"Forgive me," she said. "I did not know that it was you."

And she bent down and touched his forehead with her lips.

"What have you done?" he cried, with a look in his eyes as if she had struck him.

"I want you to understand that I do not feel toward you as all the others do," she said.

And, stepping ashore, she walked across the sand without looking back, and in through the pass between the rocks.

But before she had gone many steps, Sven Elversson was at her side, and laid one hand on her arm, that she should stop.

"Thank you . . . God bless you . . ." he said softly, brokenly. "But remember," he went on, "you must never, never do such a thing again. And you must not tell your husband what you have done. If you told him, then in his jealousy he might kill you."

Sven Elversson was gone, and the young wife walked on alone through the fields, with his last words still in her ears.

"Jealousy!"—could it be true that her husband was jealous? "Oh, heavens, no!" she thought to herself. "It is impossible. He *must* know that I am his with all my soul, with all my thoughts and feelings."

It seemed so cruelly unjust that any one should ever think her husband jealous; the tears rose to her eyes again.

"Heaven knows how it is with that Sven Elversson," she said to herself. "There are many that cannot bear the sight of him, but they all say he is a good man. But perhaps, after all, he is not suffering undeservedly. How could Edward ever be jealous about me? And that was what he was reckoning out to himself while I was talking to him in the boat.

"I wish he were here, so that I could tell him the truth. And the truth is just this—that Edward does not love me any more. It is his misfortune, and mine. But he is not jealous. Oh, a man such as he, so far above all others, who is there he could be jealous of? And that fellow actually thought he could be jealous of him!

"He has ceased to love me," she told herself once

more. "He can't help not loving me any more, but he cannot have ceased to believe in me, and in my love for him. It would be too unjust, too blind—it would be almost ridiculous."

On reaching home, the maid came to meet her in the hall, with an anxious face. The service was over already, the Pastor had come back, and was terrified at hearing that his wife was not at home. He had looked for her everywhere; had even been down to the sea to look. He was sitting in his room now—perhaps it would be best to go to him at once.

Fru Rhånge opened the door to the study. What was this?—was he ill? There sat this great strong man, with his face hidden in his arms, rocking to and fro and moaning as if in pain.

She went in, and asked in astonishment what was the matter. But when he looked up, his face was so changed that she hardly knew him—pale and drawn, with dull, bloodshot eyes, and his black beard in ragged wisps about his cheeks. She could hardly have believed such a change was possible in so short a time.

He looked at her with wide eyes, as if not knowing her. Then he passed his hands over his face, trying to control himself, to regain his customary dignity and confident ease. But to no purpose; his emotion was too much for him, and the tears streamed from his eyes.

He stretched out an arm toward her and, without rising, drew her to him. Not a kiss, not a caress; he leaned his head against her breast and sobbed, heart-rending to see.

Again and again she begged him to tell her what it was that hurt him, but it was long before he could speak.

And then—nothing more than that he had come home from church and had not found her there; had looked for her about the place, even down to the sea, and, finding her nowhere, he had thought she had given him up and stolen away.

Sigrun could not help giving a little laugh of triumph and satisfaction.

"You must never go away from me again," he said. "You must promise me, now, that you will never leave me. Always let me know where I can find you—you have seen now; I shall go out of my mind if you do not."

And she promised all that he asked. Promised that nothing but death should take her from him.

And then she stood beside him, stroking his hair, till he was himself again. She felt light at heart now that she had had proof of his love. But at the same time there was something strange, something she could not share, in this. It was a love she did not understand—a thing too hot and fierce.

She asked him how he could ever believe she would leave him. And then, impulsively, he told her his thought; she was so far above him. She was from another world, was good in herself, without having to think about it. And he was always fearing that one day she would disappear—he was not good enough to keep her long.

"He does not mean it," she thought to herself. He could not really mean it. It was only his love that exalted her, as love ever will. And in the same way she herself had hitherto exalted him in her heart.

She was no longer miserable and despairing, as she had been in the morning. But there rose up in her a sense of fear toward her husband. And she said no word of having been out sailing with Sven Elversson that day.

Meantime, Sven Elversson and his father were on their way back to Grimön. Old Joel took the tiller, and his son lay in the bows, making himself as comfortable as could be.

Joel had told him of the fire at the school, having heard the news at church. He looked old and bowed and sad; it seemed that now, after this last failure, all ways were closed to his son's advancement.

Sven Elversson stroked his forehead softly as he lay, now with his finger-tips, now with the whole of his slender, delicate hand.

There was a strange sense of freedom and ease in his soul. His thoughts came to him clear and indisputable. He saw his way.

"Father," he said, suddenly, "this loathing is surely the strongest thing of all. No one can overcome it; no one can stand against it. Best to know it from the first. Whoever tries to fight against it must be beaten."

Joel shrugged his shoulders slightly, and grunted out something in answer, but his words were lost in the noise of wind and waves.

Sven lay as before, thinking. And in a little while, when his mind again had given him a clear and indisputable thought, he lifted his voice and cried to his father:

"But loathing is not evil in itself. It is a warning and a safeguard. And if one could use it so, turning it to good use, one might be of great service to mankind."

The old man looked up. His rheumy gray eyes lit up for a moment, and his bowed figure straightened.

Sven sprang to his feet, and, stepping across the thwarts, sat down beside his father.

"Something has happened to me to-day," he said. "Something that has helped me. I am not unhappy now about the fire at the school. I have something else to think of."

Then he went back to his place and lay down again, listening to the heavy rush of the south wind, watching the blending colour of the reefs, and stroking his forehead with his slender, delicate hand.

LESS THAN THE LEAST

JULIUS MARTIN LAMPRECHT, arrested and remanded on a charge of murder, lay on the bench in his cell in the lock-up at Knapefiord, staring into the gray gloom about him.

He was telling himself, as he had done so many times since his arrest, that he was not really guilty, and that there was really no need to confess.

"Now, if I really had been," he said to himself, recollecting his own words at his examination that same morning—"if I really had been guilty of cracking in the skulls of two old people, I should never deny it for a moment. An eye for an eye and a tooth for a tooth—I know about that. And I know that justice must be done. And better to take your punishment in this world than have it to come in the next, where it lasts through all eternity."

The accused was a man about forty-five years of age, and looked almost a giant as he lay there in his cell. His hair was fair and curly as a child's, his complexion had the delicate colouring of youth, with a touch of deeper warmth on the cheeks. A handsome face, on the whole, with well-cut features. Only the eyes, though handsome too in a way, were unprepossessing, with a look in them now staring boldly, now flitting uncertainly from floor to ceiling, from corner to corner.

"Each according to his kind," he thought. "Judges and public prosecutors and that sort must be taken their way. Have to talk a special sort of truth to them, by reason that the real truth cannot reach their hearts, unless it be interpreted unto them."

And all the time he lay here telling himself that he had really committed no murder; he saw himself cold and hungry, dressed in miserable beggar's rags, coming in late one evening to a lonely village hidden away among barren, rocky hills. The door had by accident been left unfastened; he remembered how terrified the old folk had been as they looked up and saw him come in; how hurriedly they had closed the drawer in the table at which they sat. He had spoken kindly, sat down with them by the fire, to warm himself, eaten the food they gave him without hesitation, but aware all the time that they were far from glad of his company, and wished him a thousand miles away.

"And when you happen to be an old convict, sentenced to imprisonment for life, and let out after twenty years of it for exemplary behaviour, it's only natural to be suspected. I can't blame any one for that. I might have thought the same myself." Once more he was quoting from his defence of the morning.

And all the time he saw clearly in his mind's eye how he and the two old people had settled down to rest for the night, they in their bed in one corner, and he on a straw mattress at the other end of the room. The fire was still burning when they went to bed, and he could see the two gray heads side by side. He felt by no means comfortable himself; his bed on the floor was hard and univiting; he was in ill-humour, and in particular it annoyed him to feel that these two old people grudged him the shelter they could not refuse. The axe that the old man had used to cut a few twigs to put under the pot still lay on the chopping-block; he wondered if it had been left there on purpose, with the blade gleaming in the light of the fire. Easy to find, and ready to hand—was it that?

He began to feel sleepy, but dared not sleep. Once he did so, the old couple would have him at their mercy. The old man, despite his seventy years, looked active enough still. And they were two to one.

He had told them in court that morning, a man who has done his twenty years in prison doesn't want to go back again in a hurry. And really, he ought to be less suspected than others. "But I know it's not that way, as a rule—or, at least, people don't generally act on it."

And as he repeated his well-chosen words he saw himself once more lying on the floor in the little house, straining his ears to listen to the old couple's whispering, the old man urging something, and the woman trying to dissuade him. "Wait till he's asleep," he heard her say. And the vagabond on his hard straw pallet felt more and more uneasy. It was plain that the old couple had money in the house, and were afraid he might steal it. There's a power of danger more than folk would think in the life of a poor vagabond.

And he was cautious, and pretended to go to sleep, and snored loudly, waiting to see what they would do. The old man said his prayers, and that was all; but that in itself was a masterly piece of deceit to one who knew what they had in mind—one who could see how the blade of the axe shone in the light of the dying fire, all ready to hand—one who understood well enough that they were only trying to lull his suspicion to rest.

"But," thought the accused, "you can't get a judge to believe a thing like that. Won't hear a word of self-defence, especially when it's a poor wanderer coming all unarmed and helpless into a strange house. But, for my part, I can't call it murder at all. If I hadn't got up and smashed in their skulls, they'd have smashed in mine. I don't believe they were asleep at all, though they lay quite still and never moved. It was all a sham. And if I'd been fool enough to go off to sleep myself in earnest, what would have happened then? They'd have been up and out of bed in a moment, with the axe. And after, what could be easier than to bury a body and hide it up, in a wild place like that? No, it's almost wicked to tempt people, having it all so easy."

And each time the accused went over in his mind the events of that night he felt more and more convinced that he had only killed the two old people in self-defence.

At first, he had not expected to be arrested at all. In the first place, the village where the two old people lay asleep, each with a cloven skull, was far off the high road, and he had every hope that nothing would be discovered until he was far away in safety. Then, too, he had so thoroughly persuaded himself of his innocence that he felt Providence must protect him. For the justice of Providence is other than that of courts of law on earth. It was a justice that understood how a poor vagabond might be forced to act in self-defence. With that sort of justice it was possible, so to speak, to talk as man to man.

The only thing this supreme justice could reasonably reproach him with was—he admitted it freely—a little white lie or so that he had allowed himself to tell at the examination, with regard to where he had been on the night of the crime and the days following. But for all his conscientiousness and his love of right and justice, he realized that in his case it was pardonable. For when a man had been arrested in despite of common fairness and humanity, merely because he happened to have been in prison before—and possibly also to some extent because a savings-bank book, the property of the deceased, and been found on his person—why, he was simply forced to deviate a little from the strict and literal truth. He had been obliged to confess that he had stolen the bank book from the pocket of a fellow passenger in the train. He had not endeavoured to assert that it had been honestly come by, but had freely confessed he had stolen it. As to where the other traveller had obtained it—who could say? It was too much to ask that he, the accused, show know the goings and comings of every stranger.

Again and again he went through the same arguments, each time feeling himself more and more innocent of any crime.

He had reached so far, indeed, as to be filled with an intense conviction of having barely, by a miracle of grace, escaped being murdered in his sleep himself—when the door of his cell opened, and the notary, who had conducted the proceedings of that morning, stepped in, followed by two other men. One was the warder, who had been deputed to look after him, and the other a young man, dressed like a workman of the better class.

The prisoner rose at once to his feet, with an air of respectful attention. He was resolved, as he had told the prison chaplain, on all occasions to observe a proper demeanour, and show that he himself was not only a lover of justice, but well disposed toward its servants.

"I have to inform you, Lamprecht," said the young notary, "that your case will be decided to-morrow. And once more I would ask you, while there is yet time, to ease your conscience and obtain a lighter sentence by sincere repentance and confession."

The accused answered only with a determined shake of the head, but for the rest maintained an attitude of tolerant understanding.

"I can understand, of course, that the notary finds it difficult," he said. "I have myself learned to love justice, which is the foundation of all society—the one thing in which all must trust. And I can understand that it seems hard to judge. You do not wish to condemn an innocent man, or, on the other hand, to let the guilty escape."

While he was speaking he noticed that the judge made a gesture with his hand once or twice as if to interrupt, but he took no heed. A man who has spent twenty years in prison has gained a certain amount of experience in the time, and may have various things to say which might be useful to a notary acting, perhaps for the first time, as judge.

He was allowed to finish what he had to say. Then the judge went on, entirely unmoved.

"You find it very difficult to give clear and distinct answers to questions put. And I have therefore written down these three points which you have to answer." He took up a paper, and held it toward the accused, reading out the contents at the same time:

"'Do you, Julius Martin Lamprecht, confess to having murdered Jonas Mikaelson with an axe on the night following the twelfth of February 1909?

"'Do you, Julius Martin Lamprecht, confess to having murdered Brita Gustava, wife of the aforesaid Jonas Mikaelson, with an axe on the night following the twelfth of February 1909?

"'Do you, Julius Martin Lamprecht, confess to having been aware that the two persons aforesaid possessed a bank book showing a deposit of two hundred *kronor*, and to having committed the murder in order to gain possession of the same?'"

The notary laid the paper on the table.

"You can think it over," he said. "You know that there is no prospect of your being acquitted, but a confession given of your own free will may lead to a mitigation of the sentence. Here is the paper; I will have pen and ink brought in."

The accused was by no means pleased at the manner in which his mode of expressing himself had been criticized; he was indeed altogether out of humour now. He stared blankly before him.

"You heard what I said?" the notary went on. "You understand that there are three questions here for you to answer, with your signature?"

The accused drew a deep breath. He was annoyed, and made no attempt to hide it. He spat on the paper and going back to his bench, lay down and closed his eyes.

"I will have a new copy of the paper brought in at once," said the judge as calmly as before.

"You have an hour. I shall wait in the building that time for your answer. You are too fond of delay and prevarication; I intend to show you that the time for such evasions is now past."

The accused answered only with an oath.

A moment after, he heard the door open, and imagined that the visitors had left. He did not trouble himself to open his eyes and look.

"That slip of a boy will never dare to condemn me," he thought. "Not as long as I stick to a firm denial. As for his paper, I've no need to answer that. Why should I?"

And, lying stretched on his bench, he saw in his mind's eye the same scenes as he had seen before; repeated his former arguments, growing ever more and more convinced of his entire innocence. He was certain now that the two old villagers had been in the habit of laying traps for lonely wanderers; they must have had more than one such life on their conscience.

At the same time, he found something pleasant in the thought that the judge had come in person to ask him to confess. It was proof that they regarded him as an important and dangerous man, whom they were loth to release.

"There you are!" he said to himself proudly. "That's how it is. People all round are afraid the murderer may escape after all. All that crowd there was in the court this morning. And the papers taking it up so eagerly. And the judge himself uncertain what to do; yes, it's all easy enough to understand. They'd like to condemn, but they haven't proof enough. And so they're trying to wring out a confession to help them. They know they can't condemn a man without proof as long as he denies it and sticks to it."

He felt so sure of his safety now that he began to whistle.

Perhaps, after all, it might turn out that this sore trial had not been in vain. "After this," he thought to himself, "there'll be no need to be content with cold potatoes and scrapings of porridge when you come to a lonely hut. After this, you'll only have to say your name, Julius Martin Lamprecht, and people 'll know what they've got to do. They'll get busy then, soon enough, with pots and pans on the fire, and serve up the best they've got. No more lying on a bit of mattress on the floor; no, it 'll be the visitor, the stranger within their gates, that sleeps in the best bed, and the others can sleep on the floor or out in the shed, if they like."

But here the accused was again interrupted in his train of thought. A quiet, gentle voice close by him:

"Five minutes have gone already."

He opened his eyes. The man dressed like a work-man, who had followed the others into the cell, stood by his side, watch in hand, pointing to the dial as he spoke.

"What are you doing here? Who are you?" cried the accused, unpleasantly surprised to find that he was not alone. He wondered uneasily if he had been thinking aloud.

"I—I am nobody to speak of," said the other. "My name is Sven Elversson, son of Joel Elversson from Grimön. But it just occurred to me that you might perhaps fall off to sleep, or forget about the time, until it was too late. And so I asked them to let me stay in here and talk to you."

Lamprecht could find nothing to disapprove of in the stranger. There was something extremely humble about his manner, his smile, the tone of his voice. Even the way his hair was done seemed to have something of humility about it. He was clean-shaven, too, which added to the impression. All that could indicate self-ishness, pride, superiority, was effaced. "Must be one of those well-meaning folk that go about doing good," thought the prisoner to himself. "Well, he won't get much out of me, anyhow."

"D'you think for a moment I'm ever going to write a word on that paper there?" he asked, scornfully.

"Do not say 'no' before you've had time to think," said Sven Elversson, with a glance of gentle humility and goodness. "You have had dealings with the law before, and you know well enough that you cannot be condemned in this court as long as you persist in a denial; they will have to acquit you for lack of proof. But before you decide, let me tell you that there are certain persons here who have ordered the sum of five thousand kronor to be placed at your disposal if you decide to confess. There is reason to believe that you would be glad of the money, although you will not, of course, be able to spend it yourself."

The accused felt a sudden shiver through his body from head to foot. At the same time, he could not help making a grimace. But he pulled himself together.

"What the devil is that you say?" he cried.

"Yes, it is true," said Sven Elversson. "We are ready to give you that money, if you confess. You understand that it is a matter of importance to us others that you should confess? Everyone in the district, perhaps in the whole country, is horrified. And we have resolved that you shall not go about the country asking for shelter of lonely folk if we can help it. That must not be. It is too great a temptation for a man like you. We want you imprisoned for life. We wish you no harm beyond that. We have no wish to take your life, or to hurt you at all, but we must have you in confinement. I and several others have watched you in court, and heard what you said. You are not exactly an intentional criminal, but you have fancies, and are easily frightened; you imagine that everyone is anxious to harm you. And if you think over it carefully, you will see that it is best for yourself that you should be shut up. You will be at peace then, and need have no fear of any one. I think, then, it would be better for you and for everyone else if you were to accept the five thousand kronor and confess."

"Not for a hundred thousand!" exclaimed the accused.

Sven Elversson had drawn gradually closer to the man while speaking, and sat down now on the bench beside him.

"Do not say that," he urged kindly, laying one hand on the other's sleeve. "Five thousand kronor is a good sum, and fully enough for the purpose for which you would use it. You cannot say otherwise. More would not be good for the one who is to have the money, and less would hardly do. Five thousand is as good as could be."

"I can't make you out," said the accused. "What do you think I should use it for? Who is the one I should give it to?"

"I am glad you asked me that," said Sven Elversson. "It was of that I wished to speak to you. There has been a great deal about you in the papers of late, and, among other things, how you are always asking after your daughter wherever you go. You were married, it seemed, before you committed that first murder two and twenty years ago, and on your release you tried at once to find out where your wife was. But she was dead. But you had a daughter—she would be a little over twenty now, and, as far as any one knows, she is alive, but no one could tell you where she had gone. And so you have been wandering about the country looking for her everywhere. As soon as you entered a house, the first thing you did was always to ask if any there knew anything of Julia Lamprecht. And"—here Sven lowered his voice and went on a little sadly—"it seemed to me that there was something I liked about that. There must be something good in a man who went about seeking for his daughter."

"But in the name of Heaven," cried the accused, "what have you to do with it all? Why are you here, talking to me like this? Can't you tell me what it is you want with me?"

"Thanks once more," said Sven Elversson in his gentlest voice, as if fearing to arouse the other's displeasure. "Those are just questions that I shall be only too glad to answer. I am from Grimön, as I said—a little island far out at sea, so far, at any rate, that I myself need have no fear of you, for you would hardly come there. But I have a mother who has warnings in her dreams at times. And on the morning of the thirteenth of February she asked me to go over to the mainland and see how things were with an old couple—relatives of ours—who lived in a little cottage among the stonehills, far from the high road, and with no neighbours near. She had dreamed something that made it seem best for someone to go and see how they were. And I did as she asked me. And so it came about that I was the first to discover what you had done that night. And I will not deny that it was a cruel sight, and ever since I have wished something could be done to prevent you from ever being free to go about again. And that is why I have been about collecting this money. I wish you no harm, do not think that. I have told you so already. I only want to see you imprisoned now for life."

As he spoke, he moved a little closer, and stroked the other's sleeve gently. He was evidently anxious that Lamprecht should not think he bore him any personal ill will. Had the man been a lion escaped from its cage, its keeper might have coaxed it back behind the bars in the same way.

It would be untrue to say that the accused did not regard him with uneasiness. Everyone filled him with uneasiness: judge and gaoler, magistrate and witnesses. But he could not help feeling that this Sven Elversson was little to be feared—he seemed, indeed, something weak in his mind. "One of those fellows that go about doing good," he told himself again. "Philanthropists, they call them."

"I seem to understand a little now," he said aloud. "As soon as you found out that I went about looking for my daughter you thought you could use her as a bait to catch a poor fellow again for good."

And he laughed in Sven's soft face. The lion was determined to keep its freedom, and cared nothing for the bait offered.

"Thank you," said Sven Elversson, with his humblest smile. "What you say brings me just to the very thing I wanted to tell you. Look you, last summer I was doing some building work in the district. Not for myself, you understand, but to order. And I had to get some stone from a quarry just above the fishing village of Knapefiord, where we are now, and in that way I came into contact with a good many of the people there. And among them was a young woman named Julia Lamprecht. It was an unusual name, and as soon as I saw your name in the papers I remembered her."

The accused rose to his feet. Again he felt that shiver through his body. His face twitched, his eyelids quivered; it was evident that some emotion took possession of him at the mention of his daughter, though, truth to tell, he had been seeking her hitherto less from any warmth of real feeling than in the hope that she might perhaps be well off and able to give him a home.

He thrust Sven Elversson aside carelessly, and stood up in the middle of the cell.

"Is she here?" he asked. "I want to see her."

His tone was that of a man who expects immediate obedience to his orders. But Sven Elversson did not lose countenance.

"You shall see her," he said, kindly and gently as before, but not without firmness. "You shall sit and talk with her as you are doing now with me. But there is one thing to be done first. You must write the answers on that paper. You may think, perhaps, that we are cruel in trying to separate father and daughter in this way, but we must have that paper signed first."

The accused flushed angrily. He was not accustomed to have any reasonable request refused. Ever since he had been arrested, he had been treated with the greatest leniency, to make him thrive, as it were, in captivity, and render him more willing to give the confession that would keep him there. He felt now as if he could spring at this stranger and thrash him soundly, but he controlled himself. He threw himself face downward on the bench, keeping his face hidden. He did not know himself what made him do so, but he felt it was best to conceal his feelings.

"I am glad, I am grateful to you for thinking it over," said Sven. "I must tell you that Julia Lamprecht is not very happy as she is. Her mother died early, as you know. And since then she has, as one might say, grown up in the streets. She came here in company with a workman from the quarries. They were not married, but quarrymen hereabouts do not always trouble about marrying, so no one paid much heed to that. And Julia is a good girl; there are many worse than she. But a few days back, when the man heard she was your daughter, he left her. Couldn't bear the sight of her, he said. And now she is all alone. She is handsome, like her father, with fair hair, and no doubt there will be others ready to be friends with her in a way, but it will only be the same again. Now, if she had a little money, say five thousand kroner, then she could buy a little house and be properly married. Five thousand would be just about right. More would not be well for her, and less would be hardly enough. Well, now you see how we have thought it out. As soon as you have answered the questions there, you can see her, and give her the five thousand. You would like that, I think. Then she would feel she had a father. She would feel that, whatever you might have done, you had still some affection for her."

The accused was silent for a long time. He moved to and fro restlessly on the bench, moaning from time to time. There was, after all, something in the man that cried for his child. Fair, handsome, like her father, she was. And perhaps even then sitting outside and waiting. . . .

Suddenly he sat up, brushed his hair from his forehead, and looked Sven Elversson straight in the face.

"Can you tell me," he said, "why I should write on that paper at all? I shall be acquitted to-morrow."

"Quite likely," answered Sven, "you may be acquitted of the murder. But then there is that other matter of the bank book. In any case, you will not be released yet awhile. It may be years before you are a free man again. You cannot say how long it may be. And, in the meantime, what is to happen to the girl? She may be ruined before you see her. It is not an easy thing for a girl to be the daughter of such a man as you. And I am afraid she will go from bad to worse. Five thousand now, that would help her. Let her have the money now, and you will have something to think of, something to be glad of, all your life. Then you will have done something to wipe out what you have done. You would be respected for that."

The accused rose to his feet once more.

"Stop it!" he cried, stamping his foot. "You are driving me out of my mind with your talk."

Sven was silent at once.

The accused stood thinking, searching out his soul; looking everywhere for that love for his daughter that he thought must be there. They were trying to lead him as they pleased through his love for his daughter. They asked of him to sacrifice all that was left of life for her sake. He, a man with nothing in the world but his freedom, he was to give up that for his daughter's sake! For love of her! But was there any such love in him at all? Now that he sought for it, he could find nothing. Or yes, perhaps, a little. But nothing to speak of. Not enough to make a sacrifice. It is not so easy to make sacrifices. This fellow here who talked so glibly about it all, and was trying all the time to get him shut up and put out of harm's way—would he make any sacrifice for the sake of what he sought?

"I will do as you ask," he said at last. "I will answer those three questions. But on one condition. It's all very well that my girl gets the money. But the money's not everything after all. No, the best thing she could have would be a good husband. *If you will promise me to marry her yourself, then I will sign.*"

Sven Elversson started back in consternation.

"I had not expected that," he said in a low voice.

"I am asking if you will marry my daughter," said the accused, with a sneer. "Now, what do you say to that? You ask me to give up everything for her sake, but you are not so ready to give up anything yourself."

"But—she is your daugher. It was you that brought her into the world," said Sven Elversson. "I have hardly spoken to her in my life."

"Just as you like. Only then, of course, I need not trouble about the questions. It's really a pity, though. I've quite taken a fancy to you. I'd like to have you for a son-in-law." And he laughed boisterously.

Sven Elversson passed his hand over his eyes, and drew a deep breath. "I understand now," he said to himself. "The man who would have power over others must be prepared to crucify himself. Nothing less will serve."

He looked long and searchingly at the man before him.

"He is trying to get out of it," he thought. "And

wants to lay the blame on me. He is sure I should refuse. But I will not refuse. I have him cornered now, and I will not let him go."

"Let it be as you say," he said, shortly. "If your daughter will have me, I will marry her. Now write!"

The accused man hesitated.

"Very kind of you, I'm sure," he said. "But how am I to know you will keep your word?"

"Of course," said Sven. "I was waiting for you to ask that. Now, if you think a moment, you will understand that in a place like this walls have ears. There are witnesses already to the fact that I have promised to marry Julia Lamprecht, provided that she consents. I cannot escape now. As long as I wish to be looked on as an honourable man, I cannot escape. Now, sit down at the table and write!"

Lamprecht sat down at the table. He took up the pen, dipped it in the ink, and groaned.

Sitting there, pen in hand, he sought once more for that love for his daughter. It might, perhaps, have been there in his soul at the time when he hoped to find a home with her, but now—now that he was asked to give up his freedom for her sake, it was nowhere to be found.

He wrote with the pen upright, and with the pen aslant; dipped again and again, splashed the ink about, and at last it was done.

"All I ever promised you was to *answer* the questions," he said, and handed Sven Elversson the paper.

And Sven Elversson read, and saw that the judge's three questions were answered with three crooked, straggling words: "*No*" and "*No*" and "*No*." Beneath was the signature, Julius Martin Lamprecht, and finally a single sentence, rambling and ill-spelt: "I would confess if I was guilty, but I am not."

"You will not get the five thousand kronor for that," said Sven Elversson, quietly.

"I didn't suppose so," returned the other. "But I've got you to marry my girl. I never promised you but I would answer the questions if you agreed to marry my daughter. And I've done it. I'll be acquitted, and I've got a good husband for her."

He stood there throwing out his chest, proud of his victory.

Sven Elversson flushed angrily. His humility had disappeared, and his manner toward the accused was less kind than before.

"I might have thought it," he said. "I ought to have known what a scoundrel you were. I have seen how you treated those two poor creatures after you had killed them. What made you put out their eyes?" he asked passionately.

"Put out their eyes!" cried the accused. "That's not true. Someone else must have done that. When I left them——"

He broke off, bit his lips, and staggered, pale as death, to the wall of the cell.

"Thanks," said Sven Elversson drily. "I knew how I could get you, if need should be. But I waited, as long as there was a chance, to make it easier for you."

Next moment the murderer lay on his knees before him.

"I didn't say it; I didn't say anything," he cried. "I didn't say it—it doesn't count—you tricked me!"

The man was suddenly transformed to a miserable, grovelling heap of penitence and despair. All his armour of conceit and self-deception, all his subterfuges and excuses, had been torn from him now.

"There are witnesses here, as I told you before," said Sven Elversson. "I warned you."

"I'll write it again—give me a new paper and I'll confess. I'll tell you all, I'll do all you ask, for the sake of the girl."

Sven Elversson raised his voice a little.

"I will tear up this paper," he said. "Another shall be brought directly. And if the new one is properly answered and signed, then I fancy the walls will have heard nothing of the first. We will start again from the moment you sat down to write. The hour is not yet gone. You, Julius Martin Lamprecht, have still time to make a free confession."

.   .   .   .   .

A little later, the murderer sat on a chair in his cell, facing the judge. His appearance was changed; he wore the look of a man washed and cleansed, though no such process had taken place outwardly. But he had confessed. Not only had he answered the two first questions in the affirmative, and the last in the negative, but he had delivered a full and free confession of the whole affair. He was exhausted now, and a chair had to be brought for him or he would have fallen to the floor. But for all that he looked happy and content. At that moment he bore no ill will to any living soul. He was cleansed and freed from sin. He had not felt such comfort since his first communion.

In addition to the judge, there were present in the cell a warder, a constable, the clerk, and Julia Lamprecht, and Sven Elversson. The prisoner loved them all, and most of all his daughter, to whom he had just given the sum of five thousand kronor. He found her beautiful to look at. Handsome, fair, with curly hair, and a queer shyness of manner. He had not yet spoken with her alone, but the judge had promised she should be allowed to sit in his cell as long as he pleased.

Now and again the murderer turned his eyes toward the man who had forced him to confess, and he could not help feeling a certain sympathy with him.

The very look of the man, as he stood there leaning against the cell wall, with his eyes cast down and his brow gloomily furrowed, was enough to inspire sympathy. The murderer felt he understood him better than any other. He, Lamprecht, a murderer, could confess his crime and atone for it, but this man would never be able to wipe away the stain that clung to his name.

The murderer had seen how the judge and all the other servants of the law had shaken hands with Sven Elversson and thanked him. The judge, especially, had been profoundly grateful. It was a great relief to him now to be able to give his decision without hesitation.

But Sven Elversson looked as humble and sad as ever—only more humble, if anything, than before. He looked like a man utterly weary of himself.

When Julia Lamprecht entered the cell to receive the five thousand kronor, Sven Elversson had stepped forward and declared that he had promised the prisoner to make his daughter an offer of marriage. But the girl had refused at once. She would not marry *that* man— never. And she had told him plainly what manner of man he was.

Sven Elversson had been deeply hurt at her refusal. It seemed to torture him. He drew back without a word, and stood leaning unsteadily against the cell wall. And the prisoner himself felt that he was revenged.

His daughter, whom he had never seen until that day, had taken vengeance on the man who had conquered her father. He felt she was of his blood, and he loved her.

Not that he repented of his confession. He felt clean and easy in mind, happy and respected, almost like a decent man. And he had seen his daughter, whom he would love now all his life, and who would always love him, since he had given up his freedom for her sake.

As for the true confession, the murderer passed it over, erased it from his memory. He was a man who always needed to look at himself in a good light. He was already busy in his mind with a beautiful and touching story of how it was for this daughter's sake alone he had confessed, and prayed to God and man for forgiveness. As long as he lived, he would be able to weave that story over and over again, and he would believe it, and it would serve to maintain his self-respect during the long, hard years that awaited him.

BOOK II

LOTTA HEDMAN

ONE day toward the end of September 1915 a train came down from Norrland to the south. In a third-class compartment sat a young woman, very simply and decently dressed in black, with a black hat almost devoid of trimmings. She was talking to her fellow travellers. She was not afraid of raising her voice at times, and the voice in itself being somewhat shrill, she could be heard by all those near. It was soon evident that this was the first time she had travelled on the railway. And the strangeness of it all, coming out into the world and meeting strange, kindly people, seemed to have lifted her to a sort of ecstasy. All that she had been unable to find outlet for during years of life in a confined situation broke out now. She talked unceasingly, and always of herself. She was loth to lose an opportunity of letting people know who she was, and what strange message she had to bring.

"And I'm just one that's never studied at all, beyond the Bible," said she. "My head's not heavy with knowledge. Not all confused with doctrines of error. I am as an unwritten page; as the white scroll on which God Himself writes His own thoughts. And I was born far away in Lapland, and live in a little settlement, and every day I go to work at a box factory, and I'm all alone and poor, and neither husband nor child. And nobody asks whether I live or die, and nobody comes to see after me if I'm ill, and there's no one there at home that I can talk to about what's most of all to me. And I know well enough that people make fun of me behind my back, and I'm already getting shy of going about among people."

A kindly old lady sitting opposite, who had entered into conversation with her at first, and got her to speak, now laid a hand on her knee, as if to calm her, but she went on, as if driven by an irresistible inner force.

"And all my days Death has been after me like a ravening wolf. His strivings after me have been manifold. He tried to compass me about while I was yet in my mother's womb. He sent forth a madman to frighten my mother, and I was born into the world too early, and a weak and wretched thing at birth. And once he tried to drown me when I was bathing, and once, out in the forest, he let a tree fall on me, and once he sent a serpent to bite me in the foot when I was out picking berries, and once he threw me down from a scaffold on a building. And he's plagued me with sickness beyond counting."

It was not only her opposite neighbour that listened to her now. A peasant and his wife, sitting next to her, followed her words with the greatest attention. The tone and the choice of words reminded them of mission meetings, and they put on an almost pious expression.

"And in the days of my youth," went on the girl— she could not have been more than twenty-six or twenty-seven at the most—"I stretched forth my arms to God, and asked Him why He suffered Death to persecute me with sickness and wounds, but now, these last few years, I have ceased to ask. I know now that the Evil One strove to strike me down because it was God's purpose to speak through me; yes, out of my mouth God should set a barrier against the raging of the Enemy."

She paused for breath, and looked round, but finding only kindly looks and attention among the rest, she went on again:

"And I have wondered in myself why I should live so far away in the north, and why I should always walk the same little streets and never see anything of the glories of the world. Why have I been granted so little understanding to make my way and manage for myself, and why have I so little pleasure on that which pleases others? Why does the foreman at the factory never say a kindly word to me, however hard I work? Why should it be so hard for me to get milk, and why should I live in a little room where no one else would be?

"But now I have ceased from wondering of these things, for now I know that it is God that has made all waste and miserable about me. And I may be glad that He has not sent me out into the forests, or into the mountains, or sent me to live in a Lapp tent, and wander about with reindeer in the wilderness. I must be thankful that He has suffered me to dwell in a place where others besides myself have their homes."

It was not only the three sitting nearest who now gave heed to the young woman's words. One or two of those farthest off stood up to listen. "What was it?" some asked. Or, "Who was it carrying on like that for all the carriage to hear? Some of those Salvation Army people?"

"For it is God's will that my thoughts should be for Him alone," went on the woman in black. "It is His will that I should think and consider much; that I should interpret Daniel and make clear Ezekiel, and draw forth wisdom from the Revelations. And in the evenings, when others are dancing and feasting, Lotta Hedman sits with her Bible, sits searching after knowledge of God, and things are clear to her which no other in the world can understand."

A thrill of wonder went through all those who heard, and the speaker did not fail to notice it. The attention she had awakened egged her on; even if she had wished, she could not stop now till she had finished. Her long-closed lips moved now with or against her will.

"And in the winter nights, when the clock strikes twelve, and one and all Sweden has gone to rest, and the great white land lies stretched in the calm of sleep, I sit in a poor little room, a room so mean that no other would ever live there, and I see God's finger pointing to words and figures in Holy Writ. And then it is revealed to me how it shall be with all the others, all those who lie sleeping through the winter night. A revelation to me, poor and despised as I am, yet given to no other, to none among the learned and the worldly-wise."

Her voice rose yet shriller; the woman sitting opposite laid one hand again with a kindly touch on her knee. A conductor, making his round through the train, stopped to listen, wondering if one of the passengers had been suddenly seized with a fit of madness.

"And all that I have seen and learned, I have written

down in plain words, and sealed and sent it to the King. To the great palace in Stockholm, a letter from the poor factory girl at Stenbroträsk, from one that the boys run after in the street, hunting and snarling like Lapp dogs after a wild she-wolf.

"And I have waited for many days for an answer from the King, but there has come no answer from the King. And I have written my letter all again, and sent it to the papers, and the papers would have nothing to do with my letter, but sent it back.

"And then I was greatly distressed, for my letter is more important than many things. For I know when the Great War is to end, and I know that after it shall come the great Destruction, when Nature shall lay waste the earth, but that after the Great Destruction shall come the bright Millennium. And I know that a third part of all mankind on earth shall perish in the Great War, and a third shall perish in the Great Destruction, but the last third shall be left alive in the Great Millennium, which is the Kingdom of the Lord on Earth."

The words, flung out with violent force, pierced many of the listeners like cold steel, and they shivered with dread. A few years earlier, such a speech would have been received with derision, but this was the second year of the World War, when all hearts were filled to the utmost with horror and expectation. Even in Sweden, no one could feel safe from day to day, but wondered what the Russians were about up at Haparanda.

"These things and much more—all are in my letter to the King. And I wrote to him and told him how he should act so that he and all in Sweden should escape the coming time of wrath, and how they might come to share in the Millennium of God.

"But I have prayed to God for help, and asked Him how my letter could be made known to the world, since no one will help me. And God has given me His commands, and told me what remained for me to do. For there is a great sin to be atoned for before my letter can be sent abroad and made known to all men. And it is to atone for my sin that I am going south to-day."

The excitement in the carriage was at its height. Here was one who claimed to know what all longed to know: when the war was to end. A voice from someone among those farthest off was heard asking her:

"When is the war to end?"

And many others took up the cry: "When is it to end? If you know, tell us, tell us now."

It seemed as if the end of all those horrors and perils that weighed down mankind were suddenly brought within view. Perhaps before long there might yet come a time when the murdering out in the great world was at an end; when men could think once more of other matters than of war; could live without suffering day and night from the thought of old women mourning, terrified fugitives, prisoners dying slowly in their captivity.

Peasants thought of the days when they would no longer have to send their sons and hired men to guard the still precarious neutrality of their country; small tradesmen, who had done flourishing business at the beginning of the war, but were now threatened with dearth of all commodities; workmen, who saw themselves face to face with increased cost of living and scarcity of the bare necessaries of life—all asked with one voice: "When is it to end? When is all this misery to cease?"

But the prophetess from Stenbroträsk did not seem to have expected such an effect of her words.

"It is all in my letter," she cried. "It shall be made known when I have atoned for my sin, and God lets my words be published abroad throughout the world."

There was a perceptible loss of interest among the listeners; evidently this woman knew no more than anyone else. Most of those who had risen sat down again.

And the end of her speech, the few words she uttered afterward were scarcely heard by any save the kindly woman sitting opposite, who had first spoken to her.

"And I have no time to write except at night," said the girl—"at night, when work is over, and then my fingers are stiff and unwilling, and I am not quick at writing properly. They talk differently in our parts. It makes me very tired, all the writing.

"And I live in poverty and wretchedness," she went on. "Poor and ill and alone, and living in a place where no one else would ever live, and I tremble to think of all that must come."

She had marked well enough that no one seemed to care any longer for her words. Her voice grew fainter, and there was a dreamy look in her eyes. At last she spoke only in a whisper, and lowered her glance. None but those nearest could hear what she said.

"But I pray to God to spare me, that I may live to be

one among the purified host. I pray that I may be counted among that last third, and that I, who have been chosen to proclaim its coming when all despised me, may share in the Millennium of the Lord, and stand among the elect and see this earth resplendent in the glory of righteousness."

THE WONDERFUL MUSIC

THE long train from the north rolled on unceasingly from station to station. Those in the compartment where Lotta Hedman sat gradually got out: first the peasant and his wife, then the kindly woman who had got her to speak at first of who and what she was. Then there entered a man, who, by the look of him, might have been a lay preacher of some sort, and sat down in the comfortable corner. He had been in another part of the train before, and came now to find a better seat.

The newcomer at once entered into conversation with Lotta. He asked her whether any revelations had come to her before the time of the war, or if it was only since its beginning that she had been aware of her gift. He spoke in low tones, with a soft, gentle, and very winning voice, exhibiting the warmest interest, without either expressing doubt or faith. To others, his manner of speaking might seem irritating in its extreme humility, but Lotta Hedman was pleased to be addressed with some measure of respect, now that she had for the first time shown herself among strangers and revealed her calling.

"I should be glad indeed if you would tell me something about your visions," said the man. "It is too much to ask, perhaps, seeing that I am a stranger to you, but be sure I should feel it a great honour."

The young woman could not resist such an appeal, and began at once to tell about the first time she had noticed anything strange. But she spoke now with far greater calm than before. True, she raised her voice, and found also more listeners than the one directly addressed, but the man before her seemed unwittingly to exert a calming influence, and her eagerness was restrained.

"I was only fourteen at the time," she said, "and was just recovering from a serious illness that had been sent by my persecutor Death; I was very weak, and all my body felt as if it were withering and falling to nothing. But I did not live alone then, as I do now; I lived at home with my father and mother. And they were only poor peasant folk, but they cared for me in my weakness, and let me stay at home, instead of sending me out to service among strangers. And Mother asked no more of me than that I should help her with light work and errands, and read aloud a chapter of the Bible every day.

"There was no sawmill at Stenbroträsk in those days, and no box factory, and no workmen's dwellings, nor even the beginning of a settlement. All our side of the river there were no houses beyond a couple of small farmsteads. The church and the Deanery and the big farms were all over on the other side, just as they are now.

"Then, one Sunday evening, Mother told me to row over with some milk to the Deanery, for it was summer time, and everyone there had their cows out at a distance for months together, and they could not get milk nearer than from us.

"I got into the boat, and started to row across, and it was all so easy and light of a sudden. As if the heavy boat was turned to the lightest little thing, and the water changed to smooth, fine oil, and the oars to delicate wings. And everything was very quiet and still. The oars did not creak in the rowlocks, nor splash in the water, and there was no sound from either shore. Not so much as a cow-bell anywhere. No men and girls sitting talking on the banks, and all the swallows that always used to build in the high banks and were always fluttering and flying about outside their holes, they seemed to be gone all at once, and never a sign of them.

"And when I had rowed across, and taken the milk and started up to walk to the Deanery, it wasn't hard walking at all, though it was uphill all the way, and I had the sun right in my face. The sun didn't seem hot in the least, and the milk wasn't heavy at all.

"And I thought to myself they must be waiting eagerly for me, and it must mean something good for me somehow; for I had never found it so easy to get over there before.

"And then when I came into the kitchen, it was all quiet there too, and not a soul to be seen that I could give the milk to, so I had to stay waiting at the door.

"And then, almost as soon as I came in, I heard some-one playing in one of the rooms above, and I could hear it so clearly I almost fancied it must be in the same room where I stood. And it was so beautiful, I was glad the housekeeper and the maid were not there, so I could stay quietly and listen. I was in no hurry to go now—I could have stood there the whole night and not wanted to go.

"At that time I'd never heard any sort of music but a harmonica and the old church organ at Stenbroträsk, and I wondered so much what fine instrument it could be that was playing now. And it wasn't any sort of tune I knew. Just long-drawn tones like a strong soughing of the wind, and full of sound, and so clear, it felt as if they stroked my cheek so gently, passing by.

"And I had such lovely, splendid thoughts as I listened. I felt as if I were freed from earth, and half-way up to God's heaven.

"Then someone came into the kitchen, and suddenly the wonderful music stopped.

"When the housekeeper had poured off the milk, she set out something to eat for me on the table, and told me to sit down. They had had a funeral that day, she said; it was the old lady that was dead, the Dean's mother, and they had had guests to dinner. And I was to have a little of the good things, she said.

"And because she was so kind and nice, I took courage, and asked who it could be that had played so beautifully up above.

"But the housekeeper, she was so astonished, she could hardly speak.

"'What's that you're saying, child? You can't have heard anybody playing up above. The piano's at the other end of the house, and we can't hear it out in the kitchen. And you can think for yourself there's no one likely to be playing music here the day old mistress is laid to rest!'"

"Then nobody said anything for a time. I knew, of course, that I had heard what I had heard, but I didn't like to contradict.

"And the housekeeper, she sort of thought it over to herself a little, and then she began again trying to put me right.

"'It's old mistress's room that's here above the kitchen,' she said, 'and the last place in the world any one would ever think of playing music this day.'

"The tears came into my eyes then, for I knew she thought I had been telling untruth. And I felt like running away at once, only it would look so strange to run off before I'd finished what she'd given me.

"And then, what do you think? Just as I was sitting there wishing myself a hundred miles off, the door opens, and the Dean himself looks in and asks hadn't they heard the bell for evening prayers?

"And they were abashed at that and made excuses.

"'It's Lotta Hedman there; she frightened us so we forgot everything else. She says she came into the kitchen a little while back, when there was nobody here, and hears someone playing music up above. And we can't make it out, for we know surely enough there's no one here would play a note the day of the funeral.'

"And I, poor thing, being pointed out like that, I didn't know what to do with myself. I set down my knife and fork and pushed away my plate, and was just getting ready to run out of the door.

"'Music?' says the Dean. 'Now let us all give thanks to God. This is a wonderful act of grace indeed. I

knew well that my dear mother would send a greeting
if it were in her power. She would not leave me for
all eternity without a sign to be a guidance to me living
on in darkness and uncertainty.'

"And he came up to me and laid his hand on my head.

"'So you are one of the chosen,' he said. 'One of
those appointed to bring tidings from the dead to the
living. Well, well, it may be that God Himself will
speak one day through you on earth.'

"And he said no more, only turned my face upward
and looked deep into my eyes, and sighed, and went
away.

"But when I rowed back across the water, I sat thinking of all that had happened that day. And I felt that
in some strange way I was changed now, and could never
be the same again.

"And that was the first time anything wonderful ever
happened to me; the first time I found that I was appointed to see and hear things that are hidden from the
wise and learned.

"And already I believed I was to be one of the
prophets of the Lord, such as I had read of in Holy
Writ. I believed I should one day utter forth words
that should endure as long as heaven and earth. I
believed I was to be exalted among mankind, and never
dreamed that I should come to be only a poor working
girl in a factory."

SIGRUN

THE stranger thanked Lotta Hedman sincerely for her story.

"I am more than glad that I happened to be in the train to-day," he said. "Ah, if we could only hear the heavenly music oftener! Then the world would be different in many ways."

With this remark he drew back into his corner. He pulled his hat down over his eyes, but Lotta Hedman felt sure that he had not done so in order to sleep, but to think at ease over what he had heard.

After a little she felt a powerful desire to speak with him again. "Talk to him of Sigrun. Ask his advice about your journey," said a voice within her very clearly. "But why should I speak of Sigrun to one who is a stranger to her and to me?" she protested to herself. Nevertheless, in a moment the desire was there again. "Speak to him of Sigrun! Look at him, now that his hat has slipped aside. A good man who has suffered much. And of a humble heart. Whoever he meets, however fallen and deep in sin, he holds them for greater than himself. To such a man one can speak of anything. Tell him of Sigrun!"

"No, Lotta Hedman, be careful! You are not at home in Stenbroträsk now, where you know everyone. How do you know this man is as good as you say? Perhaps he is even now laughing at you in his thoughts."

The train rolled on and on, from station to station. People got out and others entered. At a great junction where several lines met, all the passengers in the third-class carriage got out, except Lotta Hedman and the stranger sitting opposite.

Hardly were they alone when the man sat straight up in his seat, put his hat in the rack above, and began to speak.

He was kind and wise, cheerful, and, above all, gentle and humble in manner. It was this gentleness that marked him, so that people could not look at him for five minutes without longing to tell him all their troubles. "That man would understand my weakness"—so thought all who met with him. "It would be good to speak with him. He would understand how hard it is for me."

And it was not long before Lotta Hedman broke off in the middle of a conversation about the box factory and work in Stenbroträsk.

"I should like to ask you about something," she said. "I am in trouble, and you know I live all alone and have no one to ask. Perhaps you could give me good advice."

"Do not say you want me to advise you," said the man. "I am surely but ill-fitted to advise. But tell me, at least, what it is that troubles you. You speak well, and this is a long journey. I am going all the way to Dalsland myself. It will be a couple of days before I get home."

"Well, it was this way. Once I had a friend. She was the eldest daughter of the Dean at Stenbroträsk. We were both going to be confirmed, and went to classes together."

Her voice choked a moment, and her eyes reddened.

"I never cared so much for anyone on earth as I did for her," she went on, after struggling a moment with her emotion.

The man sat quite still, making no attempt to hurry or assist her. He looked, indeed, somewhat embarrassed.

"Let me tell you how it was she first came to speak to me. Then you will understand what she was like."

"Do," he said. "That will be best. And take your time. We have all the day before us."

"Well, it was when we were going to the confirmation classes, and one morning, in the interval, some of us, a dozen, perhaps, were standing in a corner of the churchyard talking about a piece in the catechism. I remember one of the boys said he was sure God loved mankind, for He had made us, and so, of course, He must be pleased with His own work.

"Now the few of us standing there together, we were the youngest at the classes, and poor folk's children, all of us. The others, who were better and finer than the rest of us, walked up and down outside the church in little groups, and now and then stopped to gather round the Dean's daughter; she was going to be confirmed that year too. She was beautiful to look at, and there was something about her that drew people to her. You could hardly help looking over to where she was.

"But we others, we knew, of course, that we couldn't expect her to take any notice of us, and so we had to be content with standing in a corner talking about the catechism.

"'If we were all like her,' I said to the others, 'then God might well be pleased with us all.'

"It was the Dean's daughter we were thinking of, and then we all turned and stood looking at her.

"She had the loveliest soft brown hair, all curling at the temples and falling in soft waves over the brow and neck. A longish face, with thin cheeks and long eyelashes, and eyes like a deep well to look down in. And she seemed to be made somehow of finer stuff than the rest of us. Like some berries you can see through. She was rather tall, and walked with her head a little drooping to one side, and it seemed to us that suited her, with her looks and manner altogether."

The listener bent forward suddenly, covering his eyes with his hand. The vision of a dearly loved face rose up before him. He saw it now as it had appeared to him that day at sea, when beauty after beauty passed before their eyes. So strangely young and questioning.

"Sigrun was her name," said Lotta Hedman. "And it was an uncommon name, but that was not the only thing uncommon about her.

"Just on that day, watching her as she stood there, in the sunlight outside the church, I understood why it was one could not help looking at her.

"True, she was a human being like the rest of us. With eyes and nose and mouth as anyone else, and born in the Deanery at Stenbroträsk, and her parents

ordinary people like everyone else's. But that could
not deceive any with eyes to see. Sigrun was of another
sort than ordinary people; she was from another world."
The man, still sitting with his head resting on his
hand, nodded involuntarily. That was the very word.
From another world—a bird of passage that had lost its
way, separated from its fellows, and somehow come
among another flock not of its kind.

"For there *are* other worlds," said Lotta Hedman.
"Many worlds besides the one we live in. And Sigrun
was from one of them. But perhaps you cannot understand?"

"Yes," said the man, "I understand. I have met
someone myself once who was from another world. At
least, I think I understand," he added, as if fearing he
had spoken too confidently.

"And I slipped away into a corner under the belfry,"
went on Lotta Hedman, covering her eyes. "I wanted
to think over what this meant; that Sigrun was different from all the rest.

"If she were from another world, then surely she must
be able to see that I was one of the chosen, appointed
one day to speak the words of God. And would she
not want to speak to me herself? She who was better
than all the rest, would she not be better able to judge
and choose than they?

"But I was not left alone with my thought for long.
The others came up, all of them from our corner, that did
not dare to go up to *her;* they came and gathered round me

"'Here's Lotta Hedman sitting crying, because
Sigrun won't look at her,' said one.

"'Of course she won't—Sigrun to look at one like you, indeed, such a sight!' said another, and tried to make me see it the same way.

"'Look at your hair—sticking out all round your head like a wild bush.'

"And I sat still and let them go on. 'If it was only that,' I thought to myself. 'But it's because Sigrun is from another world, and that's worse than all the rest.'

"'And such a figure you've got,' said the others. 'No shape at all. You can never get your clothes to sit properly like others do. And your eyes are sharp and hard, and you've a voice like a raven. . . .'

"Now I hadn't been crying before, but then I felt the tears coming, because the others were all so harsh and unkind, when they tried to comfort me.

"But then all of a sudden it seemed as if a warm, gentle light filled the air in front of me—like sunlight in a room on a cold winter's day.

"A cool, soft hand drew my hands away from my face, and when I looked up it was Sigrun standing there, and smiling at me, and asking if I would row her across in my boat later on, when we had finished lessons for the day.

"And though I knew that the others must have told her that I was only a poor girl, and always ill besides; though I knew it was only for pity's sake she asked me, still I felt so happy, so happy. Oh, you can never understand how wonderful it was to feel, and I loved her from that moment."

"And I loved her from that moment," repeated the listener to himself, and felt once more the touch of a woman's lips on his face, and a little merry laugh. "Though I knew it was only for pity's sake," he whispered to himself—"though I knew well it was only for pity's sake.

"Sigrun," he murmured half aloud, "why should you come back to me like this to-day? I thought I had sent you away for ever. Why do you come back now?"

Lotta Hedman went on with her story. "But that afternoon, when we were rowing across, she asked me, Sigrun, if it was I that had heard the wonderful music in the Deanery on the day of the funeral, and asked me to tell her all about it. And I told her that and more. All the other things I had seen and heard, I told her everything, and told her, too, that I believed I was to be a seer and a prophet of God. And she did not laugh at me. Only said quite humbly that she never saw such things herself, but her dearest wish was to be a nurse. Not for ordinary people, ill with this or that, but for those stricken by the plague, or leprosy. Or if that could not be done, then she would go and care for wit-less folk, or teach the blind to read or deaf-mutes to talk. Her greatest sorrow, she said, was that she feared her father and mother would not let her go away to such work.

"I can remember even now," said Lotta Hedman, "how beautiful she was when she spoke of that."

The man sitting opposite looked up a moment, and his eyes shone. "Your story is a great delight to me," he said. "Far more than you know."

"It is very good of you to say so," said Lotta Hedman. "I thought you would have been tired of it long ago."

"Do not think that," said he. "That girl—the Dean's daughter from Stenbroträsk—you might talk to me of her all the rest of the way, and I should not be tired of hearing. And then I suppose you were friends after the day you went out in the boat together?"

"Yes," said Lotta Hedman; "we were good friends— that is true. We went out in the boat nearly every evening, as long as the lessons lasted. Sigrun liked to sit in a boat and just drift up and down, not going anywhere, but just drifting. She did not care for steamers nor for railways, and did not care for driving with horses, but she loved to drift about in a little boat. And the thing she longed for most of all was the sea."

The man sitting opposite bowed his head once more and covered his eyes. "True," he thought to himself. "She longed to see the sea. She told me that. How she had longed for it ever since she was a child of fifteen. But it was given to me to show her that. At least, I have done one good thing in my life."

Lotta Hedman did not need much encouragement from a listener; she went on, undisturbed, with her story.

"Then I thought, as soon as the confirmation classes were over, we should never see each other again, but all that summer after, Sigrun came down to the shore nearly every day, and we rowed up and down the river for hours together. And so it went on, summer after summer; it was the happiest time in all my life."

The man sighed. "Why have you come back, Sigrun?" he whispered to himself. "You, so young and good, so beautiful and unspoiled, why do you come back to me now? I have tried to think of you as a woman ageing, a mother of children, a loving and affectionate wife. Why do you come now in all the freshness of youth?"

"And now I must tell you the end of that friendship," said Lotta Hedman.

"After it had lasted four years, I was sitting at home one Sunday afternoon in spring, looking at a big red-painted farmhouse that grew up outside the east window. One wing showed out after another, and I was wondering what sort of a house it could be, and why it was being built up so grandly just that evening.

"It was getting late, and nearing twilight already. Father and mother had been to church that morning, and were sitting on either side of the hearth, smoking and talking. But I sat at the window, watching the house grow up against the grey evening sky.

"It was a red house on two floors, set high on a hill with a lot of old apple trees on the slope in front, and on one side of the orchard I could see a cowshed and barn, and on the other, stables and outhouses and a big stone store-cellar with one little room built over.

"Close by the store-cellar was a tree, of a sort I did not know. It was all knotty and rough, with a thick trunk and wide-spreading branches, and looked ever so old—there was something misshapen and threatening about it.

"Father and mother, sitting by the hearth, sat without speaking now—just thinking together. They knew each other so well.

"'It's a pity about Lotta,' said mother. And father answered at once without asking what she meant, that it was a pity, surely. He'd been thinking of the same thing, you know.

"But I thought to myself that they did not know at all, really—for how could it be a pity about me in any way, as long as I had all my visions and voices to be happy with?

"And the big farmhouse stood there clear and plain as ever. It looked as if I could just walk in at any moment through the gate and talk to the people indoors. I could see tools and things lying about in the yard, and the bucket by the well, and the dog-kennel and the pigeon-loft, and I could see it was a fine big place, but something old and out of date about it.

"It was all very still and quiet and forsaken. Not a soul, not a beast of any kind was moving anywhere.

"And then I saw something that was more surprising than all the rest. There was a stone wall round the farm and buildings and yard, between them and the fields, and in the middle a gate. And one of the gate-posts stood up straight and firm, but the other was grey and almost rotted through, and would have tumbled down if it hadn't been for a whole lot of struts and supports round it.

"Just as I caught sight of that old gatepost, I felt a shiver through me. And I knew that there was something I was afraid of, and did not want to see any more.

"I put my hands before my eyes, and turned away from the window; it would not go away. Next time I looked out, there it was, just as before, a splendid place to see, standing out against the black hills behind. And looking at a place like that in reality, you would surely think it must be rich and powerful people that lived there. Everything was well kept, except that one gatepost.

"And I tried not to look at it, because it made me afraid, but just as I turned my eyes away from it, I saw that there was someone in the house after all. Someone sitting at the window of the little room above the cellar, almost opposite the gatepost, and looking down at it.

"It was an old woman, with a stern but beautiful face, and white hair set up under a cap—I had never seen anyone wear a cap like that before. She sat quite still, with folded hands, and her eyes fixed on the post. Sitting there like a stone, just looking and looking at it all the time.

"Now I felt more afraid of her than of the post itself, and I turned away from the window, and tried to make her go away, by thinking of Sigrun.

"I thought what good friends we had been, and still were. There was nothing that could separate us. The winter before, Sigrun had been away, to visit some relatives in the south, and stayed with them for several months, but when she came back, we were just as good friends as before.

"I never needed to do more than just call for Sigrun to make all darkness vanish away. But it did not help me this time. When I turned to the window again, there was the farmhouse, just as before, and the old woman still staring darkly and fixedly down at the same spot.

"Father and mother, sitting by the hearth, were talking the same way as before.

"'Yes, it will be hard for Lotta,' said mother. 'But she's young, and young folks soon forget.'

"'Yes, that's true. As long as you're young,' said father.

"And then they sighed, and puffed away at their pipes.

"Heavy thoughts weighed on me now. I felt that father and mother were right, and that something cruel was going to happen to me.

"Then I tried again. I thought of Sigrun, as she had been, when she came to me a few months back and told me that she was engaged to a clergyman she had met while she had been away staying with her friends.

"She had been so happy at the thought of marrying a priest. It was just the thing for her, as a clergyman's daughter. And he had a living of his own already, and his own congregation, though he was only a little over thirty. It was only a small place, but then he was not to be there long. With his powers, he would certainly end as a bishop.

"So, really, it was a fine thing that he had a home of his own already, and they could get married in the autumn.

"I was a little astonished at first, for I had always thought she was going to be a nurse, but she said it was just the same when you married a priest. Better, indeed, for now she would have a whole congregation to help and look after.

"I thought over all this, and looked out again, thinking it would be better now. But it was only worse, for now the old woman stood up, and I could see her face.

And it was dark with anger and hate, and she lifted a clenched hand and shook it toward me, pointing with the other hand toward the gatepost. It was just as if she had said, if I dared to touch it, it would be the worse for me.

"She was terrible to look at, and I was frightened, but at the same time, she was so pitifully old and helpless, I felt like crying with pity for her.

"But then, just as she raised her hand, the whole thing disappeared. All—farmhouse and gatepost and the old woman herself. As if there had never been anything there at all. And oh, I felt such a relief.

"Why should I be anxious, just because Sigrun had her lover staying on a visit for a day or so? And why should mother and father be anxious about me, just because they had seen him in church that day?

"And then at last I saw a couple of heads appear on the river bank. And I was so glad, and called out to mother and father:

"'That's Sigrun, I'm sure, coming to show me her lover. Come and look, if it isn't right—the two there coming down toward the river?'

"Then mother made haste to put away her pipe and move all the chairs about and wipe up a few drops of water spilt on the floor.

"But father came over to me by the window, and we stood looking out at the two. And now I saw the man for the first time, walking there with Sigrun on his arm. He was not so very tall, but strongly built—a broad-shouldered, powerful man. And handsome, with a fine head. I could not see anything to find fault with, unless it were that he was short-sighted and wore glasses.

"When they came in, they looked proud and happy. And I was pleased, too, with Sigrun's lover, and glad they had come to see me. He looked as if he could take care of his wife, whatever might happen. As long as she had him to support her, surely she could never be unhappy or discouraged.

"The priest spoke kindly to father and mother. But when he came to speak to me, he blinked his eyes a little behind his glasses, and looked at me with a sort of smile.

"'Aha,' said he, 'so this is the great seer, the wise young woman from Stenbroträsk. I'm quite afraid of her. She can see through people, of course, and what if she were dissatisfied with me!'

"And he laughed, and Sigrun too, and father smiled a little.

"It was as if I was just something to laugh at and make fun of.

"I went all red at first, with the blood rushing to my face. Then I felt I turned all stiff and hard. And I could not understand how anyone could talk so openly about the thing that was my holiest secret. And how could Sigrun ever have betrayed me, and told her lover, when I had told her just because I could trust her?"

Lotta Hedman's voice rose to a shriller tone, just as when she had spoken of her hard and lonely life. The pain of her thoughts rang in her words.

The man before her looked up with a sad smile.

"You might surely have known it must be so," he

~aid. "Sigrun had given herself to him with all her soul, with all her thoughts, and all she had ever known."

"That was so, perhaps," said the other, "but it was cruel to me to feel. Mother tried to answer for me, for she knew I could not say anything myself then.

"'She has but a foolish mother, has my girl,' said mother. 'But the Lord has heard my prayers. He has given me a daughter that sees and understands more than most.'

"I felt how brave it was of mother to speak out. I could have gone down on my knees and thanked her, but she was silent, she too, when the priest gave her one sharp look through his eyeglasses, and began talking with a thick and heavy voice, all important, as if he might have been standing in the pulpit.

"'We've need to be ever watchful, those of us who are Christians,' he said, 'lest we should fall back into heathen ways. And whosoever seeks to penetrate into the unknown is trying, as it were, to go their own way instead of the way that is Christ Jesus. Beware of setting up other gods; of setting up oneself as God.'

"And he preached like that for a long while. And nobody in the room dared to say a word against him now. And where was all that I had seen and heard before? It all seemed blown away in a breath, the moment that man came into the house. And I had to sit there, helpless, without a word, and hear him preaching and correcting me in front of Sigrun and mother and father.

"I looked over at Sigrun, and there she was sitting, looking up at her lover all humbly and admiring. And

I could see she was pleased that he was trying to lead me into the right way. And she, too, felt now just as he did, that all we had had to talk of together before was something wicked and harmful. He was speaking for my good, and all I had to do was to turn from my erring ways and try to be like everyone else.

"I was so miserable; it was so cruel. I would rather have died than sit there and see Sigrun turn away from me like that."

The listener looked up once more.

"Yet it was good, surely, that she had no other thought, no thought of her own, but only his thoughts," he said. "That is the beautiful thing about her."

Lotta Hedman went on without heeding.

"They stayed some time, not talking to me alone, you understand, but to mother and father too. And all that the priest man said was kind and sensible in a way; he knew how to speak. When he dropped out of the preaching tone, his voice was cheerful and bright. It was easy to understand that Sigrun was fond of him.

"I did not say a word as long as he was there, and Sigrun looked at me every now and then with a sort of surprise, and at last she asked me was I ill? But I only shook my head. She didn't seem to think anything but that I ought to be quite happy about it all.

"It was a relief when at last they were gone. But then a thing happened. Sigrun had forgotten her gloves, and came back by herself to fetch them."

The man sitting listening had changed countenance. "What right have you," he asked himself, "to sit and listen to all this talk of Sigrun? Take care! Longing will return, sorrow will return, and love wake afresh. It will be just as it was six years ago, when you sat on the rocks dreaming of love. Day after day, dreaming of her."

"And then," Lotta Hedman went on—"then she asked me if I did not think her lover was wonderful and splendid; had I ever believed there was such a man in the world? And when I still said nothing, she lost patience altogether.

"'Whatever is the matter with you to-day?' she asked. 'What makes you silent and hard all at once? I thought it would do you good to talk to a priest. And he was so eager to see you himself, and I've told him so much about you, and how strange you were. And what will he think now?'

"I sat quite still until she was out of the door. But then I ran after her.

"'Oh! Sigrun, don't marry him!' I cried. 'He will make you miserable.' And Sigrun looked at me all astonished, and I said again, 'He will kill your soul, as he has killed mine!'

"Then Sigrun drew herself up.

"'Now you are wicked and unkind,' she said, 'to speak like that just because someone says things that do not please you to hear.'

"And then she went away for good.

"And I was glad that mother and father did not say anything, did not try to comfort me or explain things. I went out into the kitchen, all cold as it was, and sat down and cried. Cried for hours together. Crying for our beautiful friendship, and for my own soul that had been taken away and could never come back; I felt myself wronged and betrayed; and for the first time in my life I tasted that bitter fruit."

Lotta Hedman had lowered her voice, just as when she had ended her long speech about the letter to the King and the Millennium. Her face showed deep suffering; she felt the agony of humiliation.

HÅNGER

OH, BUT Lotta Hedman was glad to tell her story. It was a delight to be able to speak of Sigrun.

And she tried so hard to speak properly, and not in her country dialect; tried to speak as seriously as a book of devotion. And she was grateful to her listener, who sat there still, following all she said, with a patience that seemed as if it would never end.

"And now there is only one thing more I have to tell you before you can give me the advice I want," she said.

"Do not put yourself out in any way at all," he said. "Talk as you please; we have time enough before us."

Lotta Hedman dropped back immediately into the tone of the story-teller.

"Well, then, it was in the autumn of that same year," she began again, "and it had just come on to rain so heavily that we were obliged to hurry back into the house, father and mother and myself, or we should have been drenched to the skin.

"And we had hardly got indoors when the door opened and a couple of big, burly men came rushing in. They asked quite nicely if they might stay till the rain was over. And father bade them welcome, and mother and I set out each our chair for them by the door.

"And one of them was talkative, and asked father if he thought they could get work at the new sawmills they were building at Stenbroträsk. But the other man was very quiet, and said nothing, only sat staring out of the east window all the time.

"And the rain was pouring against that window with full force. There was such a stream of water down the panes you could hardly see out.

"I wondered what it could be he was staring at. For I was quite sure he must be looking at something else besides raindrops and hailstones.

"And I went up and sat down in my old place by the window and looked out.

"But there was nothing to be seen except the little grey outhouses and the water streaming from all the roofs. And it was so thick and dark outside you could hardly see as far as the river bank. And the rainclouds hung over beyond as close as a curtain.

"I thought how I had sat at that window on dark evenings, when the darkness had not hindered me from seeing; had sat there in dense snowstorms, but the snowflakes had not hindered me; I had seen ships sailing and railway trains rushing by, and kings making entry into beautiful cities, and wedding processions and angels dancing and at play before my eyes.

"But what could it help me now, though I sat at the east window? My seeing eye was closed; I could make out nothing now but the yard and the sheds and the pouring rain. There came no warnings to me now, no message, no revelations any more.

"I fancied I could see something that looked like red houses and tall woods against the grey wall of cloud, but it was all dark and indistinct.

"And I tried to feel glad that I was like others now, but my life seemed poor now, and weighed me down, now that I no longer saw or heard anything beyond what was real. I felt no joy in living. I was like one that has sat for a long time at a feast with all things plentiful, and now had not so much as a crumb to ease my hunger.

"And there was no one now that could comfort me, for Sigrun was just about to be married, and going to move down to the husband's place at Applum, in Bohuslän. She had asked me if I would go with her to her new home, and help her there, for that was what we had agreed long before. But I told her I would rather stay with mother and father in Stenbroträsk. For I would not go with Sigrun now. She had never been the same since she heard me speak ill of her lover, and I could no longer look at her now as a strange bird that had lost the way; she seemed well enough at home now among earthly things.

"Then just when my thoughts were darkest, I heard footsteps, and the silent stranger stood beside me, leaning toward the wet panes.

"'A very strange window, this,' he said, and touched my arm to make me look. 'I wonder now if you can see the same as I do?'

"'I can't see anything,' I said. 'But why do you say it is a strange window?'

"'It must be strange,' he said, 'since I am looking at Hånger farm in Dalsand through the window of a house in Stenbroträsk, ever so far away.'

"'Is that a farm standing high on a hill, with apple

trees on a slope in front?' I asked. 'Is there a store-cellar with a little room on top, and a gate with one old rotten gatepost, and an old woman sitting at the window?'

"'Yes,' he said, leaning down to see better; 'that is right. There is an old woman sitting at the window of the cellar room; it is all as you say.'

"'And she is staring at the gatepost; isn't that right? Staring as if she could not take her eyes from it?'

"'Yes,' he said, and drew a deep breath. 'Yes, sitting there watching lest the gatepost should fall. She must hold by that till the end of the world.'

"And I could see how anxious he was about what he saw. There were big drops of sweat on his forehead, and he was deadly pale, and could hardly speak.

"But then he turned away from the window, and looked quickly at me. 'But you say you can see nothing?'

"'I can see nothing now,' I said. 'But one day last spring I saw the farmhouse as you say it is.'

"And now I noticed that father and mother and the other stranger had come closer and were listening.

"'There are many in our family who have that gift,' said the other stranger to father, in a low voice, 'but I have never heard until to-day that my brother had it too.'

"But the one who had spoken to me before turned his eyes to the window again, and next moment he started back, afraid.

"'She has seen me!' he cried. 'It is all over with me now!'

"And it was strange to see him so afraid, that great, strong man. But not even mother, who was always ready enough to laugh, so much as smiled at him now.

"'Let us sing a hymn,' I whispered to mother. And we sang the first verse that came into our heads.

"And while we were singing, the rain stopped. The grey cloud hung no longer like a wall above the river bank, and a ray of sunlight stole into the room.

"The man who had seen the vision had sat down on a chair, with his hands before his face, not daring to look up or even to move.

"But now, when it cleared up and grew bright again, his brother spoke to him sensibly.

"'Come now, Jon,' he said. 'The rain has stopped, and we can go on now. Look up; you can see it is all gone now.'

"But Jon sat huddled up in his chair, and only moved his elbow to say he would not be disturbed.

"'No, Anders, no,' he said. 'Let me be. I dare not.'

"Then Anders came over to us, and shook his head.

"It is no wonder he was afraid,' he said. 'For the thing he saw was something that once was, and the place he spoke of is the place our grandfather's father came from.'

"'I think he said it was called Hånger,' I said, seeing that none of the others spoke.

"'Yes,' he answered. 'Hånger it is, and it lies in Dalsland, and we who come from there are called the trollfolk of Hånger. We are bigger in body than most men, and they say we are ill to meet, but, for my part,

I know of nothing strange about us, beyond that we all die by our own hånd. My father did so, and his father and his father's father before him.'

"When he had spoken, all was silent again. We shuddered, and could not ask nor speak a word. But the stranger seemed to feel that when he had said so much, he must go on.

"'They say it all comes of an old story,' he said. 'In the old days, the men of Hånger were proud and rich, and would submit to none, and often they were at feud with the priests. And once it seems that one of them killed a priest in a fit of jealousy. But it was never found out who had done it. The crime was never atoned, and for the sake of that sin, it has been so ever since, that all the men from Hånger must die a violent death, by their own hand or another's.'

"'But surely that can't be,' said mother. 'That the innocent should suffer for the guilty, no.'

"It happens, for all that, and none so rarely to my mind,' said the man. 'It's not easy to say how it's managed about that. But there was a woman there at Hånger, mother to him that had murdered the priest. And they say she knew all about it, and helped the son to dig a grave under one of the gateposts and long after he was dead she used to sit watching the spot, that no one should pull it up or break it down or put another post in its place. She moved down into the little room above the store-cellar, that was closer to the gate, and there she would sit watching night and day, and some say she's watching there still. And Hånger's passed from our family now, and the trollfolk of Hånger are scattered about all parts, but it seems that all of her blood can still see her. She follows us, folk say, and sees that never one of us escapes the penalty of that crime.'

"But mother would not give in.

"'It can't be that this should go on,' she said. 'There must be something you could do to make an end of it?'

"'True,' said the man. 'And there's those that have tried. Two of us there were that thought it would be well if they themselves became priests. But I don't know if the old lady found that to her mind. One of them died when he was still young—the other is still alive.'

"I was getting more and more frightened now, and, putting together all that had passed, I knew well enough what answer I should get when I put my question.

"'And is his name Rhånge?' I asked.

"'But—heavens, child!' cried mother.

"The man answered at once:

"'That's right. Rhånge he calls himself. It's just Hånger spelt round another way. He's the Pastor at Applum in Bohuslän, and just married, so I've heard, a daughter of the priest at Stenbroträsk.'"

The listener in the corner gave a sudden start.

"Well, now, I don't mean one should always go by such old stories," said Lotta Hedman. "But there might be something in this after all, and perhaps it was wrong of me not to have gone with Sigrun to Bohuslän after I had heard all this. And perhaps that's why everything has gone wrong with me since. For though

I've got back my seeing and hearing again, there's none will ever listen to what I say, and perhaps that's because I failed in my duty to Sigrun. And would it be right now?"

She broke off; her face, that had been alive with feeling, stiffened and hardened all at once.

"I can see something," she said. "Ice and snow, all white. And a tent—a black tent—and a long sledge. . . ."

The train entered a station. Lotta Hedman's fellow traveller rose hurriedly from his seat and reached up for his luggage on the rack.

Lotta Hedman did not heed; she was full of the vision that had come to her.

The man had left the train, and was moving across the platform when he heard Lotta's voice calling him back. But he went on without turning round.

Lotta pulled at the strap of the window with all her might, but by the time she had opened it, the man had disappeared.

THE MEETING

TWO days later, Lotta Hedman sat in a hired cart, jolting on along a stony road in the parish of Algeröd, in the eastern part of Bohuslän, far from the sea, right up on the Dalsland side.

"Heavens!" she thought, looking round; "this is worse than Lappland. Bare rock everywhere—I never saw the like in all my life. How can anyone live and get their wherewithal in such a desert?"

And indeed the country she was passing through was little more than a level stretch of rocky upland. Heather and juniper, moss and stunted fir showed here and there, but the rock was everywhere.

The more she looked at her surroundings, the more her spirits sank.

"What could Sigrun and her husband have been thinking of," she wondered, "to move out to a place like this? They were not so badly off before, by all accounts. Close to the sea, with a well-to-do congregation, and people round about. What possessed them to come out to a wilderness like this?"

The stony waste seemed filling her with its own desolation.

"There's no living to be got here, for priest nor any other. Well, if they've not enough to have me with them, I'll just have to go back home again, that's all."

At the moment, she felt doubtful if she had acted wisely in coming thus to visit Sigrun without an invitation, or even sending word herself beforehand of her coming. She ought at any rate to have sent a message through Sigrun's parents, or let her know in some way.

"*Herre Gud!*" she thought to herself, as she drove on. "And six years now since Sigrun left her home at Stenbroträsk, and all that time I've hardly heard a word of her. A letter or two the first year, and then I saw her once or twice the summer she came home to visit her people, but neither of us did anything really to be friends again like we used.

"I can't forget the beautiful letter she wrote me when her little daughter was born. I was so glad. And she wanted me to come to her then and help her with the little one. But I couldn't leave them at home, and I didn't really want to, I suppose. It seemed hard to go and stay with Sigrun as a maid, and I was afraid of her husband, too. Anyhow, I've regretted it since, for when the child died I couldn't help thinking it might have lived if I had been there helping Sigrun as she asked. And perhaps she thinks so too. I've never heard a word from her since then."

She felt a weight at her heart. Perhaps, after all, the long journey would come to nothing.

She strove to repress her anxiety. "What will be, must be," she told herself. "Day after day I heard voices and had warnings telling me to go. I had no peace nor rest to work things out. 'Sigrun, Sigrun, first of all,' something was always saying, when I was trying to find out about the war and the millennium.

And then, when father and mother died, and my brother took over the place and gave me the wretched little cellar room to live in—why shouldn't I start out and see if she needed me? There, Lotta Hedman, now pull yourself together. At least, you are seeing something of the world, and not wasting your money all to nothing."

As she was thus endeavouring to raise her drooping courage, the driver lifted his whip and pointed to a dark, pointed church-tower rising from a clump of trees.

"There's the church already," he said. "We're nearly there now."

Directly after, the road began to slope down into a narrow valley, with a winding river at the bottom, some farms and houses and fields, groups of trees, and a little wooden church.

But before they reached the place, the driver lifted his whip again.

"Bless me, but I do believe it's Mistress from the parsonage herself going down the road, ahead there."

At his words Lotta Hedman felt the weight at her heart almost stifling her. She could hardly breathe, and all her courage was gone in a moment.

"Oh, why ever did I come like this?" she asked herself. "Perhaps she won't even remember me. What ever made me set off on this wild adventure? Perhaps, after all, only to be laughed at and treated with scorn."

The driver of the cart evidently thought he was driving a new servant to the vicarage; he turned to Lotta and asked if he should pull up, so that she might speak to her new mistress as they passed.

"Oh, heavens!" she thought. "If I could only turn back now."

And then, when they were within a few steps of Sigrun, Lotta felt her fears completely overwhelming her. All her faith in voices and warnings was gone; she stretched out her hand to grasp the reins.

"Turn, turn back!" she cried. "I am not going any farther. It must be the wrong way."

But they were so close now that Sigrun heard, and turned round. And at sight of a strange woman trying to take the reins from the driver, a slight smile passed over her serious face.

Next moment, however, before the smile had faded, she put her hand to her heart, and hurried up to the pair.

"Oh, Lotta—is it really you?" she said, with tears in her eyes.

But at sight of her tears, Lotta thought only that they must be for her little girl that had died because she had not come to help.

She threw herself down from the cart, and would have fallen at Sigrun's feet in the road to beg her forgiveness.

But before she could do so, Sigrun had taken her in her arms, and was telling her how glad—how glad she was to see her.

And Lotta understood that Sigrun was weeping for joy that she had come.

And she herself was very happy; this was surely the greatest thing that had ever happened in her life. But at the same time she thought to herself: "Sigrun must be unhappy, indeed, if she weeps for joy at seeing one so poor as I."

THE VICARAGE

IT WAS an evening in November, when the days were short and the nights seemed as if they would never end.

All the district round about the vicarage at Algeröd was quiet and still as in the vicarage itself. The horses had come in from the fields and were stabled, the cows had been milked, and the fowls had gone to their roost.

In the brewhouse, or, rather, in the little room beside it, sat Lotta Hedman that still evening, busy with her calculations. She had the Bible before her, and pen and ink and paper, and was searching earnestly in her dear Book of Revelation.

In the kitchen, in the main building, the fire had gone out, and cook and housemaid sat at the sewing-machine trying to reshape a blouse that the seamstress had somehow mismanaged; the man was in an adjoining room, stretched on a bench, waiting for supper-time to come.

The priest was sitting in his study, but not at his writing-table. He sat in a rocking-chair in one corner of the room. A lamp was close by, and he was reading the paper. When he raised his eyes, he could see into the next room, where his wife was sitting on a low stool by the stove. She sat with her chin in her hands staring into the fire.

Close beside her sat the Bailie, who was staying at the

vicarage by arrangement. He was in poor health, and the Rhånges had been glad to take him in, since the sum he paid for his keep was a welcome aid to their scanty resources now they had moved to this poor living up in the waste lands. He was a man of about fifty, who had never done anything but please himself all his life until at last his affairs had been taken out of his hands and he himself had been sent up to a place where he would have no opportunity of wasting the little that remained to him of money and health.

The Bailie showed traces of a stroke he had had some time before: one side of his face was drawn awry, and the left eyelid hung down and could hardly be opened but, for all that, he was a fine-looking man, of good bearing. He was a man of the world, had travelled much, and was intelligent and interesting to talk to.

He had drawn up a chair near the fire, and was telling Sigrun about foreign lands, that she had never seen and never would see, now that she sat buried here in a little parsonage in Sweden.

Sigrun was busy with her own thoughts and her restless desires, and let his words pass idly by. She wished she could have listened to what he was saying; it would have perhaps dispelled her weariness and longing if she could. But it was beyond her power.

Every now and then the Pastor raised his head and looked in to them from the room where he sat. And listening, he could hear that they were talking of great cities in the lands where now the war raged at its worst. And it seemed to him very foolish of Sigrun to sit listening to all that idle chatter.

Out in the brewhouse where Lotta Hedman sat, the milkmaid had just finished rinsing her pail with hot water, and, seeing that the work was ended and the room would not be in use any more that day, Lotta moved in there with her table, her lamp, and her Bible. She drew a pair of pink stuff curtains across, in front of the great bricked-in cauldrons, hiding all the smoky black corner and making the place look more like a living-room.

She had a comfortable wicker chair to sit in, and brought out another now from the room adjoining, placing it by the table. For it was Sigrun's custom to come out and talk to Lotta for a while during the long evenings. Now and again the Bailie would come out and sit for a long time, coaxing Lotta to talk of Sigrun, and sometimes the Pastor himself would come and tease her by asking if she had yet discovered the mystery of the seven seals and the glorious millennium.

Lotta Hedman had been asked to stay at the vicarage and help with odd work, looking after the fowls and such-like, on condition that she could be content with a room in the brewhouse. She had accepted the offer with joy. Sigrun had herself put up wall paper and curtains in the little room at the side, and given her really beautiful things to furnish it with. Lotta had had her belongings sent down from Stenbroträsk, managed her own housekeeping independently of the rest of the household, and in the evenings she had the two rooms entirely to herself. It was quite like having a real drawing-room of her own.

About the same time as Lotta moved into the scullery, the lad in the men's room went into the kitchen to find someone to talk to. The milkmaid was there as well. And now all began talking about their master and mistress, and wondering if the Pastor had not yet found out that the Bailie was in love with his wife.

"He was so jealous about her before, they say," said the milkmaid, "that he moved up here on purpose, to be somewhere where she wouldn't be likely to see anyone but him. But he doesn't seem to mind about this Bailie man."

"Thinks it's not worth worrying about, I dare say," said the lad. "An old man like that, and half dead with the stroke already."

The Bailie was sitting as before by the stove in the inner room. But he was silent now, and had drawn up his chair and sat deep in thought.

He knew that Sigrun had not been listening to what he told her. What could he find to talk about that would make her listen to him?

He had spoken of life in the great cities of the world, and of the part women played there. He had spoken of women as those whose mission it was to reconcile one to life. Said that men became humble and good when they met with beauty, personified in the likeness of a young woman. He had told her that one possessing the gift of beauty should regard it as a duty to use it for healing, reconciling, bettering her fellow creatures.

But, to tell the truth, he hardly knew whether she had heard a single word of all he had said.

It was easier to attract her attention when her husband was there. Then, he never spoke to her at all, but only to the Pastor.

And then, he felt, he was forcing her to make comparison between the experienced man of the world and the simple Priest; between one who had seen and shared in great events and one who buried himself in a wilderness, never studying, never progressing, but in a fair way to sink to the level of a common peasant.

He knew that the Priest despised him. He was often irritated and humiliated by his host's treatment. But he bore it all very patiently, knowing that nothing was more calculated to lower the husband in the eyes of his wife than his showing himself tactless and devoid of finer feeling.

The Bailie sat silent for some minutes, and then taking a subject near at hand in these days of the Great War, he commenced to talk of the Red Cross, its originators, its organization, and the brave work of the Red Cross Sisters in the war.

He noticed at once that the beautiful woman by his side became attentive; she tore herself away from her own thoughts and listened.

Just at the moment when the Bailie had begun talking about the Red Cross, it happened that Lotta Hedman lifted her eyes from her Bible. Her thoughts were suddenly restless, and she could not keep her mind concentrated on her work.

"I wonder," she thought to herself, "if Sigrun has ceased to love her husband. She hardly ever speaks of him now. And the servants say he plagues her with his jealousy. But one thing is certain: he wrongs her in that. If she does not care for him, she certainly cares for no other man."

A sudden smile lit up her face.

"And here's this foolish old invalid trying to make himself agreeable," she thought. "But that matters little; nobody bothers about him."

"It must be a great misfortune to be so beautiful as Sigrun," she told herself. "You are better off as you are, Lotta."

She turned to her Bible again and tried not to think of Sigrun any more. "I hope it doesn't mean something is going to happen to her, since I am so anxious all of a sudden."

The Pastor sat on in his room, reading by the light of the lamp. Again and again he had glanced at the pair by the stove, noting quite carelessly and easily how they sat there, while they, on their part, found nothing to disturb them in the thought that he could see them all the time. Then suddenly he noticed a change. It was impossible to say where it lay. Perhaps the speaker's voice had grown louder and warmer; perhaps the young wife's attitude was different. The Pastor laid down his paper, rose to his feet, and, leaning forward with all his senses on the alert, he watched them.

The visitor was still talking about nursing and works of mercy during the war. After a little while, he saw that a tear rolled down the woman's cheek and dropped to her knee, glistened there a moment, and disappeared; then, very gently, tear after tear fell.

For a long time he went on talking, without appearing

to notice her emotion; then, suddenly, he bent forward so that he almost touched her.

"So that is what you have been wanting—that is what you are longing for?" he said. "You want to take part in the work out there yourself?"

She folded her hands and held them out toward him.

"Oh, how can I help it?" she cried—"longing for it with all my heart. It is dreadful to live on here in comfort, doing nothing."

"But could you not get away, then?"

"There would be nothing wrong in it," said the woman, lifting her folded hands toward the speaker. "If I could only be free for just a little while. After all, I am a human being—I ought to be allowed to choose for myself for once."

The sick man took her hands in his and drew them toward him.

"True, indeed!" he said. "You have the right to live as well as the rest of us."

Just then they heard footsteps behind them, saw a fierce face in the doorway of the study, and both cried aloud in dismay. The Pastor came rushing toward them, in a violent passion, which left no possibility of any explanation.

The Bailie seemed to lose his self-possession altogether. He crouched down in his chair without moving, but Sigrun threw herself toward her husband to stop him.

"Run, quick—make haste!" she cried. And the Bailie sprang to his feet and ran toward the door, while Sigrun for a moment held her husband fast.

"Edward—what is the matter?" she asked.

He did not answer, but flung her aside. She fell to the floor, striking herself badly against a corner of the table, but the Pastor, without heeding her, rushed after the fugitive, out into the hall, down the steps, and across the courtyard.

Lotta Hedman, sitting in the scullery with her Bible, was suddenly roused by the shouting and banging of doors and hurrying feet. She rose hurriedly, opened the door, and looked out. Two men were running across the courtyard; in a moment they had disappeared in the darkness.

While Lotta stood there terrified, listening to the retreating footsteps, the lad and the maids in the kitchen had likewise heard the noise, and sprung up from their seats. And now they saw their young mistress come staggering in toward them, her hair and dress in disorder, and the blood flowing from a cut on her forehead. All four hurried to her, but she waved them off impatiently.

"Never mind about me," she cried. "Hurry after my husband and—the other one. Quick, and look after them before they kill each other."

The four stood still, too confused to act on her orders, and she cried excitedly:

"Don't sit there staring at me! After them, before they kill each other!"

At this the lad hurried out, and the milkmaid, a big strong girl, followed after him, but the two others stayed in the kitchen to look to their mistress.

They brought forward a chair and begged her to sit

down, for she was trembling as if the floor were swaying under her.

Her strength was at an end now, and she fell to crying like a child.

"Help me over to Lotta Hedman," she cried. "Help me over to Lotta."

The two servants took her under the arms and led her across the courtyard to Lotta's room.

And Lotta, standing in the doorway, saw them coming, and hurried forward to meet Sigrun. She led her to the wicker chair that had been waiting for her all the evening.

"And I have done nothing," said Sigrun. "Lotta, I have done nothing wrong. We were just talking, that was all. And he was sitting in the next room, watching."

Suddenly she turned deathly pale, and would have fainted, but Lotta dashed water in her face, and she came to herself.

Lotta made haste to wash the cut on her head, and saw it was neither deep nor serious; but what troubled her most was that Sigrun seemed hardly to be quite clear in her mind. She talked all the time, repeating the same thing over and over again.

"And I have done nothing," she said. "I have done nothing wrong. We were just talking. And he was sitting in the next room, watching."

"Oh, I know, Sigrun—I know you have done no wrong," said Lotta, addressing her now familiarly, as in the old days.

"You understand, Lotta, I know," said Sigrun again. "I have done nothing. . . ."

Lotta tried to interrupt her.

"Sigrun, I'm so afraid you will be ill," she said. "We must ask Malin to get your bed ready, and you can lie down."

But at this, the flow of words suddenly stopped.

"No, not there! I will never go back to him," said the sick woman quite briefly and clearly.

"But, dear angel," said Lotta. "You can never mean that!"

"I will lie down here," said Sigrun. "I will sleep in your bed, Lotta. I can feel I am going to be ill. And I must be in a place where I feel safe."

A moment later she began again as before:

"I have done nothing wrong. We were just talking. And he was sitting in the next room, and came rushing in. . . ."

She looked at them with her eyes all wild, as if wondering why they did not follow what she was saying.

Lotta talked over with the two servants what was best to be done. They could find nothing better than to let the sick woman have her way. The housemaid hurried into the house and came back with sheets and pillows and blankets. Sigrun began hurriedly undressing; they had scarcely got the bed done before she was ready.

And as she was getting into bed, she cried again, so that it could be heard all through the place: "I have done nothing wrong. We were just talking. And he was in the next room, and came running in. . . ."

As soon as Sigrun was well in bed, she called gently to Lotta:

"Don't go to bed yet, Lotta. Sit there by the table and read your Bible. And mind, you must not let anyone in the world come and take me away from here."

And so it was. Lotta sat down with her Bible and the two servants went into the house to see how matters were going there.

A moment later one of them came back with the news that nothing very terrible had happened. The Bailie had made his escape; the Pastor himself had fallen into a ditch in his pursuit, and they feared he had broken his leg. Bad enough, certainly, yet not by any means the worst that might have happened.

Sigrun was still crying aloud her explanation, but when Lotta had told her several times that there had been no fight between the men, she seemed to grow calmer, and went off to sleep.

PREPARATIONS

THOSE who heard, in this way or that, of the regrettable event which took place some weeks later in the vicarage of Algeröd were inclined to throw all the blame on Lotta Hedman.

"If the young mistress there hadn't had that half-mad creature about the place, turning her head completely with her visions and warnings, it would never have happened," they said.

But this was not fair to Lotta Hedman. Never in all her life had she been so quiet and sensible as during that time. Her friends in the other world left her in ignorance, and she had not the slightest inkling of what was to happen.

It is easy to understand that she must have been terribly anxious the first night, sitting watching by Sigrun's bedside. "How is this to end?" she asked herself again and again. "How are these two ever to begin life again together? Sigrun is altogether terrified, and he must have lost his senses altogether, and behaved like a wild beast.

"Anyhow," she thought, trying to comfort herself, "it can only have been his jealousy. And though Sigrun is just as much afraid of him as ever, it is easy to see she is still fond of him. If only love is there, then, surely, it will bring them together again."

About one o'clock that night, Sigrun opened her eyes and sat up in bed, looking round her in bewilderment. She seemed a little confused at first, but soon came to herself, and said to Lotta in a perfectly calm voice:

"Go and lie down now, Lotta. But do not put out the lamp, and do not undress. You must be ready to help me."

Then she sank back on the pillows and went to sleep again. "She is still frightened," thought Lotta, "but she is in her senses again now. Thank Heaven for that. To-morrow she will be well again."

She did as Sigrun had said—lay down on a small folding sofa and slept till seven o'clock, when she rose and was going out to look to the fowls. But just as she reached the door, Sigrun called her back.

Sigrun was crying and trembling at the thought of being left alone. She was terribly nervous again now, and when Lotta told her that her husband was hurt and unable to move, she did not seem to understand.

Lotta had to content herself with standing at the window looking out into the grey autumn dark, until the milkmaid came across. She called her in, told her that her mistress was very ill and could not be left alone, and asked her to attend to her work for the morning.

The milkmaid, too, had something to tell. The Bailie had not come back at all. He had taken refuge with the verger, who lived not far from the vicarage. He had stayed the night there, and next morning a boy from the house came over to fetch his belongings.

No one regretted his going; it was a relief to have him out of the way. The Pastor himself was in a bad way.

He thought his leg was broken; a doctor had been telephoned for, and had promised to come over during the day.

"That's what comes of getting mad beyond reason," said the dairymaid. "We all knew that the Bailie was taken with Mistress, but none but a fool would ever believe she could care for a broken-down old creature like him."

Lotta Hedman, for her part, was not altogether sorry about the Pastor's accident. It would force him to keep to his bed, and Sigrun would have time to get over her fright. Lotta was almost inclined to regard it as a special intervention of Providence.

"Thank Heaven," she sighed. "It will be all right now. And perhaps when it's all over they may be happier than before."

A little later in the day, the boy from the verger's came over stealthily with a letter, but Lotta sent it back unopened.

Otherwise, the day passed quietly. Sigrun did not get up, but slept for hours together. And she was not the only one. The whole of the household seemed to have fallen into the same slumber as its mistress.

"It's all so quiet about the house to-day, it's almost uncanny," said the cook and the housemaid, when they came out to the brewhouse to ask how Mistress was getting on. "Like as if someone was on a death-bed."

The Pastor sent for Lotta, to ask after his wife. And Lotta went in and told him, with perfect truth, that Sigrun was asleep, had no fever, and that the slight cut on her forehead was nothing to speak of.

But when he suggested that Sigrun should be moved back into the house, Lotta firmly refused. Much better leave her where she was. She was all of a tremble still, and nervous.

"Afraid of me, I suppose," said her husband.

His face was marked with suffering. It was not only the broken leg that caused him pain.

"She will come back of her own accord, once she is strong again," said Lotta hastily.

The sick man sighed. "She will never come back to me," he said. "Never to me. She will never have the courage to come back."

Lotta Hedman had not thought she could ever feel any pity for the man who had destroyed her beautiful dreams as a girl. But now she tried, at any rate, to comfort him.

"Oh, surely, happiness will come to the house again," she said.

And she had really no thought of separating man and wife. She did, indeed, all that lay in her power to reconcile and reunite them.

When the doctor came, late in the afternoon, he said much the same about Sigrun as Lotta had done: she was not suffering from any actual disease, but would get well if only she were left in peace. Her nerves had been upset, and a sort of crisis had occurred.

They would have to be careful with her. She must not be contradicted, nor allowed to exert herself. She must not be persuaded to do anything but what she wished.

"I can't quite make out this case," said the doctor.

"Possibly, it may be something quite different. Fru Rhånge might, for instance, have contracted some sort of infection, and have the germ of some disease in her now, to break out suddenly and seriously later on. But I cannot say for certain just at present."

These words of the doctor's were of great service to Lotta afterward; several of those at the vicarage had been present at the time, and heard what he said. And she herself was surprised when she thought of it, and believed he must have been directed from above to speak as he did.

A whole week passed without any change. Every day a messenger came stealing over from the verger's and was sent back without having gained his end. Each day Lotta was sent for by the vicar to report. And each day Sigrun lay dozing from morning till evening.

Afterward, when Lotta thought of this continuous sleep, she told herself that there must have been something within that knew what was to come. "It was not because she was tired and worn out that Sigrun slept so; no, she was just gathering strength for what she had to do."

Even when she was awake, Sigrun lay quiet and still. She would draw her eyebrows together, and nod her head now and again, as if agreeing to something she herself proposed. Lotta was convinced that she lay there making plans for the future, but as yet she had no knowledge of them.

One day Sigrun asked her to go across to the house and fetch some money—six hundred kronor—from a drawer in her bureau. "It is all my own," she said.

"I have saved up all the money father and mother gave me on my birthdays. You can understand I am anxious about it now, with no one about in the house all day."

Then one day Sigrun wanted something to read, and Lotta brought her a newspaper. She lay for a long time reading the advertisements of steamer routes and railway connections. Then she laid the paper aside. Lotta paid no heed to that at the time, but afterward she remembered.

In the course of that one quiet week, the winter had come in earnest. It was not particularly cold, but a good deal of snow had fallen, and the ground was white all round. The snow was deep enough, indeed, for sledges.

This whiteness outside her window reminded Sigrun of her home and the long winters there—and the thought seemed to cheer her. On the day when the first snow came, she got up and dressed.

"That's right, my angel," said Lotta Hedman. "You'll get strong all the sooner, if you sit up a little. I'm sure now we shall have you well by Christmas."

Sigrun stopped suddenly in her dressing.

"Will it be Christmas soon?" she asked. "I had forgotten all about Christmas." She was plainly distressed at being reminded of the coming feast. The impossibility of spending Christmas anywhere but in her home seemed to strike her. "If anything's to be done, it must be done before then," she murmured. "I must have it all over before Christmas."

Lotta Hedman heard what she said, but thought it

referred to some ordinary preparations for Christmas which must be completed in time.

One evening, Lotta Hedman told Sigrun about the man she had met in the train. She described his appearance, his gentle, pleasant voice, his humility. "He was so kind to me," she said. "But just as one of my visions was coming, he ran away."

"What sort of a vision?" asked Sigrun.

"Something from the far north," said Lotta. "I saw a field of ice, and a black tent, and a long sledge."

Sigrun lay without speaking, searching her memory.

"Lotta," she said, after a while, "this is a strange thing. It must be Sven Elversson, and no other, that you met. He is just as you said to look at, and it would be just like him to run away as soon as you began to see visions that would remind him of icefields and the Arctic."

"Who is Sven Elversson?" asked Lotta.

Sigrun roused herself a little from her dreamy state and told Lotta something of Sven Elversson's story.

"I wish I knew where he is now," she said at last. "He was a very good man, and very unhappy. I believe he felt himself so despised, so trodden underfoot, that he looked on it as his business to attend to things which others counted themselves too good for. Once he let himself be shut up in a cell with a murderer, to get him to confess. He married a woman from a children's school, one of the ugliest creatures I have ever seen. That was out of sheer humility, too, I suppose. When we lived at Applum, everybody spoke of him. But he moved away from there before we did."

Lotta Hedman remembered her travelling companion's gentle voice and the feeling of confidence with which he had inspired her.

"Be sure God has some purpose in view with that man," she said. "If only I had known of this when I met him."

"I wish I knew where he is to be found," said Sigrun. "All who are miserable and in trouble turn to him. There has been so little news of him since he left Applum. He must have hidden himself away in some place where no one knows his story."

That evening, when they spoke of Sven Elversson, Sigrun was up and dressed again. She had even been through into the next room. Lotta had moved out chairs and a table, and the great cauldron was hidden by the pink curtains. The housemaid had laid a tray with tea for Sigrun and Lotta, and they were comfortable as could be.

But when the maid asked if Mistress was not well enough now to move over into the house again, Sigrun answered quickly:

"I don't know what is the matter with me, Malin. But I think I am going to be really ill. I've a pain in my head and throat this evening. And I'm red all over my body. It must be something breaking out."

"Now, what does she mean by saying that?" thought Lotta. "She's perfectly well. And not a bit of red all over or breaking out."

She came to the conclusion that her friend was trying to make it appear impossible that she should spend Christmas in her own home. "What will come of it all?" thought Lotta anxiously. "Will she never get over this fear of her husband? Oh, but it was always like that with her. Once she is frightened of anyone, it is hopeless to try and calm her.

"And to think that she, who always wanted to be a nurse, doesn't go in now and look after him herself. She doesn't even ask how he is. It's a bad sign, that."

Lotta sat watching her friend. Sigrun looked weak and languid, as sick persons do after some days in bed.

"What unhappy fate is pursuing her?" thought Lotta. "Why should she, pure and innocent as she is, the finest, loveliest creature, sit here in a room little better than an outhouse?"

And indeed the contrast was striking enough—the delicate beauty of the young mistress and the bare wooden walls of the brewhouse, the rough plank floor and smoky ceiling.

"It's a sad pity about them both," thought Lotta. "It must be miserable for him, too, lying on a bed of pain and longing for her."

There was sadness in the air. After a while, Lotta saw how her friend covered her face with her hands and sat rocking to and fro.

"Oh, I wish I were dead!" she moaned. "It would be best. If only I could die."

"It is too dull and melancholy for you, Sigrun, to go on staying here," said Lotta. "I think you had better move over to the house to-morrow."

Sigrun started up; her face turned greyish pale.

"What do you mean?—what's that you say? Has he been bribing you?"

"Sigrun—you must be mad. How could you think of such a thing?"

"Mad—yes, Lotta. I am mad, maddened with fear. Oh, you don't know what I have suffered."

And she began to tell. Not much, but just enough to make Lotta understand. "And how can I go back to it all?" she said.

"But, Sigrun, it only shows how fond of you he is."

"I do not care for him," said Sigrun. "I have never, never been unfaithful to him, Lotta, mark my words; never in so much as a single thought. But he has never trusted me, and that hurts me. It hurts me more than anything else."

Lotta Hedman said something about jealousy being something that belonged to youth. It disappeared naturally as one grew older.

"No," said Sigrun. "Not with him. It is hereditary; all his family have been the same. He has promised me again and again to give it up. But what difference has it made? We moved up here into this wilderness, that he might be in peace. And you can see what we have gained by that.

"You think, perhaps, I have no pity for him? No one knows better than I do how he suffers. And he is going downhill, Lotta; his sermons are poor, and he is losing all interest. It is dreadful for him.

"But it is dreadful for me, too. I have been terrified. He has frightened me now so many times that I have no courage left. You would have to put me in chains to drag me in there now. But you can't understand."

"But—if you can't go back to him," said Lotta, "what are you going to do?"

The young mistress rose to her feet.

"Let us go to bed, Lotta," she said, with a bitter little laugh. "It is past ten o'clock, and you must be up early to-morrow to your work."

THE FLIGHT

NEXT day Sigrun lay in bed. She had a pain in her throat, she said. No one but Lotta was allowed to go in. And Lotta was charged to tell the Pastor that her mistress was likely to be ill for some time.

She lay in bed all that day. Not until after supper, when the servants had gone to bed, did she get up. Then she dressed, and came out to Lotta in the scullery.

"Do you feel better now?"

Sigrun smiled. "Yes, Lotta, much better."

It had been a hard day for Lotta. She was beginning to realize that Sigrun was preparing to leave her home. And she wondered what she could do to prevent such a disaster.

"I have been thinking," said Lotta. "It seems to me you ought to go home to Stenbroträsk for Christmas. It would be much better for you, and far more proper than staying over Christmas out here like this."

Sigrun did not seem altogether unwilling. She said no, at first, but when Lotta began to talk of the splendid Christmas they always had there, she appeared to think it worth considering.

They stayed up late again that night. Sigrun sat in silence, pondering over something she could not quite make out, and Lotta did not venture to disturb her.

A little after eleven, the door opened suddenly, and a woman stumbled into the room, took a step or two, and sank to her knees on the floor, holding out her hands.

"If there's any human soul here, help me!" she cried. "I'm so ill, so ill. I'm burning all over."

Sigrun's weakness and weariness were gone in a moment. She sprang to the stranger and helped her up, put one arm round her, and supported her.

"Come with me," she said gently. "Come over to the light and let me see what is the matter first."

The woman stood there shaking and trembling with fever. She could not lift her feet, but shuffled help-lessly, and would have fallen but for Sigrun's aid.

Helping her over to the light, she saw that the woman's face was terribly swollen and disfigured. Dark breaking blisters close, close together all over. And the same with her hands.

"Lotta!" said Sigrun in a low, trembling voice. "What is it?"

But there was no need for Lotta to answer. Sigrun knew as well as she did what the sickness was.

She knew, too, that it was risking death to touch the poor vagrant, yet she began resolutely stripping off her clothes, and while Lotta Hedman made the bed ready, spreading clean sheets, cool and smooth for the hot and tender skin. Sigrun gave her clean linen underclothes, and soon they had the groaning, shivering woman stretched on the bed.

And there they sat, full of pity for her, while she moaned and writhed in pain. Sigrun tried to give her water, but she seemed unable to swallow. Then the mistress turned again to Lotta, and the two sat hand in hand, silent and horrified at the power of the dreadful disease.

Soon they breathed more easily; the sick woman seemed to be quieter now, and suffering less.

And a little later, a short hour since she had first entered, she was perfectly calm and motionless. The uneven breathing stopped.

The two friends rose, laid the dead woman out where she lay, and crouched together as before, close to each other, as if petrified by the terrible dead face.

"A few days, and I shall look like that"—the same thought was in the minds of both. "Look like she does now. No one would recognize me. No one could say who it was."

"Who can she be?" asked Lotta in a whisper. And Sigrun answered in the same low voice that it must be some poor vagrant with no home to go to.

"Her clothes were not so very bad," she went on. "But sadly worn. Her boots are wet and trodden through; she has tramped a long way through the snow. The sickness must have come upon her on the road, and she has wandered about over the country in delirium. It must have been the light from our lamp that made her come here."

Again they sat in silence, watching the dead. And now it was that a dreadful thought came to Sigrun.

"If I lay there in her place," she said to herself. "Why not? Why should I not manage it so that it is Sigrun Rhånge who lies there?"

It seemed as if Lotta Hedman had read her thought;

she turned to Sigrun and stared at her in breathless fear.

"No one knows her," said Sigrun. Her voice was no longer low and whispering, but firm and decided. "No one knows where she comes from. No one can have seen her come in here. A poor vagrant without a home."

Lotta said nothing. She would not betray her suspicions. If Sigrun were not thinking of that after all, then it would be best to say nothing.

Sigrun went on as before:

"You know what it is, Lotta—the smallpox. And she lies dead in my bed, and the bed and the whole place will have to be disinfected; we shall not be able to stay here. We should have to move over into the house. And perhaps I may have caught it myself already, and die—if I did, all would be well. But I might get better, and then I should be back in all the old misery again."

"But it will be better now, after all you have gone through," said Lotta eagerly. "Your husband knows he has wronged you now. He will be more careful."

Sigrun rose, and moved the lamp into the other room.

"We must not disturb her," she said.

"You have so many happy years before you," said Lotta. "When you are both a little older, it will be calm and quiet for you again. And he is such a splendid man, clever and understanding."

Sigrun stood full in the light from the lamp, and Lotta was astonished at the change in her. In a moment she seemed to have regained all her former beauty, more. There was a splendour of majesty and power about her now. Lotta could not help feeling that Sigrun was something higher than others; that she must be loved and protected more than all others.

"Lotta," said Sigrun, "you see now that it was for this you were sent here from Stenbroträsk—to help me with this?"

This was speaking in a language Lotta understood. But she would not be won over so easily.

"Dear angel, it might be I was sent to hinder you," she said.

Sigrun made Lotta sit down in one of the wicker chairs, and then, kneeling at her feet, took her hands and said in a voice of earnest conviction:

"I promised Edward once that nothing but death should make me leave him. And that is why I have not gone away before. And all this week I have prayed to God that I might die rather than be forced to break my promise. Now, though I am in fear of him, and cannot stay, it has held me back. Lotta, you understand?"

Lotta nodded reluctantly.

"And now, Lotta, God has heard my prayers. He has sent Death to me. And so I can go without breaking my word. Lotta, surely *you* should understand that this is God's will?"

"No more of this, Sigrun," said Lotta, trying to rise. But her mistress held her back.

"It is God Himself helping me, Lotta," she said. "Now I can go away without making Edward unhappy. Oh, I don't mean he would not mourn for me a year or two, perhaps, but it would be without bitter-

ness. But if I ran away from him—do you think he
would ever allow it? He would go out to search for me
everywhere, and when he found me, he might kill me.
Or if I got a divorce? It would be the death of him.
But to go this way—out of life altogether. . . .

"It would only be a quiet sorrow. He could not be jealous of Death. Don't you see, Lotta, how much better it
would be for him than anything else?"

"For him, perhaps," said Lotta. "But for you?"

"For me," said the young wife, with a smile that was
like a light from heaven—"for me, all is good that is
best for him."

"The best thing for him would be to keep you," said
Lotta decidedly.

"But I cannot!" cried Sigrun despairingly. "You
don't know what it means to be watched every hour,
never to be free. You don't know what it is, with all
these terrible scenes and quarrels and promises to be
better, when it never is better, and ill-humour and
misery. You don't know what it is to go in constant
fear of something dreadful happening. To be always
forced to lie and hide things, though you have done nothing but what was good and right. Oh, you don't know
what it is like, or you would not ask me to go back."

"No," said Lotta—"no, angel dear, I did not know
you had suffered like that. You have never spoken of
it until yesterday and to-day. But is there no other
way?"

Sigrun rose to her feet. "There is one way. And
God has sent it. But Lotta Hedman will not let me take
that way."

Nothing could describe the torturing power of Sigrun's beauty as she spoke such words as these. A witchery seemed to emanate from her being, and she knew it, and never, perhaps, had she used it so mercilessly, so victoriously as to-night.

"I am doing no wrong, Lotta," she said. "I am going to the war, to help the wounded. That is my one desire. I am ashamed to stay at home doing nothing. You know it is what I have longed for all my life. And God is helping me, Lotta. Why will you not help me?"

What could poor Lotta Hedman say? She had never loved Sigrun as she did this night. She resisted still, knowing that Rhånge came of a family of suicides. Perhaps he would kill himself if he lost his wife. But she dared not say anything of this to Sigrun; it might only increase her fear of him.

"But you have your father and mother at home," was all she could find to say.

"You forget the infection. I cannot go home to them now."

She went over to Lotta and made her sit down again in the chair.

"Lotta, I am so unhappy," she said. "Every day is an agony. Am I to suffer like this all my life?"

"But, Sigrun, how can you bring this sorrow on us all?"

"Sorrow?" said Sigrun—"sorrow? What is it, after all, to sorrow for the dead? What is it compared with sorrowing for the living? I must do it, Lotta, for Edward's sake. Think what a man he was when I first met him. Calm, happy, eager to make his way. A good preacher, and loved by his congregation. Now—can you not see how he has changed? He is going to ruin here in poverty and loneliness. I must leave him, Lotta. If I were dead, he would find another place, another living, where he could rise to all that he meant to do when he had the ill-fortune to meet me."

"You cannot make me see that you need do anything so dreadful."

Sigrun shrugged her shoulders.

"I am not trying to make you believe that it is only for his sake. I do it because I am miserable, and must free myself from my misery. Oh, Lotta, if only I could really die! I know that would be the best. But, next to that, the best thing is for me to disappear. I am going to pieces; it is driving me mad. Perhaps I am mad already."

"But do you ask me to help you go away so that I shall never see you again?" said Lotta despairingly. She had not thought to speak of herself, but she felt driven to use every argument she could find.

"Why should you not see me again, after a few years?" said Sigrun. "Listen, and I will tell you all my plan. I will go on foot the first few miles, till I come to a parish where no one knows me. There I can get a cart to take me to the nearest station. Then by train to Göteborg, and from there to America. There I can enter a training school for nurses, and then go to the war. You see, there is nothing impossible about it. And when a few years have passed, I can write for you."

"Do not try to persuade me," said Lotta. "I should have to tell all sorts of lies, and I could never do it."

With indescribable bitterness Sigrun answered:

"I have had to lie every day since I was married."

Lotta Hedman was overwhelmed; her heart was wrung with pity. "Let her have her will," she said to herself. And at the same time, she was so full of anxiety at what Sigrun was about to do that she began to weep.

"God was willing to help me," said Sigrun, "but Lotta Hedman would not."

"But, Sigrun," cried Lotta, dashing away a tear with the back of her hand, "will you force me to help you ruin yourself? You ask me to help you in something so dreadful that I tremble at the very thought. You will no longer have a name among the living. You will go out into the world without friends, or parents, without even being able to say where you come from. It will be misery if you succeed, and shameful and terrible if you are found out."

But her words were of no avail. The young mistress was as firmly resolved as before. But she ceased begging and persuading now; she began to threaten.

"Lotta, mark my words; if you will not help me as I ask, then to-morrow I go to the verger's to him who is waiting for me there."

"You would never do that," said Lotta.

"I would do anything. Anything but go back to the old life."

Before Lotta could reply to this, something happened. There was a sound of footsteps approaching from outside—a cautious tread, but heavy and distinct. The sound did not stop at the entrance, but continued round the house. Once or twice again it was heard; then it died away.

Sigrun made a sign to Lotta, who hurried to a window, drew aside the curtain, and looked out into the snowy-clear night.

"It was the farm lad," she said.

The beautiful woman drew herself up. Her eyebrows contracted, her head was raised, her eyes shot a furious glance at someone who was not there.

"He has done that every night," she said, "since I moved over here. It is by his master's orders. He is watching. Listening to hear if I have a lover with me."

Lotta said nothing. She was beginning to give up all further resistance.

"And you, Lotta; you think Edward will change? Well, there you can see. Does he trust me now any more than before? Sending a boy to spy on me?"

She raised her voice as she spoke; the insult of her husband's suspicion wounded every fibre of her being.

"It can never come right between them after this," thought Lotta. "He has killed all the love that was in her. Perhaps it is best that she should go."

And so it was that Lotta Hedman gave way before the sudden conviction that Sigrun's love for her husband was dead or dying, though she would not admit it herself—was not even, perhaps, aware of it.

Lotta protested no more. She did not assent in words, but she ceased to oppose.

Some time passed in hasty preparations. Sigrun took off her rings and borrowed a change of clothing from Lotta. A little underclothing and the six hundred kronor she packed away in a leather bag, likewise belonging to Lotta, who further had to provide a cloak and kerchief. It was essential that nothing of Sigrun's own clothing should be missing.

When Sigrun was nearly ready, she turned suddenly to Lotta and stood still.

"Lotta, you understand that all this has been brought about by the hand of God? Do not fear either for me or for yourself."

Her courage and presence of mind were admirable in their way. She showed not the least hesitation or fear.

But when all was ready, there came a hard moment at the last.

"I am leaving so much that is dear to me," she said. The tears flowed down her cheeks; she seemed to realize at once the full seriousness of the irrevocable step she was about to take.

"Now I shall never look at the little picture of Stenroträsk again, that comforted me so many times. And the locket with the portrait of my little girl—I dare not take that either."

"That, at least, you might take, I think," said Lotta. "But you need not go at all," she added.

"And, Lotta, you know there is one of the cows I was so fond of. Look after her a little when you can."

She moved toward the door.

"Don't forget, Lotta, when my Christmas rose comes out, to put it on Edward's writing-table."

Then she kissed Lotta Hedman for the first time, and went away.

Sigrun had not been gone more than a quarter of an hour when Lotta again heard footsteps outside—a light, careful tread, not the heavy tramp of the farm lad. The moment she heard it, she thought to herself: "What a mercy! It is Sigrun come back again after all."

But no sooner had she drawn the bolt and opened the door than she found herself face to face with a strange man. No wonder the poor girl was terrified. Never in her life had she felt so sinful and conscience-stricken as now.

"Eh, Lotta, Lotta," she thought to herself. "It is beginning already."

The fellow was poorly dressed, with a big slouch hat. Evidently, some sort of a vagabond. "For Heaven's sake, don't come in here," said Lotta, placing herself in his way. "We've smallpox in the house, and there's one lying dead inside there."

The man did not make off at once, as Lotta had expected. He stood in the doorway, looking round the room.

And before she could guess his intention, he had thrust her aside, and strode across to the entrance of the little room beyond, looking in at the bed where the dead woman lay.

But Lotta gave him no time for close observation. She rushed after him and threw her arms about him, pulled him away, and closed the bedroom door.

The man made no resistance. He seemed to think she was anxious to keep him away from infection.

"It won't hurt me," he said. "I've got it already if I'm to have it. The woman in there is my wife. She was taken bad a couple of days ago, and this morning she was delirious and ran off."

It was evident that he was speaking the truth—and the whole of Sigrun's plan was thus of no avail. Lotta felt as if the place were falling about her ears.

"But—who are you, then?" she asked.

"I'm not exactly a stranger here," said the man in a calm, quiet voice. "I'm a knife-grinder, and they know me here at the vicarage. I was here only a week ago, doing the scissors and knives. I go about with my horse and cart and grindstone from place to place, and I've not what you could call a proper house of my own for nursing sick folk. When Ruth was taken bad, I was going to get her down to a hospital, but then she ran away, poor creature. I've been wandering about looking for her all day. I wonder how she managed to get here."

Worse and worse. Lotta felt as if the ground beneath her feet were giving way. But, in her confusion, she yet made one more endeavour to save her friend.

"But it's not your wife lying there," she said. "It's my dear mistress."

"Eh?" said the knife-grinder. "The pretty mistress—is she dead? Did they let her lie out here in an outhouse and die?"

"She wished it so herself," said Lotta Hedman.

"Why, then, I beg pardon for tramping in like I did,"

said the man. "I'll have to be seeking Ruth somewhere else."

He was a little, withered man, with a dark skin and one shoulder constantly thrust up, which gave him a look of sullenness and discontent. Lotta remembered well that the last time he had been at the vicarage he had been rude and troublesome. But now, in the presence of sickness and death, he was quiet and humble.

To Lotta's great relief, he moved toward the door. But then he stopped. There before him lay a pair of wet, downtrodden boots.

"But—these are Ruth's," he said. "What does this mean?"

Lotta's resourcefulness was at an end. She could find nothing for it now but to tell him the truth.

Sigrun had reached beyond the church and cemetery of Algeröd, and was just crossing the bridge over the little stream when she heard Lotta Hedman's voice calling to her.

A moment later a sledge drew up beside her, and Lotta came forward and told her what had happened, telling her, at the same time, that the knife-grinder had promised to say nothing.

The man himself was sitting on the sledge, looking sullen and angry, but he spoke as calmly and peaceably as before.

"It's this way," he said. "I don't like the fashion of it, having Ruth put away and buried under another name. But I'll stick by what I've said for the rest. Young mistress can get up in the sledge here, and I'll drive her back to the vicarage, and nobody the wiser. I'll be as silent as a stone wall."

Sigrun walked over to the man. She had tied a black kerchief round her head, but now she thrust it back.

"And all for that, I'm to go back to my misery?" she asked.

The man seemed uneasy. He cast a hasty glance at her and looked away.

"She is dead. What does it matter in whose name she is buried?" said Sigrun, in a voice trembling with desperation.

"I don't see it's acting fairly by Ruth," said the man stubbornly.

"No," said Sigrun. "It is not, I know. But do not think that I am going back home after this. That I shall not do."

She pointed toward the river, gleaming darkly between the snow-covered banks.

"I will go that way, if need be," she said.

She stood before him, firm and resolute. And the stern earnestness of her face told him clearly enough that she would do as she said.

He turned his face away, as if fearing to look at her.

"I know she'd have a better sort of burial and all that," he said. "And it's no great matter to me, after all, seeing she wasn't my lawful wife, so to speak, though she'd been going about with me these two months. But it seems to me . . ."

Lotta gave a cry. Sigrun had hurried away, and stood now crouching by the rail at the side of the bridge, trying to get under.

"For the Lord's sake!" cried the man, rushing toward her. "Don't go and harm yourself! I'll do as you say."

"Remember, I will never go back to it all again," said Sigrun.

"No; you'll have no need. I'll keep silent all right."

"Sigrun is wonderful to-night," thought Lotta. "No one can resist her; she does as she pleases with us all."

And indeed it seemed so. The little ill-humoured fellow could not do enough for her.

"I haven't my proper cart with me to-night," he said. "I borrowed a sledge this morning to go out looking for Ruth. But that'll make it the easier, perhaps, for me to drive you on a bit of the way. It's not so easy to go tramping in the snow for them that's used to sitting warm and comfortable at home."

THE LONG DAY

THE day that had begun with Sigrun's flight from her home was, for many, a sad and weary day—a day so long that it seemed as if it would never reach an end.

So it was for Lotta Hedman. Coming back to the outhouse at three in the morning, she found all as she had left it, and began as well as she could to make preparations for what was to come. She gathered the dead woman's clothes together, thrust them into the stove, with an armful of wood, and burned all to ashes. Then she washed out the stove and drew her curtains across, leaving all looking as it had done the evening before.

Trembling and terrified, she went into the adjoining room where the dead woman lay. She was not afraid of the dead, as a rule, but she felt it here. Sigrun and she had sorely wronged the dead, and she could not approach the bedside without a shudder. Nevertheless, she carried out her plan—took out a sheet and laid it over the body, hiding it completely, and with deep feeling read a prayer or two.

This gave her comfort. She felt now with certainty that the dead woman was no longer an enemy to herself and her mistress, but their faithful helper and ally, of whom she need have no fear.

Lotta endeavoured also to prepare herself for what

she must say to those in the house. She called to mind that no one had seen Sigrun all the previous day; she could therefore say that her new illness had begun the night before that. Sigrun had not wished a doctor to be sent for on her account; she thought it was only a little rash breaking out, and nothing dangerous. Then . . . what was she to say next?

Lotta walked up and down the room, thinking it over. But after a while she felt too weary and discouraged to move about, and sat down in a chair instead. Soon this too seemed uncomfortable; she rose, and stood leaning against a wall. At last she sank to the floor, close by the bed where the dead woman lay, and stayed there so.

"I ought to go in to the Pastor," she thought. "I ought to wake the servants." But she did neither, only sat still, repeating her explanations to herself and turning them over every way.

"It will all be found out some way or other," she told herself. "And we shall be miserable and shamed, both Sigrun and I. It is terrible to sit and wait like this."

An unexpected comfort relieved her for a little while from her fears and anxiety.

As she sat there on the floor, bowed down by dread of what was to come, her soul took flight from her body, and, rising, hovered away into space between the worlds.

Soon it had risen so far that Lotta Hedman could see earthly things in their proportion; she saw now, not fragments of things, but things themselves in their whole extent. Not merely a stretch of river and stream, but the whole course of the waters from source to mouth. Not a little corner of the forest only, but the mighty expanse of trees in its whole extent. She could follow the line of a mountain chain from end to end. Plains spread out beneath her, and the contours of the land showed clearly marked against the glittering surface of the seas.

It was a beautiful and exalting sight, thought Lotta, but her soul did not stop to watch; it rose still higher.

And soon it had reached a point in space from where it could see the fates of mankind in their relation. Lotta could follow the wanderings of men through the valley of life. And it passed in what seemed to her less than seconds. She saw them enter life, go their brief way, and pass again, out into the unknown. She saw her friend Sigrun on her journey, and the way marked out for her, and the roads that crossed it.

She saw, too, the road which the woman lying dead beside her now had had to traverse. A dark and poor and difficult way, and already it was growing smoother, not smoothed, however, by a covering of darkness, but vanishing in a gleam of light.

At the end of the road stood the dead woman herself, still looking back over her course, that was now transformed into a ribbon of light, and Lotta saw that the woman's spirit rejoiced.

The dead woman pointed to Sigrun's road, and to one of those that crossed it.

"Look," she said, "the thing I longed for most of all in life is now fulfilled by my death!"

And with these words, she vanished in a great

splendour, so great that Lotta's soul could not follow there, but must wait without.

And at once it returned to her body, and Lotta Hedman felt now relieved from all her fear a while, believing that what had happened was something that rightly should and must have happened so.

She retained this calm of mind until the door opened and someone asked her if she knew it was half-past seven already.

At this Lotta tried to rise, but now her confidence was gone. She thought of all the troubles that awaited her, and had not the strength to get on her feet, but remained sitting.

The door closed again, no one entered, and for a few minutes she was left in peace.

"It will all be found out very soon now," thought Lotta. "It must be."

And the shame that would come upon Sigrun and herself weighed her down.

A little later, the housemaid entered, with early breakfast for her mistress.

She saw the lamp still alight, the wick smoking and nearly spent, the room full of smoke and almost in darkness. She called out, but no one answered. Then she realized that something must be wrong. She set down the tray, struck a match, and discovered Lotta sitting in a heap beside the bed; she saw, too, that the figure lying on it had a sheet spread over, as over a corpse. She came closer, lifted the sheet a little, and saw a pair of swollen hands.

At this Lotta came to life.

"For Heaven's sake, be careful. It is smallpox."

The girl dropped the sheet and started back.

And she it was who spread the news, telling the Pastor and the rest of the household.

Lotta herself, protected as she was by the dread of infection, was scarcely questioned at all.

A messenger was sent to fetch the verger, a man of strength and authority, and he arranged everything as well as could be done.

He gave orders that Lotta Hedman should stay where she was on account of the infection, and no one was to go near her. Even if the Pastor himself were to send for her, she was not to go.

He and Lotta together laid the body in the coffin, which was afterward carried away to a hastily dug grave.

No investigation was made, hardly a question asked. The vicarage was for a time cut off from all the rest of the district. That the vicar's wife should give out that she was dead while in fact still alive was a thing too unheard of for any to suspect.

"It is that knife-grinder that has been going about the district these last few weeks—he must have brought the infection over from Norway," was the general view. "His wife was ill, too, and ran away from him in her delirium."

The doctor's words were also called to mind; the disease must have been there before any knew of it.

And the longest and most agonizing day Lotta Hedman had ever known came to an end without any discovery of what had been done.

Sigrun glanced now and again at the driver sitting on the edge of the sledge. It was still dark night, and she could only vaguely distinguish the outline of the figure—the broad-brimmed hat, the upraised shoulder, the short nose, and the sullen mouth.

"It is not a man sitting there," she told herself, "but Death. I did not know him when he came first, but I know him now. And who else could it be? I have given myself up into his power. And he has come to fetch me and carry me away to his own land."

They drove on over wide and desolate mountain tracts, covered with snow. A few scattered, stunted trees and bushes here and there rendered the barrenness of the country still more marked.

"It is the kingdom of Death," she said to herself.

And she, who had a while ago been so eager, active, and commanding, felt herself now sinking into a quiet calm. The effort of will was at an end, hopes and desires were gone.

It is dangerous, perhaps, for a mortal to make an ally of Death. For Death may take it in earnest.

And Sigrun seemed really to feel a change taking place in herself. All the links that bound her to her former life were being loosened one by one.

Love of her husband, the sorrow and misery of her married life, had filled all her thoughts before. But now, all this faded and disappeared. A great void was where it had been, but no regrets, no bitterness.

"The dead must feel like this," she thought. "Thus it must be to be freed from all earthly things. Love and sorrow disappear."

Little foolish things she had said as a child, and had been ashamed of ever since, little offences that had troubled her long, little humiliations she had never forgotten—all these vanished now in a moment. Hereafter, she would think of these as things that no longer concerned her.

She thought of her parents, and the help they had always given her—now she would never have to trouble them again for aid. All was new about her now; she was in another world. "They cannot reach me here," she thought. "They have stood by me up to now, as far as they could. Now I am gone from them for ever. I am driving into the kingdom of Death."

She was like a climbing plant, fastened with many threads to a trellis. Now, one after another was loosed, and soon the whole growth would fall to the ground.

"It must be like this to die," said Sigrun to herself. "It is not hard or painful at all, only a deep rest."

Gradually it grew light. The man on the side of the sledge became once more an ordinary vagabond, with a sullen, unkindly face. The landscape was a stony, barren, poor, but altogether earthly tract, and Sigrun herself awoke to life with its insistent demands for courage and strength of mind. . . .

The horse had had no rest all night, and they were going very slowly. They had to halt for some hours at a peasant's hut to give the animal food and rest. At last, however, they came in sight of a village where there was an inn.

As they were thus approaching the end of their journey, the knife-grinder turned to Sigrun.

"A man like me," he said, "going about the country all ways, sees many strange things in his time. But I will say, this business to-night's the strangest I've ever had a hand in."

"You think so?" Sigrun turned to the little dark man with a friendly smile.

"I'll take my oath I've never seen nor heard the like. And I can't for the life of me see what it was made me soft enough to help with it at all. I can't make it out."

"Neither can I," said Sigrun. "But be sure you will never regret it."

"Why, as to that, you never know," said the man. "But, anyhow, I don't like to let you go on now without knowing how you're going to manage, and where you're making for."

"I am going to America," said Sigrun.

"It costs a heap of money to get to America," said the man.

"You surely do not think I should start on such a journey without money," she returned.

At this the man pulled up, went to the horse, and began lifting and fingering the harness.

"Well," he said, after a pause, "I've nothing much to do this way or that myself. Might be best, perhaps, to drive past the inn here, and I could take you on a few miles farther. There might be someone here that knew you."

For the last half-hour Sigrun had been troubled by that very thought. And the offer was welcome indeed.

"When I do a thing, I believe in doing it thoroughly," said the man, taking his place on the sledge once more.

The next few miles, however, were toilsome. Again they had to stop and rest and feed the horse. And soon they found that the snowfall in these parts had been lighter than where they had come from; the going became so bad after a time that they were forced to walk long stretches of the way.

And time went on. It was nearly noon before they came within sight of the second inn.

Just as they were near enough to distinguish the buildings, a man came driving up with a milk-cart.

"You'd better be careful, Gustavsson," he called to the knife-grinder. "They've telephoned up to the inn to be on the look-out for you. Say you're carrying infection. Vicar's wife at Algeröd died last night of the smallpox, and they say it's you and your woman brought it with you from Norway."

Again they halted, and considered what was best to be done. At last they decided to turn back. Neither cared to drive on to the inn; it was too dangerous.

The knife-grinder suggested making to the eastward, up toward Dalsland. "There's the railway runs from there to Göteborg, too, and nobody 'll know you there."

They turned off accordingly, along a road running east, leading up again through a wild and barren mountain tract.

The going was better here, but the poor beast was nearly spent. And after a third halt for rest and food, it had come to the bottom of its fodder bag.

The knife-grinder brought out some bread and butter and fell to. Sigrun had nothing to eat with her, but she was not hungry.

Afterward, when she looked back on that day, she wondered at herself.

"It was strange. I was altogether calm, and felt nothing at all. No uneasiness, no weariness, not even hunger. I knew all the time all would turn out as it should. I was numbed, as it were, in a way, but I was strong and able to hold out all the time. There must have been something at hand, too, that helped me."

While on the long road up to the plateau she asked a question.

"Did you not say this morning that the woman who died was not your wife?"

"I said so, yes. And it's the truth. She has a good husband and a decent home, but she liked better to go off with me."

And Sigrun questioned him further; not that the matter interested her at all—nothing in the world interested her that day. But talking made the time pass more easily.

"She liked you more than her husband, then?"

"Well, I don't know rightly about that. She was married to a man named Sven Elversson. Mayhap you've heard of him?"

Sigrun nodded.

"I thought at first she'd wearied of him because of—that old business, you know," the man went on. "But after, I found out it was because she thought he didn't care about her himself."

"She wasn't nice at all," said Sigrun. "And he only married her out of pity."

"She was no beauty, that's true," said the man, "but

she was a good soul for all that. She was that sort that'd do anything for one they cared about."

Despite her indifference, Sigrun could not help feeling uneasy at these words. She asked no more about the woman.

"Do you know where Sven Elversson is now?"

"He lives at a place in Dalsland, called Hånger. A big place it was once, but there's so many ugly things happened there that no one would live in it, and it was let go to ruin. Sven Elversson bought it for next to nothing. And he lives there now with only his old folks, now that his wife's gone, but he's always taking in someone to help and look after, children and poor folk, as many as he can have there."

Surely there must have been some strange influence at work to-day—something affecting the vagabond knife-grinder as it had done Sigrun. This man, whose habit it was to roam about the country growling and cursing, a terror to all, was quiet and gentle now, and spoke well of everyone.

They started off again, Sigrun sitting in the sledge, and the man on the side as before, with his legs hanging down. Then suddenly he slipped, and fell down in the road.

The horse stopped at once. The man picked himself up and climbed to his seat once more. But a little after, he slipped off again.

"Queer," he said. "I don't know what's the matter with me. My head seems going round."

Sigrun suggested he should sit in the sledge beside her. He did so, and they drove on again. A little later, the reins fell from his hands.

"I must be ill," he said confusedly. "Going the same way as Ruth, by the look of it."

But Sigrun hastened to reassure him.

"You have not slept all night," she said. "Sit there in the corner, and let me drive while you sleep a little."

Again something seemed to give her courage. "He is not ill," it whispered to her, "only tired out. There, he is asleep already."

When she had driven a little way, the horse stopped and refused to go farther.

Sigrun shook her companion by the arm.

"Do you know if there is any place near where we can put up? The horse is quite exhausted now, and it is getting dark already."

The man looked up, dull and heavy with sleep.

"Do you think it's the smallpox?" he asked.

"No, you are only sleepy," said Sigrun.

"It's the smallpox, I doubt, all the same," said the man.

But a moment after he pulled himself together.

"There's no help for it," he said resolutely. "There's a place a couple of miles farther on—a 'vagabonds' hostel,' as they call it. We must try to get on to there."

"We must find shelter somewhere," said Sigrun.

"It's the only thing we can do," said the man. "Though I'd rather have kept from showing myself there again. We're across the boundary now," he went on. "We're in Dalsland, and once we're over the next rise, it's downhill the rest of the way. Turn off to the left at the cross-roads, and drive on to the first house you see."

When at last Sigrun had got the horse up over the rise, she saw in the fading daylight a broad landscape spread out before them, gently sloping, and pleasant to see, with many lakes and long wooded ridges, showing up clearly against the heavy, snow-laden air. The beauty of the sight cheered her, and she drove on with renewed vigour, reached the cross-roads, and turned off to the left.

Several times she had a view of the landscape first seen, but the country seemed as uninhabited as before. At last, however, she sighted a farmhouse just below. The house itself was fairly large, as if belonging to a rich estate, but all the outbuildings were small and mean, little better than any peasant's dwelling might possess.

She roused the sick man anew.

"Are we there now?"

"Yes," he answered, shaking off his drowsiness. "We're at Hånger now. I never thought to come seeking shelter here again."

Sigrun gave a cry. "Hånger!" For a moment she felt like a shipwrecked soul, with the waves already closing over her. "Hånger—that was where you said Sven Elversson . . ."

"Ay," said the man. "And I'd never have come here by choice, but there's no help for it now."

"But—if he asked about his wife?"

"Why, I'll have to find something or other to say."

"That he should live here, of all places in the world," said Sigrun despairingly.

"He took the place because it's lonely like, and far

away from folk. Ordinary people never come this way, but all sorts of tramps and vagabonds and poor folk, they go to him."

Sigrun drove down a hill toward the house. And her despair passed from her almost at once. Again the same numbness came over her, and something whispered that there was no need to fear; all would go well.

Just at the entrance to the drive stood a little red-painted hut.

"Here it is. Just go in there," said the knife-grinder. He roused himself.

"I'll drive up to the house and get the horse in," he said. "You can go in meantime. There's nobody in the traveller's hut, it seems. You'll find a key just down under the step."

Sigrun did as he said, and found herself in a little cottage divided midway by a passage running through, with a room on either side. Both rooms were arranged and furnished in the same manner. Bare walls, fixed bedsteads with straw mattresses, a stove, a big, heavy table, and a few heavy chairs. A bucket of water and a bundle of firewood were there, but there were no pillows, no sheets, cooking-pots or plates, no towels or washing basins—nothing that could be taken away. A great cupboard stood in one of the rooms, but the key was not in the lock.

It was not altogether cold in the rooms; there had evidently been a fire there during the day. And they were clean and well aired.

"I must try to light a fire," thought Sigrun.

While she was busy with this, the knife-grinder entered. He could hardly stand upright. Without a word, he threw himself on a bed, and in a moment was fast asleep.

"I do not think he is ill," said Sigrun to herself. "He will be all right when he has had a night's rest. No need to call for help."

She lit a fire in the other room also, and sat down before it, thinking over her plans. Suddenly she realized that she was tired—she was indeed nearly falling from her seat. Also, she was hungry. "I ought to have brought some food with me," she murmured. And then, suddenly, she remembered her bag. Where was it? It was not in the room. She must have left it in the sledge.

She hurried out. The sledge was standing outside, and the bag was there. She picked it up, and was just going back into the house when a voice hailed her.

"Is that you, Ruth?"

Darkness had fallen quickly. She could vaguely distinguish the figure of an old, bowed man, slowly approaching.

"Do not come near us," she cried; "we are infected."

"I know," answered the man. "We had a telephone message to-day, but I never thought you would come back here again. Well, well, needs must, they say, when the devil drives."

"This must be Joel Elversson," thought Sigrun— "Sven Elversson's father. He is grown old and weak; he takes me for his son's wife."

"Sven is not at home to-day," said Joel in his solemn way. "But we will receive you, Ruth, I and Thala, as he would have done if he had known you came here in need and in peril of death. Here is the key of the cupboard. You know where to find all you need there. And we will bring down food for you and set it outside the door."

He handed her a small key, which she took without a word. He did not seem to expect any answer.

"There's none here bears any grudge against you, Ruth," he said. "We know what it was that made you go. Make yourself as easy as you can, and sleep in peace."

He walked away, and Sigrun hurried into the house. In the cupboard she found pillows and sheets—all that was needed for the night. And, shortly afterward, food was brought.

Sigrun took a part of it and set it in the next room for her companion, then, barring her door carefully, she ate something herself, and went to bed.

"I must have a few hours' sleep now," she thought. "And then I can go on again. I must get away from here before anyone learns who I am."

Almost before she had framed the thought she was fast asleep.

MORNING

WHEN Sigrun awoke, a little ray of red winter sun was shining into the poor chamber where she lay. She had slept, not for a few hours only, but the whole night through. She made haste to get up and set the room in order before going on her way.

The rest had strengthened her; she felt well and resolute now, and without regret for the step she had taken. The only thing that troubled her now was her fear lest she might be discovered. If only she could get away from Hånger without any one learning who she was, she felt sure the danger would be past.

Again she found a tray of food outside her door, and with it a paper, on which was written:

"We understand that you are remaining here, since the man has gone away alone. Do not doubt but that you will be welcome."

She went into the room opposite, and saw that her companion had indeed gone. It was one more source of anxiety removed. She was rested now, and would far rather go on foot than drive in his sledge. All she need do was to ask her way to a town where she could get a proper conveyance. It could not be far to the nearest railway station; she could be in Göteborg that evening.

She fastened the black kerchief round her head, put

on Lotta Hedman's cloak, and, taking up her bag, prepared to start.

Before leaving the room, however, she opened her bag to see if the money and other things were safe. Then she gave a cry of dismay. The six hundred kronor were gone.

She felt in the pocket of her cloak, and in her dress. The money was not there.

She understood at once that they had been stolen. The knife-grinder had taken them out of the bag while it was in the sledge.

She staggered to a seat. This was a terrible blow. She could not go to America now. All roads were barred. Oh, Heaven!

She bowed her head on the table and tried to think. Yes, she had told the man yesterday that she had money. And he perhaps had been thinking all along how he could get hold of what she had. Tired and exhausted as he was, he had yet been able to carry out his plan.

And in so doing he had rendered life impossible for her.

"It is a hard world to go out in for one that is poor and alone," she thought. "A hard world."

She felt not exactly penitent; but she realized now the utter impossibility of accomplishing her purpose.

"I might go out as a beggar on the high road," she thought. "But what would be the good of that? I did not leave my home to be an adventuress."

To return home seemed equally impossible. How could she tell her husband that she had given herself out

as dead in order to escape from him? It was impossible
—not to be thought of.

She knew that for the time being she was among good
people. Should she ask them to help her? Again the
same difficulty arose. She would have to confess her
deceit, her shame. And these honest souls would feel
compelled to inform her husband at once that she was
alive.

"It was no fancy, after all, that of yesterday," she told
herself. "It was Death that sat beside me on the sledge.
And Death will not release one who has once given herself into his hands."

"But he is not a hard master," her restless thought
went on. "He loosed the bonds that held me to earthly
things, and in a gentle way. Why should I not trust
him now?"

And so she remained sitting at the table for about an
hour, trying to familiarize herself with the thought of
death.

"God will be merciful," she said. "He knows all. He
knows I did not mean harm to any one. And He knows
that this is the one way open to me now."

Just then someone entered the room. But Sigrun did
not move. It was utterly indifferent to her now, whoever saw her. Her decision was taken, and she knew
what she had to do.

She lay still bowed over the table with her face in her
hands, and could not see who had come in. The step,
however, told her that it was a man, and not an old, but
a young man.

"It is Sven Elversson himself," she thought.

She heard him approaching her at first; then he drew back. He went to the stove, lit a fire there, and returned to the table where she sat.

"Is it so hard for you, Ruth?" he said. "Let me send some of the children to you. Is there nothing here that you might be glad to see again?"

At these words she raised her head, and turned toward him, with a look of fixed despair.

"I am not the one you thought to see," she said. "I am Sigrun Rhånge, wife of the vicar of Algeröd."

Sven Elversson drew back a step or two. But he had so trained himself to preserve the same calm, whatever news might be brought him, that he did not even utter a cry. Only his face turned pale. But his confusion was evident from the fact that he began thinking aloud.

"Sigrun Rhånge is dead," he said. "She died the night before last. When I heard she was dead, I went to Algeröd myself, to see her once more for the last time, but it was too late. She was already laid in her coffin and buried in her grave."

Sigrun sat gazing at him. There was a solemnity of grief in his words that almost touched her. She was convinced that he was unaware of having spoken aloud.

"Would it were so," she said in answer to his thought. "Would that Sigrun Rhånge were truly dead and in her grave."

"Sigrun Rhånge is dead," he repeated in a low, monotonous voice, still unable to collect himself. "I shall never see her again on earth."

"Yes," she agreed. "We may surely say that Sigrun

Rhånge is dead. But I, unhappy creature that I am, I am living yet."

Something within him seemed to grasp the inner meaning of all this quicker than thought, and set his heart in fierce commotion. His cheeks flushed, and his eyes glittered.

He came toward her, took her hand and held it in one of his, while the other stroked her cheek with a swift, momentary touch. He seemed trying to convince himself that it was indeed a living woman here before him.

"You, alive!" he said, and his voice rose to a cry of joy, only to sink next moment to a low, gentle tone. "You here, in my house! What does it mean?"

There was much in his manner that astonished her. But at the same time, it gave her a little courage. Here at least was one who did not look on her misfortune with cold indifference.

"You wrote so kindly to your wife this morning," she said. "And I have always heard so much good of you. Will you help me now? I am in the greatest need that ever any could be."

The tears flowed from her eyes. And in her extremity, her desperate need of help, she threw herself on her knees before him.

He did not help her to rise at once. Instead, he laid one hand on either shoulder, and bent over her, his face almost touching her.

"You helped me once," he said, "when I was in my sorest need. Do you not think I should be glad to repay you that a thousand thousand times, if it were in my power?"

Suddenly he checked himself, and, regaining calmness, moved quietly away from her and drew up a chair.

"Will you not tell me how all this came about?"

She stood up beside him, and began hesitatingly:

"There is so much to say. . I hardly know how to begin." For a moment she was on the point of giving way to tears, but restrained herself. "We were not very happy in our marriage, my husband and I."

He did not seem to notice that she was standing while he was seated. But he understood that she needed help to tell her story.

"My wife was not happy either," he said.

He rested one elbow on the table and leaned forward so as to cover his eyes.

Sigrun understood that he was encouraging her to go on.

"There's been talk about us here and there, I dare say," she continued. "If you were in Algeröd yesterday, no doubt you heard about the scene with the man who was staying with us. . . ."

"Yes," he said, "I heard that and more. But there was no ill-will in what was said. Only sorrow—nothing but sorrow."

His voice was almost a sob. He felt the old fierce pain once more. It hurt him beyond words to speak to her like this, when his one desire was to lay his head in her lap and tell her of the sorrow that had racked him the day before and the misery of this morning, when he learned that his wife had come back now—now that his heart longed only to be left to its sorrow for another.

"And no one doubted that I was dead?" asked Sigrun.

"No," he said. "No one doubted that you had died of the smallpox."

She grasped his arm hastily.

"You—you do not know who it was that died. It must have been . . ."

She stopped, with open mouth, not daring to go on.

"Was it my wife?" he asked.

"Yes," she said. "I think it must have been . . . your wife."

Sven Elversson said nothing, but rose and walked across the room.

Now Sigrun in her turn sank down on a chair. "Death," she thought—"Death will not let me go. I had forgotten that the dead woman was Sven Elversson's wife when I asked him to help me."

She sat crying quietly, and pulling at a handkerchief. The eerie, drowsy, death-like feeling came over her again.

A few moments later, Sven Elversson came back to the table and sat down in the same position as before.

"Now tell me everything," he said.

And she obeyed. She told him all that had passed from the moment when the strange woman had come to her door, until now, when she herself sat in the vagabonds' hostel at Hånger.

He listened with all his soul, and was filled with sorrow for the desperate thing she had done, and all the misery she had brought on herself. He understood better than she did herself that, as she was, all ways in the world were closed to her now. That if she stayed in this world at all, she must be condemned by her own act to endless unrest, endless anxiety, endless penitence and shame.

But despite his sorrow and deep sympathy for her, he could not repress a feeling of rejoicing in himself, that repeated over and over again: "At least she is alive. And she has come to you. Sits here beside you, talking to you. What does all the rest matter now that she is alive?"

Sigrun had long finished her story, and Sven Elversson sat silent, thinking what to say, what must be done. And watching him as he sat, she felt clearly that such a man as he could do nothing else but send her back to her husband. "This man cannot be led to any wrongful deed," she thought.

"And so it has all been in vain," she told herself. "All to no purpose. Death will not let me go."

She looked her fate bravely in the face. And she made no attempt to influence Sven Elversson by speaking of what she had resolved.

"This is a big thing," he said, and was surprised to find himself talking to Sigrun just as he did to others whom he helped. "But the one thing clear to me at the moment is that you must not go about the country now carrying infection. You will have to stay on here at Hånger for a time."

She looked up at him. It was so simple, and she had never thought of it. A few days' respite at least. The thought of death slipped aside.

"There is no one here but my father and mother," he went on. "And I do not think they will be afraid. But I forgot, there are some children staying here too, that I took in a while ago. But we can send them down to the village. And then we can shut up the place to travellers for a while. You can move over to the house and have one of the guest rooms to yourself."

"And after?" she asked almost harshly.

He bowed his head, and tried to think. Because he loved her, he could read her thoughts, and he knew that his answer now meant life or death to her.

He could find only strength to say:

"It must be in the hand of God."

"I cannot drive her to despair," he thought to himself; "but it may be that her own mind will change. Her love for her husband may wake anew. Surely all will go well, all will come right in time."

She understood that this was only a respite, but she gave a sigh of relief.

"The way I look at it is this," he said. "It is never well to lie, and hide things. There's no denying that. But then, again, it is not well to torture a creature to death. That's no less true. But the heart may change. Or, better, may become itself again. And then it will be easy, all that seems so difficult now. May I not believe that?"

She shook her head decisively, but said nothing.

"Nay, let us believe it," he said. "Let us trust to that. And now you will not mind if I tell my father and mother all about it. They are not the sort to tell more than they should. And then we will try not to make this more hard and serious than we need. Just think that it will all come right again in time."

Sigrun felt as if he were playing with her. At any other time his manner would have annoyed her, but now it was indescribably soothing and comforting. She felt as if this man had taken all her burden, all her trouble and misfortune, on himself, to bear it in her stead.

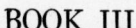

BOOK III

THE BEREAVED

IT WAS Sigrun's mother, the old Dean's wife from Stenbroträsk. Early in May, 1916, she was on a visit to some relatives in Bohuslän, and, being so near, thought she ought to go over to her son-in-law at Algeröd and see how he was.

On arriving at the humble little vicarage, she found that Pastor Rhånge had brought his mother over to keep house for him. A simple and straightforward soul, this mother, who, as the widow of a pilot, and in straitened circumstances, had pinched and saved to get her son into the priesthood. The visitor noticed that she was proud and happy at being able to live with her son and look after him, as was reasonable enough. Nothing to take offence at in that.

But the income arising from the living was so pitifully small that the old lady had likewise found herself obliged to eke out the money by taking paying guests. She had staying with her now two young girls, in delicate health, who had been sent there in the hope of benefiting by the fresh mountain air.

At first the two girls had been a little afraid of the dark and gloomy master of the house, who was in mourning for his wife, but when Sigrun's mother came to Algeröd they had got over their fear. It was a great surprise to her. Instead of a house full of sorrow and mourning, she found a place full of laughter and play and merriment.

The afternoon seemed long to her; she was in dread of losing her patience before it ended. Wherever she went, the vision of her daughter was before her eyes, and she could not but wonder how Rhånge ever could endure these two young girls about the place, showing off as they did, and courting his attention, so evidently that it must have annoyed and incensed him had he been as he was before.

But he was changed—that was evident in every way. He was a different man altogether.

His voice, his laugh, had grown loud and shrill, and he had, too, a strange way of boasting about his own excellence.

Before, his manner had always been marked by great dignity and seriousness. No one could be in his company for two minutes without discovering the priest in him. But now, all that had disappeared. Before, he had seemed to leave it to others to find out that he was a gifted and distinguished man; now, he took it upon himself to tell them so.

He spoke of how clever he had been at school, how easily and well he had passed his examination, of the great and wonderful things he had done among his congregations; kept on with story after story, as if he would never end.

And the two girls clapped their hands in evident admiration.

It seemed, indeed, as if he were pleased to show his mother-in-law how they looked up to him, and how completely he could do as he pleased with them. He was like a man who has made one great failure, and seeks desperately in every way to reinstate himself.

He was not in any way pleasant or obliging toward the two young girls, and there was contempt in every word he gave them. But he could not keep away from them. He spoke of work he had to do, but he did not leave the company. Sigrun's mother was hurt at first, thinking that her daughter was already forgotten. But in the course of the evening, another idea came into her mind. She began to think he felt the loss of his wife so keenly that it was driving him to ruin.

She was to stay the night, and when it was late enough for her to retire, she could not refrain from saying a few words to him: that she understood he would have to marry again soon, but she sincerely hoped he would be careful in his choice, and not take the first that came to hand.

At this he asked her to go with him into his room, but said nothing to the others.

And there he showed her how he had collected all Sigrun's belongings—things she had brought with her from her own home, as well as those from after her marriage.

Portraits of her in all sizes were spread about the room, and her books were foremost on the book-shelf.

One book there was which her mother recognized particularly; a little book of devotion which had been given her before her confirmation. It lay on the table beside the bed.

"I read in it every evening," said the Pastor—"that book and no other."

He opened the middle compartment in a large cabinet. Here he had put away a couple of little ivory boxes, which Sigrun had had as a little girl. And, taking them out, he laid them caressingly against his cheek.

"She was fond of them," he said, "and they are never touched by any hand but mine. Those others out there are never allowed to see anything of all this."

He showed her the little picture of the home at Stenbroträsk, which had comforted Sigrun so many times. It was wrapped in several layers of tissue paper, rolled up in a cloth, and packed away at the back of a drawer, as if it had been something precious.

"You don't think I would ever let any one else look at this?" he said.

He brought out a little cloth which Sigrun had worked for him.

"It is always on that table," he said, "because Sigrun herself put it there. But I have another that I put over it when the sun shines in—you can see it is not faded."

Sigrun had made a cushion for his rocking-chair, and the fringe at the bottom had come loose in one or two places. He had tried to mend it himself, sewing with coarse thread and big stitches. He held it up now to show—clumsily done it was, but he could not entrust the work to any other hand.

Sigrun's mother offered to take it up with her to her room and mend it properly. He allowed her to do so, but held the cushion long in his hands, turning it over and over, before he could let it go.

The dearest treasures of all, Sigrun's two plain rings and one other ring, and one or two little gold trinkets, he had put away in a little leather bag.

"I carry that about with me all day in my waistcoat pocket," he said. "And at night it is under my pillow. It never leaves me night or day."

Sigrun's mother was moved to deep sympathy. She saw how his sorrow was tearing at him, threatening to rend him asunder. And she understood that he strove against it in the presence of others, tried to be as he had been, but could not, and that it was this which made such discord in his being.

She sat down on a sofa and beckoned him to her.

"Come and sit down by me," she said in a gentle, motherly voice. "And tell me all your trouble."

At this he broke out into violent weeping.

"I don't know," he cried—"I don't know what is to become of me. I can find nothing in life, now that Sigrun is gone.

"She is gone," he said again, "and yet I cannot feel that she is dead. To me it seems as if she had gone from me because she was afraid of me.

"I could not make her happy, but it was only because I loved her so, beyond all bounds or reason. I wanted her all to myself. And I hemmed her in and shut her off from everything. And now it tortures me beyond measure that I let her suffer. If I had known she was going to leave me so soon, I would have kept myself in check. What would it have mattered if I had perished, as long as she was happy in her brief earthly life?

"I know they say she died of the smallpox. But I

dare not believe that was it. And I dare not ask how it was that she went. I dread to hear that she died because I had made her so unhappy that she could not stay with me."

Sigrun's mother sat still and let him give vent to his feelings. She was not surprised at anything he said, for she knew, being old, that no human being ever stood beside the grave of a loved one without being torn by remorse and the pangs of conscience.

A LETTER

A FEW days later, Lotta Hedman came in to the Pastor in his study in the middle of the day.

She had a letter in her hand, and stared straight before her; her hair was as smooth as Lotta's hair could ever be, and her brow was clear as if Heaven had opened above her and shed over her something of its glory.

The Pastor was somewhat surprised himself to see that she came in so calmly and coolly to speak to him, for Lotta Hedman had been strange and confused in her manner ever since the night when Sigrun had gone. She was restless always, and often talked aloud to herself. It was supposed that she saw visions, and those who heard anything of what she said noticed that it was always about the great destruction and a horseman on a red horse, and the great beast, the dreadful end of the world.

She avoided everyone as far as she could, and most of all her master. He had often noticed how she would go a long way round to keep out of his way.

Her hair stood up, as a rule, all about her head, her eyes rolled about, her clothes were ill-cared-for, and her work was done as best might be.

Whenever she encountered the two young ladies, she would call to them with stern words from the Scriptures, that sounded like threats.

They had tried to persuade the Pastor to send Lotta back to her own country, but he understood that it was her sorrow for Sigrun that troubled her, and so he had protected her and retained her in his service.

To-day, noticing the change in her appearance, he said to himself: "I see, now, that her mourning is over. There is no one but myself in the home that remembers Sigrun now."

But Lotta begged him to listen to her with patience, for she had much to say.

And to his great surprise, for she was in the highest degree solemn and earnest, she began by telling him a saga.

"There was once a homestead," she said, "where honest peasant folk lived, but close by was a mountain, and there were trollfolk there. And the peasant's wife had once been into the dwelling of the trollfolk, to help one of their wives in childbirth. And as she bathed the child, it splashed a drop of the water into her eye, and that drop of water gave her the gift of sight in that eye, so that ever after she could see all that the trollfolk were doing about her own place. She came on them many a time when they were stealing things, or laying traps for man and beast to their hurt.

"Then one day it chanced that the peasant's wife was going out to the fair at harvest-time, and walking there among the booths she met the troll from her home. And she forgot herself, and passed the time of day with him. 'Good-day to you, gaffer,' she said, shaking hands with him; 'that's a fine piece of cloth you've bought there.'

"'Ay,' said the troll, 'and cheap too. There were two peasants quarrelling about the piece, and while they fought, I took up the parcel and made off.'

"After that they stood a bit talking easily together, but then suddenly the troll said: 'But how is this, old lady—how is it you can see me at all?'

"'Why, it's this way,' said she, 'I got a drop of water in my eye last time I came to your place, and ever since I can see you, whether you like it or not.'

"'Well, now, to be sure. And which eye was it, then?'

"'In the left,' said the woman. And quick as light he raised his hand and struck out her left eye. Took the eye clean out, never leaving a bit of it. And after that she could never all her life see anything out of ordinary.

"And that was what Pastor did to me the first time we met," said Lotta in a high, shrill voice. "Pastor struck out my eye with the gift of sight out of my face, and ever since, my life's been all confusion. I can see, but only darkly; I can hear, but indistinctly, and I get no further, and find no one to listen to me. I'm poor and homeless, and I shall never be more than a poor working girl."

The Pastor sat quietly listening, and when Lotta stopped a moment for breath, he said, without a trace of anger:

"Go on with what you have to say, Lotta. I am sure you did not come to me to-day only to speak of these old things."

"No," said Lotta, "but I want Pastor to remember that, because I have wronged you greatly afterward, in my turn. It may be well now and then to know that there are old debts owing, so one can ask for payment. And I have great need of mercy and forgiveness, as you will see."

The Pastor shook his head.

"Now I cannot see what you are thinking of."

But Lotta answered steadily:

"I know what it is I have to say, and it is no easy thing to confess, but before I come to that, there is one thing more I must tell you first.

"I am not one to go tale-bearing about," she said, "and I have never said a word to Sigrun about it, but I know there is a place called Hånger. And I have heard the whole story of the priest who was murdered there, and the gatepost and the old woman at the window and the curse that lies on the men of Hånger. And it seems to me that a man who knows he is come of a strong, wild race, that has always been hard to get on with, and who knows, too, what manner of death awaits him—I think that man must have asked himself at times if he did right in taking for his wife a girl innocent and delicate as a newly opened leaf, and knowing nothing of all the dark within him."

"Lotta Hedman!"

The Pastor's voice was still calm enough; he was but warning Lotta not to go too far.

"Let me go on, Pastor," she begged. "For I do not say this in any reproach, but only to remind you that there are faults on both sides, though the fault on ours, on Sigrun's and mine, is so much the greater that it will need much mercy and forgiveness in your scale to balance it.

"And now I have only to tell you how it was Sigrun left us. And it is by her own wish that I tell you this. I have had a letter from her to-day, telling me to do it, and it has loosed me from my abasement and lifted me up out of my deceit, so that I can once more look my fellows in the face."

The fact that it was Lotta Hedman speaking, rendered her words less surprising to the Pastor than if it had been another. He thought she was about to tell him that Sigrun had not died of the smallpox, but had taken her own life, and that Lotta fancied she had received some sort of permission to tell him about it now

And Lotta began her story.

But as she went on, her courage faded, for she saw how the man before her grew darker in mind, as the sky darkens before the coming of a great storm. Clouds drew up from every side. A terrible cold and a terrible darkness spread abroad. And at last she could hardly utter a word.

Nevertheless, she managed to relate, without any circumspection, that she had had several messages from Sigrun, and that the latter, after her arrival at Hånger, had been ill with the smallpox. It had not been dangerous, but a long illness.

And all through her illness, and ever since, she had stayed with the good folk at Hånger. She had been out into the world on her own resources for a single day, and the things she had met with then had so terrified her that nothing could persuade her now to leave her friends and her sheltered life to go out among strange things and people.

But the eloquent words with which Lotta had intended to describe her own misery and shame, and her joy that Sigrun had changed her mind and would return to her home, all this remained for the most part unsaid.

All she did was to lay before the Pastor the letter she had that day received, dated from Hånger, the 15th of May, 1916, and with these few lines:

"Lotta, you must go to Edward and tell him everything. And ask him to come here to Hånger and fetch me, if he considers me worthy to be his wife again."

Inside was a small envelope addressed to the Pastor himself. He tore it open, and found the one word:

"Forgive!"

When he had seen it, he broke out into a bitter, heart-rending laugh. It was like the first gust of the storm bursting through the clouds and flinging them aside to commence its fierce play.

"You can telephone to Hånger and tell Sigrun I will come and fetch her to-morrow," said the Pastor. "To-day I have to go to an examination at the school."

Lotta did as she was asked. And just after noon the Pastor drove off alone. He had a long journey before him to a distant school. But on coming to the cross-roads, he did not turn off along the way that led to the school. He turned eastward, up toward the Dalsland boundary, in the direction of Hånger.

THE TROLLFOLK OF HÅNGER

OH, THERE is surely no need to believe that any supernatural influence was at work. But for one who has heard close to his ear the low-toned whispering of the beloved dead, or marked, with an unrest so great that the heart seems ready to break under it, how a soft tide of gentle thoughts comes sweeping through the soul; has felt the softest hands guiding the weary pen to its end—such an one finds it hard to believe that there were not invisible hosts this day gathered about the unfortunate man who drove along over the broad, desolate mountain tracts.

For however hurt and betrayed, however deceived and humiliated he felt, however his thoughts turned toward vengeance and punishment, they were yet led again and again toward something else that seemed to draw them with even greater power.

And the thing that drew them so was Hånger, the home of his fathers, that he had never seen, with its red buildings set far up among the pine-woods, looking out over a landscape with ten long ridges, ten high peaks, ten glittering lakes, ten parishes—and hardly ten homesteads in all.

To him, the vision had never yet appeared—the vision of the old house at Hånger, with gatepost and orchard and cellar, as he knew it had appeared to others of his race. But over him, too, lay its secret power. And his thoughts turned now to his childhood, when he had dreamed that it should fall to his lot to lift the curse that rested on Hånger and the race of Hånger. He recalled his argument of the old days, that since the curse had come upon them through the murder of a priest, so it might be lifted from their heads if one of the Hånger folk became a priest and a holy man of God.

Later, in youth and manhood, he had lost those thoughts, it is true; yet, after all, it was that original idea which had determined the direction of his life.

When he had commenced his studies, and all had gone well in what he touched, he had ceased to believe that any ill-fate especially threatened the men of his race. It was all nothing but a wayward, unruly character, and a gloomy inability to keep what was their own. If a man were but wise, and knew how to control himself, the thought of suicide would surely disappear. "And I shall be the one to show them that a Rhånge from Hånger can die as others do," he had sometimes thought. "And so, after all, it may be my lot to make an end of the old superstition."

And indeed he had succeeded in resisting all the temptations common to youth, and in leading an orderly and blameless life, in all save his relations with his wife.

He started in his seat as if suddenly awakening. For a moment or two he had been freed from the consciousness of his misfortune, but now, at the thought of his wife, it came back to him in all its horror. The very fact that he was a priest, and should live blamelessly, made the coming shame more intolerable; the gossip and scandal cut him like the lash of ironbound thongs. "Better if she had never, never returned," he thought in his bitterness of heart. "She has made life impossible for me at home here. We shall have to go and live abroad."

Strangely enough, however, his thoughts soon turned from his wife, and settled again on the old homestead with its uncanny story.

It was his father who had told him of Hånger, and there was much besides the murder and the curse in what he said.

He had told how none knew where the Hånger folk had come from. Five brothers had suddenly appeared in the parish, all big, handsome, strong men, but of unknown family, from an unknown land, speaking an unknown tongue. It was generally believed that they were the offspring of trollfolk, by some woman who had fallen into their power, and, in truth, their wildness and violent character, their courage and sharpness, their strange ways and obstinate will, and, more than all, their extraordinary success in acquiring goods and property, gave further credence to the legend.

These men, who had come into the district as poor labourers, had in the course of a few years made themselves, first, masters of Hånger, where the eldest brother had settled down, and afterward, of four other estates.

It was comforting to think of those forefathers of his. They had never been like the other peasants round them. They had dressed grandly, and walked proudly; they might have been gentry themselves, but had never cared about it. He felt to-day the need of something to increase his self-respect, and he found a certain dignity in belonging to a richly gifted and famous race.

And all things considered, he was perhaps not so very unlike them after all. Lotta Hedman had herself compared him to a troll, and reminded him that he came of a race of wild men.

If only he had not been a priest, and forced to hold his own powerful nature constantly in check!

He called to mind the night when he had gone in pursuit of the frightened Bailie—it must have been the old trollfolk blood breaking out in him.

And this again brought him back to his home and his wife, and an agonizing pain wrung his soul anew. He remembered how he had suffered all that spring from sorrow and pangs of conscience. But bitter as this suffering had been, it was yet even more bitter to know that Sigrun had condemned him to it in cold blood, without any compelling reason. No, the bitterest and worst of all was that she had lowered herself to deceit, that she had freed herself in such a ghastly manner; had taken a miserable vagabond into her confidence, and fallen at last into the hands of such a man as Sven Elversson—a man whom he had himself driven forth from among his congregation. This it was that filled his cup of shame to overflowing.

"She came to the right man at last," he thought. "She is dead, and he is an outcast, who dare not show himself among his fellows."

But again he was led from the agony of his thoughts by the recollection of his forefathers and their home.

Over the treeless wastes where he now drove, the west wind, the strong wind from the sea, whined sharp and biting. "It is very cold up here," he thought. "It must be better on the other side of the range. Hånger lies in shelter of the eastern slopes; it would be warm and spring-like on such an evening as this."

Once again he was thinking of his race.

All of them had been marked by some trait which distinguished them from those around them.

One of them had had a horse which he loved beyond all else, and he was rarely seen except in the saddle. He went to his work and to his pleasures on horseback, and had even one Sunday ridden into the church and demanded to receive the Holy Sacrament without dismounting.

A faint smile passed over the priest's face at the thought of that remarkable scene. It had often amused him in former days to imagine it to himself. But he had never thought such a thing could be true; he had always regarded it as invention and fable.

That same horseman had once had a quarrel with his wife. "Folks should use their wits at times," she had said, "and not trust only to their strength." But this had angered him, and he had hoisted her up and set her to ride astride of the roof-beam. "Now I've set you there by strength," he said. "Let's see if you can get down again by your wits."

It must have been no easy matter at times to be the wife of one of those Hånger folk. They had been violent, jealous, and obstinate. Strong and able men, indeed, hospitable and magnificent, but given to coarse jesting that might well prove more trying than many other faults.

One of them once took it into his head to have everything he owned in pairs. It was not sufficient to have one bell in his room; he must have two. One window was never enough for a room; there must be two or four or six. Two chimneys, two doors, two barns, two haylofts. Never one lad or girl, but always two or four of them. It might seem an innocent whim enough, but he had nearly brought Hånger to ruin with his alterations and rebuilding.

Among the cattle, too, he would have as many bulls as cows, and he ordered his wife to bear him a boy and a girl, a boy and a girl, and so on in regular succession And when she did not obey him, he was not to be trifled with.

Again the Pastor smiled. No, clearly it was no light matter at times to be mistress of Hånger.

One of the men there had been who was always singing. He came to church singing, and went away singing; he sang when he answered any who spoke to him; sang when he went to bed and when he got up.

But for all his singing, he had been a hard and unreasonable man, and it was with him that the misfortune had come. He had once tried to cheat his brother over some inheritance, but his own wife had discovered the fraud, and asked their priest to come to Hånger to talk over the matter with him. But the Master of Hånger thought there was something more behind the visit, and, inflamed with jealousy, had lain in wait for the priest on the way home and killed him.

Yes, it was true, as he had just said: no easy matter to be wife to one of the ancient race of Hånger.

And yet, none of their womenfolk had ever given themselves out for dead in order to escape.

He laughed a short, harsh laugh. It might seem as if he had been the worst of them all. Otherwise, his wife would hardly have had recourse to such desperate means.

And what had she to reproach him for after all? Nothing but having loved her too much. He had asked nothing of her but the one thing, that she should be his alone, entirely and without reserve.

But suppose that had been in itself too much to ask? If it had been harder to fulfil than that of the mad demands of those wild forefathers of his? Can one human being demand of another such utter and complete surrender of self? Not only in love, but in all else?

Pastor Rhånge remembered how he had often thought Sigrun was a being of a different sort, unlike all others; that she had seemed to have a nature of her own, though she could never find expression for it.

And that nature of hers, he knew now, was pity. To do good, to sacrifice herself for others, to care for the sick, that had been all her natural craving, but he had set himself against it. He could not endure it. He would have her all to himself, and not share her with any besides.

And the thing that had happened, that had seemed so abominable to him before, was there, after all, anything in it but what must necessarily come? It was the steel spring, long compressed, which had unfolded as soon as the pressure was released.

"Sigrun is pity itself," he thought. "Mercy is her aim, her task. I should have realized it."

The sudden acknowledgment of his own fault comforted him now. Sigrun no longer appeared to have sunk so low, to be so unspeakably hard and without feeling.

He turned the thought over in his mind. "Yes," he said to himself. "That must be why we were never happy together. I hindered her from being what her nature commanded her to be."

Then, suddenly, the old agony returned. "This fellow, Sven Elversson, he cares for her better than I. He too is given up to works of charity. And that is why she stays with him."

He had not thought of Sven Elversson with any jealousy before. "Sigrun knows what he has done," he had said to himself. "She could never love him."

But now, the whole thing seemed more than suspicious. Why had Sven Elversson not told him at once that Sigrun had come to Hånger? Was he in love with her, and had he thought to keep her for himself?

But in the midst of his anger came one of those thoughts that seemed to hover in the air above that desolate land, and refreshed the soul of the unhappy man like cool summer rain.

"Have you any right to expect service and aid from Sven Elversson?" said the thought.

And the priest remembered how he had sinned against Sven Elversson, and ruined his life, and condemned him to nameless misery.

But this consciousness of his own guilt brought a strange soothing calm in the midst of his anger at the wrong he had suffered from others.   It was like a cooling drink to one in fever.

And a new humility, a self-knowledge, woke in his mind.

He no longer felt himself as the punishing avenger with all right on his side.

He was prepared now, not to forgive, but to search and examine with care before passing his final judgment.

THE LIFTING OF THE CURSE

THE priest checked his horse. There below him, in the glow of the evening sun, was Hånger itself.

For a moment he doubted whether it could be right. He had always heard the place described as consisting of large buildings. Here, the main part was certainly of decent size, but all the rest seemed small and insignificant.

But the orchard was there. On the slope between the small houses grew tall, century-old apple trees, now in their finest bloom, making a roof of delicate white and pink above the lawn.

And the old oak was there, not yet in full leaf, but well on the way to clothe its wrinkled, knotty branches with soft, leafy green.

And the view was there, too. A view out over a marvellously fine and light and softly drawn landscape, where the ten mountain ridges and the ten lakes lay now, at the hour of sunset, decked in every imaginable hue, one height a brilliant white, and another threateningly dark; one lake like a sheet of polished steel, and its fellow behind the next hill glittering all in gold.

It was impossible to think that men who had lived all their lives within sight of such beauty could remain harsh, rough, and wild; without any thought beyond gaining riches and lands. Here, in the wonder of these surroundings, he seemed to find the explanation of all that joyous delight in splendour and magnificence that had marked his forefathers.

He sat for a long while looking at it all; at last, however, he jumped down from his seat and walked into the wood close by. Here he tied up his horse to a tree, spread out some fodder before it, and set off quietly and thoughtfully toward the house.

When he was near enough to see in between the buildings, he noticed a man and a woman sitting in the soft, bright spring evening under the great oak, on either side of a garden table. The man was reading aloud, the woman sewing. Neither had noticed him as yet.

He stopped, and walked round behind one of the out-buildings, approaching them from another direction. Close by where the two were sitting, there grew a hedge of fir trees, thick and tall. He stole along under shelter of this, coming up noiselessly and unseen. When he was near enough to hear distinctly the voice of the man reading, he lay down quietly on the ground, and moved a few twigs cautiously aside, so as to see all he wished.

He had not the slightest qualm of conscience in listening thus. "Sigrun's whole future and my own are at stake," he thought. "I must know the truth, by whatever means."

At first, however, he found himself listening to nothing more than a little poem by Snoilsky. It was the story of the prisoner of war, who, when released at last, after a toilsome journey over unknown ways, finds himself one dark evening outside the poor cottage where years ago he had left his wife. Then, looking in through the window, he sees another man by her side. He understands that she has believed him dead, and he goes away into the night, preferring to disappear rather than cause her suffering. And before he goes, he fastens to the door a small leather pouch containing all the little money he has, as a gift to the poor home.

Sven Elversson read this story of love and resignation very beautifully, but the Pastor heard the words without properly grasping their meaning. His whole soul was concentrated on his wife.

Sigrun was sitting so that he could not see her face. But it was at least herself, he saw. He recognized her hair, the pretty curve of the neck; every movement of hand and arm as she sat at her work was familiar to him.

"She lives!" he said to himself, folding his hands. "It is true—it is true that she is alive."

His heart melted with emotion. He had seen her again, but it was not as he had thought it would be. He felt no anger, no wish to call her to account for all she had made him suffer; he would not speak to her of the shame she had brought upon herself; he could only thank God with tears that she was alive, and wished to return to him.

He laid one hand over his eyes, and thought what would have become of him if Sigrun had really been dead. A bitter misanthrope, dragging through life without hope, with no interest beyond guarding his memories; a man who sought the society of other women only to deride them for not being as she, the only one in the world for him. He could see no bottom to the depth into which he must have sunk.

On the way here, he had wished in his despair that Sigrun had never made herself known. A cruel and senseless thought—how could he ever have entertained it for a moment?

All this passed through his soul now like a storm. And the voice of the reader was lost in its fury.

In the first transport of joy he had been almost on the point of springing up and hurrying forward to his wife. But he restrained himself. "No," he thought; "there must be no trace of doubt or suspicion between us. For the sake of our happiness, I must stay here now."

"We will not read any more this evening," said Sigrun, when Sven Elversson had finished the poem. "I have something to say to you."

And her voice reached the listener behind the trees, full of the ring of life. Sweet as before, low and touching, with the faint little lisp.

Sven Elversson raised his head from the book and turned toward her. The Pastor saw at once that he was greatly changed. He carried his head as high as any other, and had the easy, untroubled bearing of an educated man. The slight stamp of the lay preacher, the exaggerated humility that had marked him before, were gone now.

"Yes, it is almost a pity to sit over a book on such an evening as this," said Sven Elversson. "Better to talk."

Sigrun hesitated a little before beginning what she had to say. She folded up her work, and put it away carefully. Then in a firm and resolute voice she said:

"It is done now, Herr Elversson."

"What is done?" he asked carelessly. "Your work, you mean?"

"No. The thing you have asked me to do every day since I have lived under your roof. I have done it now."

"You have . . ."

He had risen, greatly moved, and did not complete his sentence.

But Sigrun's voice answered him firmly and clearly, without a tremor:

"I have written to Lotta Hedman and asked her to tell Edward the whole story. At this moment he knows I am alive. And to-morrow he is coming here to fetch me."

"He is coming here?" Sven Elversson repeated. His voice was not firm and clear. It was faint and troubled.

"Yes," she answered. "I have asked him to come here to Hånger. I will tell you why later on. But, first of all, I want you to tell me now if you are pleased."

To the watcher it seemed as if the man before him changed his form and appearance before his eyes. He seemed to shrink, and the patient smile showed full and distinctly about his mouth. His eyes, that had shone so cheerfully a moment before, looked down at the ground; his arms hung loosely at his sides. And as he spoke, in answer to Sigrun's question, his voice had the old ring of painful humility.

"Surely I am pleased, Fru Rhånge," he said. "But it is overkind of you to speak of this as if it were my doing. I know—or I should say, I have always believed, that after the first excitement had passed over, there had not been a day but you have repented, and longed to go back. But you are thinking, perhaps, of your fear of your husband's anger, and the harsh judgment of the world, and how I have tried to give you courage to face it all. That is all I can claim credit for."

The listener heard and understood now, not with his ears alone, but with his whole soul. "What is true, and what is false in this?" he wondered. "God help me to find out the truth!"

Sigrun's face he could not see, but he fancied she shrugged her shoulders a little.

"Yes, of course," she said. "What else could there be for you to help me with?"

"It is good to remember that it is so," said Sven Elversson, in his gentle voice. "You realized, almost at once, the great wrong you had done your husband. It was impossible that you could condemn one who loved you to a whole life of solitude and longing. I am sure, I am convinced, that you would have taken this step months before, if it had not been for your illness. You have not, until now, had strength to face the gossip and scandal it would mean. And I should be the last to blame you for the delay. I know what it is to be an outcast and disowned by one's equals."

There was something in Sigrun's manner suggestive of impatience. Her voice had a touch of mischief as she answered:

"Oh, yes, I knew, Herr Elversson, that you would be pleased. But since this is the last time we shall speak together alone, I should like to tell you that it was not you alone who persuaded me to go back to my home. Your wife, too, has helped me very greatly—more, perhaps, than you yourself. I think she must have loved unspeakably," Sigrun continued in a gentle voice; "and I have tried to learn from her how one should love."

Sven Elversson's face darkened.

"She was a good woman," he said, simply, without his usual wealth of words. "We were very fond of her while she lived here among us."

"Mor Thala has told me a great deal about her," said Sigrun. "She went out to Grimön, it seems, the day after the schoolhouse was burnt down. She wanted to tell you that both she and the schoolmaster had done their best to make the children comfortable there. And she begged you not to take the misfortune too much to heart. You had already gained friends through that work; people had begun to realize what sort of man you were."

Sven Elversson made a gesture as if to indicate that he would rather hear no more of this. But Sigrun went on:

"I saw your wife at Applum, and I remember she was very plain to look at. Perhaps it was this, or perhaps something else that annoyed you, for Mor Thala says you spoke to her unkindly; more so than you had ever done to anyone else. 'If I came to you and asked you to be my wife,' you said scornfully, 'then we should see how much you respected me yourself.' And she neither blushed nor paled, but her face went ashen gray, and she stood up. 'You say that to me in jest and without

meaning,' she said. 'But if ever you asked me in earnest, it would be the happiest day of my life.' And that
seemed to touch you, and a couple of years after, you
married her in reality, because her answer then had
shown you she was a good and noble woman."

"True, she was good and noble," said Sven Elversson.
"I must do her justice. It was strange that she should
be willing to marry a man like me."

"Mor Thala has told me," went on Sigrun, "that it
was she who advised you to move out here to Hånger.
She knew the place, and knew it was all going to ruin,
so you could buy it for next to nothing. She made
peace about you, looked after your business, sold timber, I think it was, so that you should have money
enough to live on, arranged all things in your home so as
to answer more or less to the habits and needs of your
upbringing, and she took in all those in need whenever
you found them, and looked after them until you could
find them work elsewhere. Do you not think that
woman loved you?"

"No," said Sven Elversson. "I think she was trying
to love me. She fought against all that she disliked in
me, but at last it was beyond her power to go on, and
then she went off with Gustavsson."

"It was not so," said Sigrun—"not that way at all.
That was not why she went. But she knew you loved
someone else. You had betrayed it somehow or other.
There is a book of poems that is always on your table.
Mor Thala says you often read in it, but only one of
them all, an Icelandic love song, by Bjarni Thorarensen."

Sven Elversson sprang to his feet, and clutched at

his breast. "What do you mean?" he cried, almost threateningly.

Sigrun lifted her hand. "I wanted to talk to you about your wife," she said. "I shall be gone to-morrow," she added appealingly.

He sat down once more, humble and resigned. But his eyes had lost their wonted brightness; they looked at Sigrun solemnly and sternly.

The listener bent forward in tense eagerness. He recognized Sigrun's voice, but there was much in her manner that was strange to him. There was something about her now, a calm self-possession, a mature woman-liness, that she had not had before. "She has gone through much since I last saw her," he thought. "She never had that power of control over one who spoke with her before. No one can resist her now."

"Let us say," went on Sigrun again, "that your wife noticed last autumn, more distinctly than before, that you did not love her. Perhaps you read that poem oftener—how can I tell? And so she went away, but she did it in such a manner that you should not think she had gone for love of you, to make life easier for you. That was why she went with Gustavsson. I have spoken of this with your mother, and she agrees with me entirely. And Gustavsson himself told me so. 'She came to me because Sven Elversson did not care for her'—that was what he said."

Sven Elversson raised his hands deprecatingly.

"Why must I hear all this?" he said. "How can you think it will make me happier to know it?"

"Yes," said Sigrun; "it is always good to know that

one has been loved by one who was good. And well too, that you need not now suspect her of deceit or fickleness. You see what it was: she was made of the same stuff as that soldier we have just read of, who came home from the wars. And so you see," Sigrun went on, "it was she who taught me how to love. How love can pass all understanding, how it can fill one's soul to such a degree that it lets its own body be destroyed."

She rose up, and stood behind Sven Elversson's chair. And in so doing, she turned so that her husband, from where he was, could see her face. At sight of it, he almost started back, before the supernatural beauty that shone in her lovely features.

She spoke quickly now, following up her thoughts without waiting for reply.

"The poem in that book of yours, Herr Elversson, that you are always reading, is called 'A Song to Sigrun.' And whether it were because of the name, or for some other reason, your wife believed she knew who it was you loved."

Sven Elversson would have spoken, made some protest, or assurance, but she stopped him.

"Let me finish, that you may know how your wife could love in death as in life. Try to imagine her as a soul that is nothing but love, right down to the most unconscious depths, nothing but love, and that this soul determines to sacrifice itself for the one she loves. Finds ways and means that another would never have thought of, takes possession of another human being's will, leads, guides, accomplishes, whispering thoughts, dictating speech, compelling all things to her wish."

Sven Elversson shook his head. Very gently, but unmovably, he said:

"Now you are talking like Lotta Hedman."

"Yes," said Sigrun, "I am talking like Lotta Hedman. I know it. And I will not deny that it was Lotta Hedman who taught me to believe in the power of the dead. But how do you know she is not right? What star was it that led the dying woman to me of all others? And whence came the thought that so compelled me? You know how timid and sensitive I am. It is true that I had been lying there thinking of flight, but what made me do it in such a way? There were other means I could have chosen. But from the moment your wife lay there dead in my bed, I could not think of any other. And why was Lotta Hedman unable to resist? Why did Gustavsson come after I had gone, and not before? What made him so quiet and submissive all that day? Why were we not discovered? Why was my money stolen? Why was nothing found out after? I had certainly no deep-laid plans of my own. How did all this come about, Herr Elversson, unless it were that the woman who loved you, in the power of her endless love, had resolved to lead the woman you loved to you?"

She had spoken eagerly, as one inspired, overwhelmed by the miracle she felt she had shared. But there was no trace of passion in her voice. The listener behind the trees marked that well. Sigrun was speaking to the man who loved her in the firm assurance that he understood she did not love him.

Sven Elversson felt the same. His voice was thick with emotion, but it never changed into the tone of passion

"Be it so then! Let us talk like Lotta Hedman, if you wish. But if the dead woman's soul sent you here, might it not be as well for torture and punishment? She knew that my love could only increase, just as she knew that you could never come to love me in return."

"Yes," said Sigrun, with the same strange note of lofty inspiration, almost as if she were speaking to one from another world, "she knew that, yes. And she knew, too, that, if there had not been something in you that protected you against all love but hers, you would not have allowed me to stay here at Hånger. But she believed, perhaps, that some sweetness might come into your life by your teaching me how life should be lived. Might not that have been her aim? Afterward, when you are old, when all that flames and burns now is cooled, then you will think of this winter at Hånger as a time of happiness."

He shook his head.

"Not now," she said, "but after, and to your last hour. For I believe, as I said just now, that it was all to this one end, that you might teach me how life should be lived. What was I, a few months back, before I came here? I was not wicked; I meant well to all, but I was timid; I tried to do well, but mostly it went as best might be. There was no plan in my life. I did not know that one could be good and true, faithful and kind, under whatever circumstances. And that is what I have learned here with you; to detest all that pollutes the soul. That is what I take with me now, back to my home and my husband. He shall see that I am changed, and he will have more trust in me than before.

We shall be happy now, and we have you to thank for our happiness. And you must think of us and be glad."

He took one of her hands in his, bent over it, and wept.

"To-morrow, when Edward comes," she said, "I will tell him all this, and he will understand and thank you."

Sven Elversson started up in dismay.

"Is he to know . . ."

"Yes," she said. "I shall tell him that you love me, and he shall learn how she who is dead loved you. I will tell him all. You must see that there can be no more darkness, no more secrets between us. He shall know how it was I learned the secret of love. I will tell him that it does not care for promises and commandments, but knows its own law only. It cares for nothing, thinks of nothing, but the beloved. And it goes away when it is best; when it would bring suffering to stay. And I will tell Edward of all this here, at Hånger, where his fathers lived, in a place where nature itself is at once gentle and great. For he can be so, too—gentle and great."

The listener moved in his place. He felt shame at spying thus upon these two. He would have stepped forward and spoken openly and freely with Sigrun and the man who loved her, whom she tried to comfort and give courage now she was about to leave him.

But as he looked about for a way to go, he noticed something he had not seen before; out of a heap of stones immediately before him stood an old gatepost.

There was no gate, and no post on the other side.

The thing stood there alone, so rotten and decayed that it needed all the struts and supports about it to keep it standing.

Pastor Rhånge started.   He had not seen the thing before, but he had not been looking that way.   At first, he was convinced that it must be hallucination; that there was no gatepost there in reality; then it occurred to him that it might have been left standing as a curiosity.

But while he was looking at the post, the opportunity for declaring himself had passed.

The two had gone on speaking; he perceived now that Sigrun was talking of another subject altogether.

"But is it possible," she was saying, "that you do not know how it all happened?   Mor Thala told me once that you were ill with fever at the time, and delirious; that you could remember nothing of it all."

Sven Elversson made no answer.

"I understand you do not wish me to speak of this at all," said Sigrun, "but I do so want to speak to you about it.   Remember, to-morrow I shall not be here."

"I took my part in it, of course," said Sven Elversson, "but I was so ill I remember nothing.   Afterward, I heard the others talking about it, and I reproached them.   But then they said I had no call to say anything, for I had been in it, too.   And then I remembered, that they had forced me to   .   .   ."

He had spoken with the greatest effort, the words seeming to force themselves painfully through his lips. And he could not finish.

"You fancied you remembered," said Sigrun.   "You

know well enough it is impossible that you should have done it really. You would rather have died."

"I did it," he said. "Do not try to think otherwise."

"But I do think otherwise," said Sigrun, "and I want you to know that. All the time I have been here under your roof, I have felt convinced that it was not true. No one who knows you could believe it."

Sven Elversson bent forward and grasped her hand. And very earnestly and simply he said:

"You have been very good to me this evening. I can never thank you enough for this hour."

She understood his meaning, and refrained from pursuing the subject further.

"But at least you must let me thank you for these months at Hånger. I shall always think of this as the true home of charity. And I will try to make my own home like yours."

"You can leave that till to-morrow," he said.

She rose to her feet.

"Do not go yet. It is the last evening."

"Then read a little of Snoilsky."

He opened the book, but closed it again.

"It is too dark to read."

"Then say something you know without the book. Let me hear Bjarni Thorarensen's 'Song to Sigrun.' I have often wanted to ask you, but I never dared."

Sven Elversson made a gesture as if to refuse.

"I shall not be here to-morrow," she said again, with a note in her voice impossible to resist.

And he began to recite the Icelandic poet's passionate prayer to his love not to forsake him even though she should die and go to dwell in the mansions of heaven. "'Do not think I could not kiss a dead bride, or that I could not lay my arm about the waist of one pale in death and wrapped for burial.'"

He sat with his face turned away from her, his head bowed forward, his eyes resting on some point in the far distance.

But all that he had kept in check so well while they had been speaking, all that the soft enchantment of the evening, and the presence of the woman he loved, had not availed to loose, was freed in him now by the wild and powerful fervour of love that glowed through the poet's word. All his pent-up feeling poured out now in his voice.

"'Does not the summer sun kiss with like warmth the ice-clad mountain peak and the reddest rose? Are not white lilies loveliest of all flowers?'" Sven Elversson's voice trembled in the rush of the storm of love that raged within him.

Sigrun listened tensely for a few moments. Then suddenly she turned away, so that he should not see her face.

It was turned now toward the listener behind the trees. And he saw how, with features convulsed with passion, she, too, gave way to an outburst of feeling. Her eyes closed in pain, her hands were clenched together and her lips moved in silent plaint. Her husband could not hear the words, but from the movement of her lips he fancied he could read what she said.

"And I can never tell him—never!"

"'Come to me in autumn, when the winds rage over

black waters,'" Sven Elversson went on, his voice one impassioned cry. "'At midnight, when the moon is hidden in stormy clouds.'"

The listener in his hiding-place shuddered with chilly dread. He saw Sigrun lift her arms with a gesture of intense longing. He saw how the whispering lips again and again shaped their cry of agony:

"And I can never tell him—never!"

"'Sink with thy snow-cold breast to my heart,'" murmured Sven Elversson, in a breaking voice, "'and rest there, maiden from the grave, till thou hast loosed my soul from the fetters of life.'"

The Pastor glanced away from his wife, and looked toward the post. It seemed as if it had stood there till this hour for a single purpose—to remind him that he came of a race never known to endure a wrong—a race that knew how to take vengeance.

The two by the table said no word after the poem was finished. Sigrun rose hurriedly and went into the house. Sven Elversson walked the opposite way, through the trees, and past the gatepost, down to a little quiet pool, where he stood, looking down into the water. He had passed within a few steps of the listener, but without noticing him.

And Rhånge felt that this man who loved Sigrun must die.

It would be easy enough. Just creep up behind him and throw him into the water. He felt, too, that this man would not even attempt to defend himself. He would greet death as a welcome friend.

It was a perilous moment. Then to the mind of the

excited man came a thought which saved him. It had lain, no doubt, all ready in the depths of his soul for long, but only now did it rise up to his consciousness.

"Once you drove out that man from your church because of what he had done to the dead; what is this you would do yourself to the living?"

This thought it was that restrained him in that difficult hour. Was not life a thousand times more sacred than death? How could he, who had refused to admit Sven Elversson into his church, be now so savage as to entertain the thought of ending a fellow creature's life, of separating soul from body, to commit an act which held more than any could understand, and the consequences of which might go on through an eternity of eternities?

When he looked again toward the pool where Sven Elversson had stood, he was gone.

And something more was gone—the gatepost. Afterward, he thought that, in the struggle with temptation, he must have gone over to it himself, and flung it down with its supports; that it had fallen, and had been so utterly rotten and decayed that it had dropped with out a sound, leaving nothing but crumbling dust behind.

But he was not sure that it was so. He thought also that the thing had stood in his own soul; that it was his own violent, reckless, savage nature, with its supports of inherited habit and ingrown prejudice and sense of rights long held, that had fallen.

For that it had fallen, he felt now with wonder and relief. He knew it, from the mighty train of gentle thoughts that flowed through his soul.

He knew it, from the power of self-sacrificing love that filled him now.

He realized it from the joy he now felt in being a priest. He thought of his life, how he was at once a husbandman tending the fruits of the earth, and a shepherd of souls, head of a household and leader of a congregation, master and ruler and the helping minister of all—and now, for the first time, he felt that he truly loved his work, as the noblest and greatest and happiest of all.

He was happy, on this lovely evening in spring, as he drove back alone over the desolate, barren, unbeautiful mountain tract, toward his own poor home.

And he looked back, marvelling, at the thing which had saved him; for it was not his love, nor his priestly office, but the thought of the sacredness and majesty of life. A thought that had grown up slowly out of Sven Elversson's ill-fate and now stood firm and clear in its maturity.

. . . .

When Sigrun came out next morning into the garden, she saw that the book of poems had been left on the table, and went to fetch it in.

But, on taking it up, she found something between the leaves. And, looking to see, she found a small purse of yellow leather.

It was thrust in just at the page where stood the verses of the prisoner returned from the wars, and it contained her two plain rings, one other ring, also her husband's gift, and a few small trinkets.

She wondered at this, trying to think what it could

mean. And then at last she understood. And, trembling with emotion, she began to weep.

So it was Sven Elversson found her.

At first she could make no answer to his anxious questioning. Then at last she sobbed out:

"Edward was here last night, and heard all we said. He saw that I loved you, and he left this for me."

"Love me!" cried Sven Elversson. "You love me?"

"Yes," said Sigrun. "And Edward saw it, but he is not angry with me. My love, he will not come to fetch me now. He tells me to stay here and be yours now."

.   .   .   .

Later in the day, Lotta Hedman came over to Hånger with a message from the Pastor, asking Sigrun how she wished matters now to be arranged.

And she had much to tell, and among other things this: that, on the previous night, she had seen the old homestead of Hånger for the first time rise up in all its ancient grandeur. She had seen the old woman sitting at the window, and the gatepost, and all the rest.

Then, suddenly, she saw the old woman lift her hands to Heaven, and her face shone with joy.

And a voice was heard declaring:

"The trollfolk of Hånger are loosed from the curse."

And at the same moment, the old woman who had watched so long sank into dust and vanished, and the gatepost fell, and house after house collapsed, and Lotta Hedman knew that deliverance had come at last, and that she would never see that vision again.

UNG–JOEL

EVERYONE knows how strange thoughts can be. It is as if they were sown about the earth by an unseen hand. And one can go about fancying one has found something rare and fine, and be glad and proud of it, until one day it appears that the same had grown up in hundreds of other minds as well.

So it was with Pastor Rhånge's thought of the sacredness of life. He was by no means the only one who had found it. . . .

It was in the month of June, the time of year when people in Bohuslän, or, rather, in the coast tract of Bohuslän and on the islands near, made ready for the coming of visitors.

There had been a great to-do everywhere in making preparations. Houses and boats were newly painted, rooms swept out, gardens tidied up, bathing-huts warmed, and refuse cleared away. And now the trains began to come in, laden with visitors from all parts of the country. Invalids and the overworked, loads of children and loads of aged folk, those seeking rest and those in search of amusement. It seemed as if all Sweden were on the road to the cool reef-belts and the boisterous sea.

But the visitors for whose sake all this was done were to come from the eastward, from up inland. From the west, from the sea, no visitors were looked for. No preparations had been made for any coming from there. No orders, no instructions, had come regarding visitors from the sea.

And so, when visitors did come from the sea, naturally enough, their reception could not be the same as in the case of those from inland. Also, they brought with them horror and confusion and gloom, but no pleasure at all.

One week of the month of June, 1916, had passed when Sven Elversson was constrained to make a journey to Applum, all for the sake of those same visitors. His brother, Ung-Joel, who had been at sea the last few years, sailing between Holland and the Swedish ports, had come home to Knapefiord, sick and strange in mind after having met with some of those strangers out at sea, while they were yet on their way. And he had told his young wife she must send for his brother to come and see him.

When Sven Elversson came to Ung-Joel he found him walking up and down the little room behind the kitchen, where the young couple had set all their best furniture, and which they never used as a rule. He was pale and weary, but not exactly ill. His eyes were blood-shot, and looked as if ready to close at any moment for lack of sleep, but he gave himself no rest, to sit or lie down.

"How is all with you, Ung-Joel?" asked Sven Elversson.

Ung-Joel made no answer to the question, nor did he seem in any way aware of his brother's presence. He walked up and down as before, beating the air now and again with both arms.

"The seagulls—that is the worst, you know," he said.

"If we could only do something to make him sleep," whispered his wife. "But he is afraid to lie down; he is afraid to close his eyes. Just walks up and down, up and down. . . ."

"The seagulls—that is the worst," said Ung-Joel again, and waved his arms as before.

"Ung-Joel," said Sven Elversson, trying to bring up some old memory to turn his brother's mind from his trouble. "Do you remember when you and the fellows from the *Naiad* came over to Grimön that day with a snake for me to eat?"

And at that Ung-Joel stopped in his walk.

"Is that you, Sven?" he said. And the tears began to flow from his tired eyes. "It's a good thing you came. So I can ask you to forgive me, before I go mad."

"No need to talk like that," said Sven Elversson.

But now Ung-Joel began to tell how one day, after the great fight in the North Sea, he had come sailing round the Skaw, and had seen the hosts of the dead floating on the surface of the sea.

They did not lie flat on the water, but were held upright by their lifebelts, with heads above water, so their features could be seen.

And Ung-Joel told how the vessel had sailed for hours among the dead—thousands and thousands of dead. The sea was covered with them.

He described many terrible sights he had seen, but what seemed most terrible of all to him was that all those dead men had their eyes torn out by the innumerable seagulls that hovered about their heads.

"And I'll tell you what happened to the second mate," said Joel. "He'd been standing looking at all this ghastliness a while, and then suddenly he shut his eyes and jumped overboard. We never saw him again. He knew he would never be able to live in peace after what he had seen. And I wish now I had done the same."

"Do not think so, Joel," said Sven Elversson.

"I've got those horrors fixed in my eyes now," said Joel—"fixed there so I can see it all if I shut them only for a moment. I daren't lie down; I must be on my feet day and night, to keep my eyes from closing."

"You must think of other things," said Sven Elversson. "You've a wife and children."

"I'll tell you what we did," said Ung-Joel. "We got out a couple of guns we had on board, and started firing at the gulls. It was a sort of relief: something to vent our rage on. And I think it was that that saved us.

"But it was a silly thing to do, all the same. For it was no fault of the gulls. And they did no more than harm the dead—what's that against what was done to the living? And it was that I wanted to say to you, Sven. When I think how men deal so with men, that thousands of young lives are strewn about the sea, I can only cry for shame.

"And, Sven, I know I used to look down on you before and reckon myself better than you. But I want to ask your forgiveness for that. I used to think how you and your comrades up there had done a wrong to the dead, and I myself—I've never done a single thing to help the living."

"That you have, Joel," said his brother.

"No," said Joel, weeping, and threw himself on his knees beside an upholstered armchair, covered with pieces of embroidery, where his brother was sitting. "I've never helped a single soul, not even father or mother, or any one. And that's why the world's so cruel as it is."

"It could be better, Joel," said Sven, stroking his brother's hair. "And you can help to make it so."

"It's too late now," said Ung-Joel. "Now that I've got that sight in my eyes. I'm going mad now."

Sven Elversson laid one hand gently over his brother's eyes.

"Try now, Joel," he said. "You cannot see anything cruel now, with my hand over your eyes."

"That's true," said Ung-Joel. "There's blessing in your hand, Sven, from all the good you've done for others."

"Close your eyes now, Joel," said Sven Elversson. "And just think of how we can work together and help each other from now on."

And Ung-Joel closed his eyes, and in a moment he had fallen forward against his brother's knees, asleep.

It was a strange day, indeed, for Sven Elversson, that day in Knapefiord. It seemed as if every living soul in the place had hit on the same thought as Ung-Joel.

When his brother had been put to bed, and was quietly and healthily asleep, Sven Elversson went for a walk through the fishing village. He had gone but a little way down the smooth rocky slope when he met a woman. It was the wife of that Hjelmfeldt who had been one of the crew of the *Naiad*.

As soon as she saw who it was, she came up and shook hands with him, and begged him to go in and speak to her husband. Hjelmfeldt had been one of a party that fished up a mine at the beginning of the war, with the result that he had now but one arm and two half-legs remaining.

"And I said to myself," said his wife, "that if ever I came across you again, I'd ask your forgiveness for what we'd done to you. I've been thinking of them that sit making those mines and things. And if one of them heard about you, I dare say he'd think he was a fine fellow compared to you."

"That may be," said Sven Elversson.

"But I say no!" cried Hjelmfeldt's wife, with loud-voiced eagerness. "If he thinks it's wrong to harm the dead, then let him think how it's a thousand times worse to make up such devil's tools to cripple the living, and leave a man helpless and miserable all his life. You've never done that. You only tried all you could to help us."

Sven Elversson went into the house to see her husband, and sat with him for a good while, listening to his troubles. Then he went on his way again.

The next he met of those he knew before was Julia Lamprecht. She, too, came up and spoke to him.

"You offered to marry me once," she said. "And I said I would never marry such a one as you. I have thought of that many a time since this war began. And

I'd like you now to know I've been sorry for it. For what right had I to judge you for how you've acted by the dead? But those whose doings have left all the quarries in Bohuslän empty, and the workers idle, and their wives and children starving—they've wronged the living, and that's worse."

Sven Elversson went on, and after a little while a young man whom he did not remember having seen before came up to him.

"You won't know me, I dare say," said he. "I was only a boy when you left Grimön. But I was one of those that called after you in the street that time. And I'd like to ask your pardon for that now, for I've come to see how it's worse to wrong the living than to wrong the dead. I've been a pilot in the war, and been torpedoed three times, and each time some lives were lost. And I thought of you, and wondered why we that used to be so hard on you are so patient now. Seems as if it was only right for human beings to turn on one another like savages. And yet it can't be right, somehow. . . ."

On leaving the pilot, Sven Elversson climbed up to the top of a hill behind the village and stood for a long time looking out over the sea.

"If the trouble of my life," he said, "could bring people to remember that life should be inviolable; that a living man should not be robbed of his life or hindered in its use, then, after all, some good would have grown up out of the bitter seed of my misery."

IN THE NETS

SOME days later, when Ung-Joel had slept his fill and was nearly recovered, Sven Elversson came down in the afternoon to Knapefiord harbour, and found the *Naiad* lying in its usual place. Olaus from Farön and Corfitzson and the others whom he knew were on board, making ready, like the rest of the fishing fleet, to put to sea. They were going out with the drift nets, far into the Kattegat. And Sven Elversson felt a sudden desire to go with them, and spend a night at sea.

Olaus looked as if he were minded to refuse, but finding no good reason, he agreed. And as soon as a suit of oilskins had been found for Sven Elversson, they put off. The weather was better than they had had most of that summer, and they might hope to make a good haul. But Sven Elversson soon noticed that all on board were in ill-humour. They spoke unkindly to one another and to him. When he asked about the yield of the mackerel fishery early in the summer, they answered with oaths that a fisherman's life was the poorest that could be.

They reached the fishing grounds, and got the huge nets out, without a single pleasant word being spoken; the same gloom was noticeable later, when they had their meal. That night, Sven Elversson sat up on deck;

the watches relieved each other in turn, but none took the opportunity of having a chat with him. The men walked up and down, silent, bitter, and sullen, all of them.

Sven Elversson felt depressed and unhappy over all this unfriendliness, but hoped the spirits of those on board would improve when the morning came and it was time to haul in the catch. Something approaching cheerfulness was also apparent when the motor was started, and the two ends of the net were brought on board ready to haul.

Olaus and Corfitzson were hauling, the others stood ready to disengage the fish from the meshes as the net came in. And as the fish appeared, a full catch of splendid mackerel, glistening all colours of the rainbow, their faces brightened.

"You see, they won't have troubled us the night," said Corfitzson.

"Keep quiet, can't you!" snapped out Olaus, with an oath. "Want to tell them we're here? They'll find us soon enough without that. Feel here!"

He hoisted the net a little out of water, and all saw, among the glittering fish, something big and dark. There was dead silence on board, and next moment the body of a man came on deck with the net.

One young fellow, who had taken Hjelmfeldt's place on board, tried to get the corpse free of the net, but the skipper's voice called to him sharply:

"Leave it alone. There's another of them here."

And a moment later a new command:

"Let them alone. There's more of them coming."

Just then Corfitzson and Olaus lifted on board a dreadful mass: two bodies twined together.

And when the last of the net was hauled in, there lay a huge mound of dead men, brown meshes, and fish in one confusion. The fish, still living, flapped and slithered about, making the whole horrible mass seem alive.

When the bodies were lifted on board, Sven Elversson was so affected that he wept. He wiped the tears away with the back of his hand, but could not stop them. He stamped his foot, but the tears still came. He was forced to leave his work at the net and walk away far astern.

There he stood until the net was in and the motor started for the homeward run. The silent crew, sullen, unwilling, and gloomy as before, had begun once more the work of clearing fish and mussels from the net, and getting loose the rest.

"All in the net to be thrown over," commanded Olaus.

When Sven Elversson heard the order, he went up to the rest. The tears still flowed from his eyes, but he did not heed them. He took his place with the crew, and set to work, helping with their dreadful task.

They came to one of the dead. Sven Elversson lifted him up, and loosened some of the meshes that had caught in the buttons of his uniform. It was an elderly man with a sailor's beard under his chin. Someone suggested that he was an Englishman. When he had got the body loose, Sven Elversson began hoisting it to the deck.

"All that's in the net to go overboard," said the skipper, bending down toward the corpse.

But Sven Elversson restrained him.

"Will you not let this be laid to rest in holy ground, Olaus?" he said.

Olaus did not answer directly.

"Best to get these horrors away from the ship," he said.

Sven Elversson clenched his teeth in the endeavour to keep back his tears, and said as firmly as he could:

"If you throw this overboard, you will have to throw me, too."

He was astonished to hear himself speaking so, but he could not help it. He felt that he would stand by his word.

The others, too, saw that he meant what he said, and would never let the dead man go while he himself lived.

The skipper swore, and turned away, but made no direct refusal, and the others understood that he agreed.

Sven Elversson tried to lift the body, but it was too heavy for him. Then the young fellow newly joined came to his help, and together they laid the dead man by the bulwarks.

The next body was loosed from the net, and laid beside the first without question. Two men carried it up to where Sven Elversson stood. "This one's a German," they said.

To his surprise, Sven Elversson noted that the men on board had suddenly changed to a different expression, a different humour. They swore no longer, but spoke calmly and quietly. They no longer felt hatred toward these hosts of dead, that came and stole away their livelihood. They were accustomed to show respect and reverence to the dead, and something in their nature was more at ease to know that these drowned men of war were to be given decent burial.

Sven Elversson, too, felt strangely easier in mind. His soul felt more at rest now than ever since the first day of his misfortune.

He seemed to hear voices about him, thanking him for his charity to the bodies that once had been the dwellings of immortal souls.

"Now you are loosed from the burden that was laid upon you," said the voices. "Thus it was to come about. Your guilt is taken from you. You have risked your life to save the dead, and you have atoned for all."

His heart beat lightly and strongly, and he thought: "Let others condemn me now if they will, it will not matter, for in myself I know that I have fulfilled my penance and conquered."

THE SERMON OF THE SACREDNESS OF LIFE

SVEN ELVERSSON, his mother Thala, his brother Ung-Joel, and Ung-Joel's wife, stood among the crowd in the little burial ground outside the church at Applum.

It was the day when the dead sailors brought into Applum after the great fight in the North Sea were to be laid to rest. A great grave had been dug, to receive no less than seventeen coffins. So great a funeral had never before been seen in the little parish, and it might safely be said that never before had so many people been gathered in the little churchyard.

Not for eight years had Sven Elversson been so near a church as now. He had even hesitated a little about going to the funeral now, but his mother, who had come down to Applum to see to Ung-Joel, had persuaded him to go with them.

"Look you, Sven," said she, "I'd not set my foot in Applum church any more than you, but to-day's a week-day, so there's no question of that. And after all you've done to have those poor dead bodies laid in Christian ground, you'd not be leaving them the last of the way?"

It was as she said. All that last week, ever since the day he had been out with the *Naiad*, Sven Elversson and his brother Joel had sailed about among the reefs and islands in a light craft, looking for stranded bodies. Some had also been brought in from other parts, but the two brothers themselves had collected no less than eight and ferried in to the stone quay at Applum.

"Besides," said Mor Thala, "you can see yourself that folk look at you differently now to what they did."

This was, perhaps, what weighed most. The war, its horrors, all the misfortunes that had come upon the fisherfolk, had made them look more gently at Sven Elversson and his offence. They were more inclined now to notice his striving to help and restore.

"He must be a good man, anyway," they said. "He tries to help any one that's hard put. And, after all, helping the living's the greatest thing."

When it was then seen that Sven Elversson himself was doing more than all the rest to secure proper burial for the poor sailors, there were some who fancied they understood what made him do so, but most felt that, after all, it was not needed so.

It was otherwise with Sven Elversson himself. Each day he went to this new task of his with a strange delight. Every hour of it gave him more peace, more calm of mind. He felt a lightness of heart, a happiness, that he could not express, but the reflection of it shone in his face.

Not the joy of love, not the noblest deed, no word of praise could have given him the inner security he felt now, since he had taken the body of a dead English seaman on the *Naiad* under his protection.

He could not understand how it had come about, for

it was no great heroic deed he had done. The risk, the chance that Olaus would throw him overboard together with the dead, had not been great. Nevertheless, he felt that the great change had come, and that after this he could once more dare to feel happy. Now for the first time he began to think of a future that might hold days and years of happiness for him.

There was a strength in him now that he had not suspected before. He hardly needed sleep. His heart beat so easily, so untroubled; he felt it a joy to be alive.

"Oh, but I was miserable indeed before," he thought. "Every breath was an effort to me then. I did not know what life was."

That he found himself regarded more kindly by his fellows than before was, of course, an added satisfaction, but he thought at the same time that even if they had continued to hate him, it could not have made him feel unhappy now. He was freed, he had atoned.

The day after the burial he was to go back to Hånger. "I shall go back to Sigrun as a new man," he thought. For her sake more than all else his deliverance was a joy to him. What a glorious fullness of happiness awaited them now!

Standing there in the churchyard, following the service, he thought with emotion of these men who had given their lives for their country, but his joy was not lost for that. He saw that the former Pastor of Applum, Edward Rhånge, had also come to be present at this celebration for the dead. For a moment he felt anxious and uneasy, but it passed off at once, and his heart beat again with the same wonderful lightness as before.

"That man is my friend," he thought. "Who could have given me so great a gift as he has?"

When the burial was over, and the last hymn had been sung, Rhange stepped forward to the grave to speak.

At sight of him standing thus above the crowd, Sven Elversson felt an indescribable sympathy for this man, whom he had so disliked before. The fine head was indeed the same, but the features were thinner, giving a more spiritual appearance. "A splendid man," thought Sven Elversson. "He bears the mark of self-sacrifice upon his face."

As Pastor Rhånge, in a few introductory words, was greeting his former parishioners, someone pulled Sven Elversson by the sleeve.

He turned, and perceived Lotta Hedman standing beside him. She was pale, with glowing eyes, and her hair so unruly and wild that it seemed as if it would lift the hat from her head.

"No, I did not come with him," whispered Lotta, in answer to Sven's question. "He has been here some days already. I came alone. I was 'called.'"

Just then the speaker by the grave said a few words which claimed Sven Elversson's attention.

"Here, on the verge of this wide grave," he was saying, "I would speak to you, my friends, of the sacredness of death and of life.

"And I venture to say that there is none here among us who has not from youth up realized the sacredness of death. If any sinned against the inviolable holiness of death, he should be visited with the severest punishment.

"There was once a man here in Applum named Sven Elversson. His sin was that he had violated the sacredness of death. And we felt that he was more to be contemned than any amongst us. There may perhaps be some now present who were in the church that day when his sin was declared from the puplit; some who remember how he looked as he stole away, humiliated and wretched. Some may, perhaps, have been among those who sent him on his way with words of scorn. He was a man who almost seemed to invite such treatment. Seeing how he smiled with the same patience whatever was done to him, how he moved aside and humbled himself in every way, one felt perhaps it was almost a duty to add a little to his shame.

"And so it was that at last we made him leave the place. And I do not think anyone missed him greatly when he went. For there was something about him that was always asking our respect. Whenever anything difficult had to be done, and none of us were very willing to undertake it, that man stepped forward. He was trying to persuade us to give him back his honour as a man. And we could not do it, for we felt he was under the judgment of God.

"And so he went on his way through life, as a man under the judgment of God. Always with the same humility, always fearing to stand in the way of others. And he kept apart from us, choosing rather those who were less hard to please—the vagabonds of the roads, and children, who had less knowledge of right and wrong. We found nothing strange in this; it was natural that the man should wish for some company of his fellows. And when we heard time after time how some poor child from the streets had been placed in a good home through his help, or that vagabonds and tramps had begun to seek honest work, we found nothing very strange in that, thinking only that the man had no doubt his own end in view all the time. He was always trying to win back some honour and respect for himself. And we were growing almost tired of his constant endeavours.

"For what could we do for him after all? He had not sinned against any of us. He had not sinned in such a way that his crime could be atoned for by punishment. He had sinned against a sacred custom, and we had no power to grant him absolution. Moreover, we seemed to feel that God had condemned him as we ourselves had done.

"And so, while he was striving to help his fellow men upward in life, I can imagine Death standing behind his chair, leering scornfully at him, knowing the man was in his power, was his prisoner and could not escape. Who was there in all the world that could deliver him?"

Sven Elversson noticed that Mor Thala was crying. He himself felt, as he listened to the preacher's words, as if he were living over again all his past efforts to regain the goodwill of his fellows, but he did not weep. He stood there with untroubled eyes and easy bearing, and looked the speaker in the face.

"But now, of late," went on the Pastor, "we have

seen that Death has gained more power in the world even than before. He rules over us and oppresses us. He reaps his harvest before the time. He takes violence and cruelty to his aid. He lets loose crime and evil-doing. There is no misdeed he does not suffer on earth, and we can see no end to his power.

"And now that we are suffering under the harsh tyranny of Death, we begin to ask: Is there, then, nothing on earth strong enough to take up arms against Death?

"And we know that there is but one thing on earth that dares to resist the power of Death—the constant, unflinching enemy of Death—and that is Life.

"And in the midst of this war, when dreadful things are done, such as the shipwreck of tens of thousands at sea as if it were a trifle, the sending of tens of thousands into captivity as if it were nothing to speak of, the slaughter of tens of thousands at the cannon's mouth as if it were a praiseworthy deed, the driving forth of tens of thousands from their homes as if it were but a natural and customary thing—in the midst of all this, I still believe that there is growing up amongst us a greater love of life than we had known before.

"For Life, Life has been only the poor handmaiden at the service of all, asking nothing for itself. Life has been just the daily bread that was eaten, as it were, without a thought. There was nothing solemn about Life, to be painted in pictures and hovering as a ghost in the gloom. Life has not even any form or figure of its own whereby we may know it.

"Now you may think," the speaker broke off, turning more directly to his listeners, "that I am speaking empty words, seeing that all of us well know Life is the thing we love most of all. But, my friends, it is not enough that we love Life. Life, I would say, is like a child ill-cared for. It may be brought up with more love than understanding, to be a shame and a thorn in the flesh, until we hardly know how to bear with it.

"Or, my friends, we may liken Life to a young bride, whom we take into our house and give all our love. But this is not enough. We must surround her also with peace and holiness, and give her her due and show her kindliness; if not, then the young wife will forsake us, and leave us to loneliness and despair, because the ways whereby we would have led her were not the true ways.

"But of this I might go on speaking to you all day and night until another day, without coming to an end. I must not let this lead me from the thing I am charged to tell you now.

"I will only take it, as I have said, that, during these last years, Life has begun to be a thing more sacred and precious to us than before. And for every day of all this misery, we feel this the more.

"And so it is that we are beginning to look with greater kindliness toward those who are the true servants of Life; who seek to keep Life a good and noble thing, and render aid and protection to the living.

"I have heard many here in Applum say that they repent of the unkindliness and scorn they showed toward Sven Elversson. And I believe it is because they have begun to understand the greatness and holiness of

Life. They realize that to save the children of the streets and the vagabonds of the road is a noble work. They see that Life is greater than Death.

"And to you, Sven Elversson, faithful servant of Life, I can now say that we, your former neighbours, no longer look on you as one stamped with a shameful mark. And we repent of ever having done so. We repent of the suffering we have caused you."

The speaker waved a hand toward the listening crowd.

"Is it not true that I speak for all here present?"

No voice was raised in protest. Many of the listeners had tears in their eyes.

Sven Elversson stood calmly, with the same inward happiness glowing in his mind. "It is good that this should come," he said to himself. "But it is not the greatest thing, after all. The greatest is that I have been freed from guilt in myself, in my heart."

"I am glad that you suffer me to say this in your name," the Pastor went on. "I am glad that you have declared Sven Elversson innocent in your hearts, before his innocence is established by other means."

And then the Pastor went on to tell how several of the bodies of the seamen brought to land had on them letters and papers still legible. These had, of course, been taken charge of, to be returned where possible to the relatives of the dead. But in one case, that of the English sailor first brought on board the *Naiad*, a letter had been found consisting only of some few lines, without address, and unfinished, yet of such remarkable content that he, the vicar of Algeröd, had been called in to give his opinion on it. This letter he would now read, translating it into Swedish, to those present.

And this was the letter.

"They say we are going into action to-morrow. And this is to ask you, Mary dear, to go to Springfields at Handley Park and tell them something about their foster-son. He took no part in the wicked thing we others did. He was delirious before. Then we thought he was dead, and nobody troubled about him. Then when we found he was alive, we made him believe he had been in it, so he could not give evidence against us after. I must write this now; I shall have no peace until. . . ."

"Now, since we know," said the Pastor, very quietly and earnestly, "that Springfield is the name of the people who adopted Sven Elversson as a child, and also that he himself never had any clear recollection of what happened, but only trusted to the word of his companions, we must say that his innocence is clearly proved by this message from the dead."

The speaker's voice trembled a moment, but rose again to its full power. He turned now directly to Sven Elversson.

"We did not wish to tell you of this, Sven Elversson," he said, "until now, when we could at the same time make it known to all. But now I, your parish priest in former days, who once laid you under the ban of contempt and abhorrence, I have come to declare your innocence at the door of that church from which I once drove you forth. And I count it the greatest mercy of God that I myself am suffered to say these words. You are known to all now as an innocent man, and the disgrace that clung to your name is gone for ever. You can walk with uplifted head among your fellows."

A wave of emotion swept through the crowd. The listeners turned to ask one another what it was they had heard. Many wept for joy that a man's innocence should have come to light after so many years of suffering.

"You will have no need to hide yourself away and humble yourself any more," said the Pastor. "No need to receive ill words with a patient smile. No need to fear that even those who love you must shudder at what you have done. You will be greeted as one of the best among us, and those who are near to you likewise."

"He is thinking of Sigrun," said Sven Elversson to himself. "Thinking of her joy in this. And it is right. It will make her very happy."

When the Pastor had spoken these last words, he turned from the side where Sven Elversson stood, and addressed the crowd on the other hand.

"All that this man has suffered has been suffered for no crime," he said. Sven Elversson felt his heart beat faster, with increasing violence. "My poor heart is better used to bearing sorrow than joy," he thought.

"But since this is so," the Pastor went on, "you will all ask now, I know, 'Why, then, has God dealt so hardly with him, and why were we so misled?' I have asked myself the same. And I believe I have found the answer.

"As for the man himself, I will say no more than this, that I believe it is through his very misfortunes that

God has given him such joy that he would not be without it now."

At these words Sven Elversson thought once more of Sigrun and all the joy that waited him. He felt his heart leap in his breast with delight, but at the same moment, something seemed to break. He could no longer stand upright, but sank to his knees.

"And I believe, too, that Sven Elversson has been sent us as a sign. For God speaks to us in these days not by words, but by the actions of men, and in the deeds of every human being we should read a thought of God."

The speaker drew a deep breath and looked out over the crowd. He saw that all were looking anxiously, expectantly, to him for some word of hope and deliverance from the great distress that weighed them down.

"And when I remember how this man has come to us in this time, I think it is that God had tried through him to show us how we can find a way out of our misery, if not at once, still within a span of time that human thought can embrace."

Sven Elversson slipped to the ground. He had made no cry or moan. His mother, standing near, thought he had sat down to avoid the curious glances of those round him. And he might well need to rest after the excitement of the day.

"For I have learned," said the Pastor, "that this man made to himself a weapon and an instrument of that which troubled him most of all. He had often noticed, in trying to help some creature aside from evil ways, that good words were of little avail, and little could be done by noble example or the prospect of winning praise and living an orderly and respected life. The first thing, he found, was to give the vicious man a hatred and horror of vice, to make him loathe it so that the loathing sank into his soul and body and made it unendurable.

"And now that I have said this, I ask you all here gathered about the grave of these dead seamen to follow me in thought out to sea, beyond the reef belt, yet not so very far, for those whom I wish you to meet are very near us now.

"I went out myself yesterday to see them; those who have made the voyage from Horns Reef up to our very shores, held up by their lifebelts that would not let them sink, those thousands flung into the sea like refuse that none would touch.

"And I ask you now, all of you, to follow me in thought at least, and try to see that sight. You shall see the black holes in place of eyes in the gray faces of the dead. You shall see the sunken cheeks, the hands held up in some strange way, beckoning and waving with the movement of the water; you shall see those that float about lying with swollen bellies; those that lie feet uppermost, and turn over now and again to thrust up their heads, like acrobats turning somersaults. You shall see those who were thrown into the water torn apart and shot to pieces already.

"There are heads that turn from side to side, as if they had something to tell you. And a shrieking, greedy flock of birds about them, and fishes leaping joyfully in the water. All this you shall see, and fix the vision in your minds so that it never can fade.

"But now you ask me: 'Why should we see all this?

"'We are quiet and decent folk, living peaceably among ourselves, and we have no share in the guilt that caused this war; we can do nothing to hinder what is done by either side.'

"But I say to you, that you should see these messengers of dread—should see them and never forget it. For surely it was not without some purpose that they have been cast up on our shores. All the thoughts of sorrow and pity which that sight could wake in you, those thoughts you should not thrust aside; no, nor the bodily horror and disgust of things left to perish.

"Let the horror and hatred of it fix itself in every fibre of your bodies, and give birth to an abhorrence of war that nothing ever can overcome.

"For remember, that though we here are not responsible for the war, yet we have read of it every day in the papers. We may perhaps have found it interesting that such great events should happen in our time. We have stood aghast, perhaps, in admiration of the great deeds. We have had our sympathies with one side or the other, and rejoiced at their success.

"But now these dead are come to us, that we may see how abominable a thing is war.

"And some of you have profited by the war, and some have believed that it would lead to great and beneficial changes, and some think that nations are strengthened and exalted by war. And none can hold their own or their children's thoughts away from the war.

"But now these dead are come, to show us what we

could not see and realize so inwardly before; that war is an abominable thing, a ghastly thing.

"These bodies floating in our waters, they are no ghostly vision, no story of imagination, but reality and truth. And the same may come again after a time, in reality and truth as now.

"And therefore I ask you in thought at least to follow me out to sea, and learn to know these dreadful things, and fix them in your minds and never forget.

"And you shall bring the knowledge of these things to others, so that they, too, may feel unconquerable abhorrence at the very mention of war; so that the word 'war' shall never more be uttered, but become a sound so intolerable to human ears that none dare speak it.

"There are others, perhaps, who have seen even more dreadful things than this. And they, too, shall speak and write of war, until there is woven about it a ghostly fear and shuddering, a dread that nothing can overcome.

"For how can we know what else may come?

"In a few years the memory of this war's sorrow and agony and destruction may be forgotten, and a new generation may once more set out to war with the joy of battle in their hearts. It lies with us now to fix in the minds of all humanity so great a horror of war that no talk of glory and brave deeds can ever take its place.

"For though great words have been spoken against war, and great examples have been set by men of peace, and the wisest calculations proved its madness, still the war is yet alive.

"But out of the very horror and gruesomeness of war

itself we can make ourselves weapons and armour and cure, and leave these as a legacy to our children, that they may overcome the greatest enemy of all mankind.

"And now at last I would say some words of the holiness of Life in the time when war shall no longer exist on earth. . . ."

But the words were never spoken. Someone pulled the speaker by the sleeve.

"Sven Elversson is ill. He is dying. It has been too much for him."

The Pastor stepped down from his place and made his way through the crowd to where Sven Elversson had stood. He lay now on the grass, with his head on his mother's knee, not dead, but very ill. His breast trembled with the violent beating of his heart.

When the sick man saw the Pastor approaching, he greeted him with an indescribable smile, full of love and free from fear, as he might have greeted the one dearest to him of all. He tried to reach out his hand toward him, and murmured something either in thanks or asking pardon.

The Pastor knelt beside him; he, too, was filled with a great tenderness now, and anxiety at the thought of losing such a friend as Sven Elversson had now become.

"Sven Elversson, brother," he said. "Live! You must live now for her sake."

They carried the sick man in to the vicarage. A doctor who was present hastened to him. He examined the patient, and declared that he might live a little while—a day, a week, perhaps a year, but that was all.

Meanwhile, the crowd stood round the grave, waiting. They knew that Pastor Rhånge had had more to say; that he wished to tell them something that would give them peace and comfort at parting. They could not do without it now.

A messenger was sent in to the vicarage, and returned with the answer that the Pastor could not leave Sven Elversson now. He was sitting with his arm round the sick man, and nothing else could give him strength to live, or hinder the spark of life from dying out.

THE FIFTH COMMANDMENT

WHILE the crowd still waited for the conclusion of the sermon, a voice was heard, not from the graveside, but from somewhere farther out. A woman's voice, thin and shrill, yet strangely audible and distinct.

They gathered round the speaker, and saw a young woman on her knees, with arms outstretched, head thrown back, and eyes closed. She seemed unconscious of herself, and spoke as in a trance.

"I see the dead," she said—"I see those whom we have buried here. I see them move toward the land of Death, and enter in. And now, after they have gone a little way, I see them coming toward a building, like a schoolhouse, and asking admittance there.

"'We are souls that have passed through the school of earth,' they say to the keeper at the gate, 'and we have come hither to show what we have learned of knowledge there.'

"But the keeper of the gate shakes his head. He tells them that they have ended their schooling too quickly. But all the same he opens the gate and lets them in.

"And I see them go into a great hall. I can see their fear. They are afraid and trembling, like all who are to be questioned so.

"Then a man comes forward to meet them. He wears

a long robe, and his hair lies in smooth locks about his head.

"'Ye souls that have passed through the school of earth,' says the man to them, 'can you say my Ten Commandments as they are said on earth to-day?'

"I see the souls of the dead rejoicing that no harder question is asked than this. And all together answer:

"'Thou shalt not worship false gods.

"'Thou shalt not take the name of the Lord thy God in vain.

"'Thou shalt keep holy the Sabbath day.

"'Thou shalt honour thy father and thy mother.'

"I hear them say this, but haltingly, and with great difficulty. And they are wondering in their minds why it should be so hard to say the words. They do not know themselves what makes them stammer and speak so faintly.

"'You have learned this in some manner, albeit with faults and errors,' says the teacher. 'Now say the rest!'

"And then the souls of the dead speak out clearly and without difficulty:

"'Thou shalt kill!

"'Thou shalt commit adultery,

"'Thou shalt steal.

"'Thou shalt bear false witness.

"'Thou shalt covet they neighbour's house.

"'Thou shalt lay waste they neighbour's field, and his wife and his servant, his goods and all that is his.'

"And when all this is said, I can see that the dead are glad to have passed the test so well.

"But the teacher asks them:

"'Who has taught you so to misread my law, that I had set to be a guard about the sacredness of human life?'

"And they answer him:

"'We are soldiers. We are the subjects and servants of Death.'

"Then the teacher cries to them:

"'Wake up, ye dead, and see who is this that ye honour, and who is your master!'

"And I see them waken up out of the error of earthly life as from a long dream. And they see then with dread that they are immortal souls, whose place is in heaven, and they begin to sorrow for all that they have done on earth, and to fear for the punishment to come.

"But then the teacher speaks to them again:

"'I am he that is Lord of Death and of Life.

"'And I sent Death upon earth to be the servant of Life.

"'I let the withered leaves fall to the ground, that new fresh leaves may grow again next year.

"'I let the stars in the firmament burn out and die that new stars may arise in their stead.

"'I let the bodies of those who have lived their life be laid in the grave, that new life may bloom upon earth.

"'But since Death has made himself master instead of servant, I will pursue him.

"'For it is not my will that the harvest should be reaped before its time, nor the young fowl bird be taken by the fowler before it has built its nest and brought forth its young.

"'And I will set a boundary and a landmark between

the time that is now and the time that is to come; in a few years I will mark it. And this time shall be called the time of darkness.

"'But ye souls, go back again to earth, and teach mankind to keep my Fifth Commandment, which is the Commandment to love thy neighbour, and is the key to all the rest.

"'Tell them that my Millennium hangs in the east like a dawn. But how shall it rise in the sky and give light to the world, as long as ye let Death take the Great Beast in his service?

"'For the Great Beast is War.'". . .

Lotta Hedman came to herself. She looked round and saw a close circle of people. Many faces shone with a great content.

"Where have I been?" she said. "What have I said? Has God at last spoken through my mouth?"

Tears of joy and thankfulness flowed from her eyes.

CONCLUSION

NEARLY a year had passed when, one day, a woman in mourning came driving to the vicarage at Algeröd.

Her coming occasioned no great surprise, for though it had never become generally known that she still lived, there were yet a few of those visiting Hånger who had seen and recognized her, and the rumour had spread.

She had never been separated from her husband by any legal act. Sven Elversson's illness had forced him to live quietly, without any excitement, and the others had done all they could to spare him.

Now that she had come, she went very quietly up to one of the small rooms and made herself at home there.

She did not force herself into the place of the old lady who had been mistress in her absence, but her nature was such that no one could resist her, and by the power of affection she began to rule over her and the servants and brought back peace and content to the home.

Her husband let her come and go as she pleased, and live her own life, as he did his.

But after a few months had passed, she came into his room one day with a letter in her hand.

And, looking round, she saw that the room was full of pictures of herself, and all the things she had worked and embroidered during her marriage were collected there.

Her books were on the bookshelf and her prayer-book lay on the table beside the bed. She seemed to feel herself in an atmosphere warm with love.

"You did not know, perhaps, that Sven Elversson has left a considerable sum of money," said Sigrun to her husband. "When his adopted father in England heard the news of his innocence, he kept his promise and made him his heir. He died at the beginning of the year, and now the legacy is due. It all goes to Sven Elversson's old parents."

"That man left a great happiness behind him," said the Pastor.

"And now they write to me, Joel and Thala, to ask if we will accept Hånger as a gift from them. It was their idea that we should carry on Sven Elversson's charitable work. The means would be at our disposal. . . ."

She noticed that her husband's face darkened.

"It would be a much greater field of work for you," she added.

Pastor Rhånge rose to his feet and walked up and down.

"If you wish to move to Hånger," he said, "I will not try to keep you here."

She answered quickly: "No, I will never leave your house again."

"But, Sigrun," he said, "you understand what I mean. I am glad to have you living in my house—but that is not enough for me."

"You are my first love, Edward," she said quickly.

She broke off, took his hand, and led him to the window.

"Look out on the lawn," she said. "There was a corner over there that was covered with pansies when we first came. They were at home there, and grew up every year by themselves. Once I had a proper flower-bed made there, and planted other flowers, and they grew and throve too. But now the bed with the strange flowers is gone, and look—the pansies are beginning to grow up again in their old place."

THE END

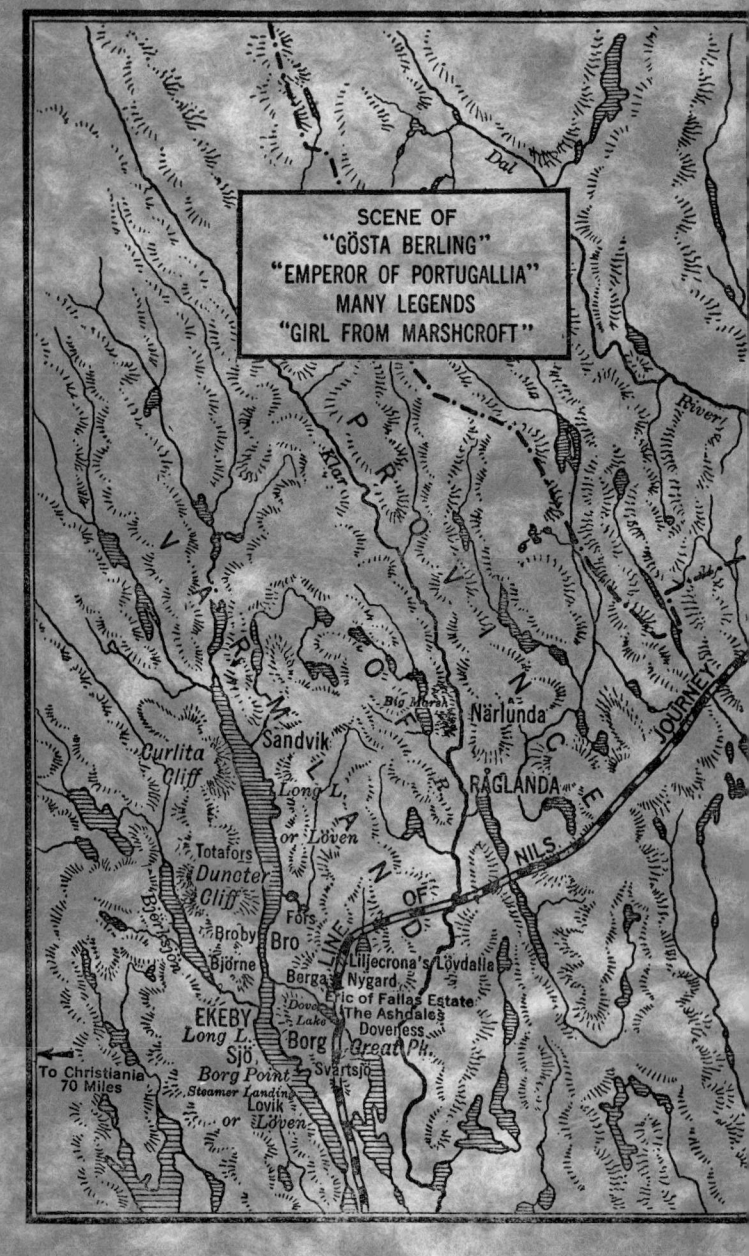

SCENE OF
"GÖSTA BERLING"
"EMPEROR OF PORTUGALLIA"
MANY LEGENDS
"GIRL FROM MARSHCROFT"